AN
OXFORD
TRAGEDY

AN
OXFORD
TRAGEDY

NORMAN RUSSELL

ROBERT HALE · LONDON

ISBN 978-0-7198-1608-6

Robert Hale Limited
Clerkenwell House
Clerkenwell Green
London EC1R 0HT

www.halebooks.com

2 4 6 8 10 9 7 5 3 1

Typeset in Palatino
Printed in Great Britain by Berforts Information Press Ltd.

CONTENTS

PROLOGUE

Two Scenes of London Life

May Day, 1894

URSULA FORREST, HOLDING a letter in her hand, stood at one of the windows of her first-floor millinery establishment in Old Bond Street, and looked at the stream of traffic pouring down from Piccadilly. She noted one of the Dark Green Line Holloway omnibuses from Victoria struggling to make its way through the snarl of lorries, vans and cabs, and thought of the girl sitting silently in the room behind her.

Rosalie had arrived half an hour earlier by one of those Dark Green Line vehicles. She rented rooms in Holloway, but her photographic salon was in Regent Street, where she often worked far into the night, and then slept on a camp bed until the next day's business dawned.

Ursula turned from the window, pausing to examine her reflection in a long cheval glass. At thirty-five, she had lost the delicacy of youth, but was still what was sometimes described as 'a fine figure of a woman'. Her naturally blonde hair was, as always, expertly coiffeured, because it was attended to every morning by a visiting stylist from Monsieur DuPont's hairdressing establishment in Oxford Street. A 'fine figure'? A more apt description, she thought, would be 'majestic'. Her grey morning dress, by Worth of Paris, fitted her to perfection.

'Our sweet ring-dove fears that she will no longer be able to help fund our little coterie,' she said, holding up the opened letter for the girl to see. 'The general tenor of her letter is that economies have to be made. Still, she expresses her undying love, and adds a few lines from Keats. Shall I read them to you?'

'Oh, yes, please, Ursula!'

> '"Of all its wreathéd pearls her hair she frees,
> Unclasps her warméd jewels one by one;
> Loosens her fragrant bodice – by degrees
> Her rich attire creeps rustling to her knees."'

Ursula Forrest laughed, and it was a hard, heartless sound. The ring-dove had been a wonderful, exhilarating conquest, but there were others. No one was indispensible. She looked at the girl sitting on the banquette in the centre of the elegantly furnished sitting-room. Slim and darkly handsome, with her hair pulled back and fixed with a satin bow, she wore a well-tailored jacket and a long, close-fitting skirt, that gave her a boyish look. Dear, amusing, cynical Rosalie!

Beside the young woman stood a camera mounted on a tripod. She rose from her seat and began to prepare one of the frames that would house a glass slide.

'I can't associate the ring-dove with Keats's timid Madeline,' she said. 'Strength, and a positive attitude – those are the things that belong to her – or so it would seem.'

'Oh, she is strong enough,' Ursula agreed. 'But whenever she has to deal with me, she reveals her sentimental side. Hence that drivel from *Saint Agnes' Eve.*'

'Dear Ursula,' said Rosalie, 'what will you do? I know how much you esteem our dear ring-dove. Surely you'll give her time to find some money somewhere?'

'Today is May Day,' said Ursula Forrest. 'I'll give her till the end of this month, and if the money's not forthcoming, then she need not call here again – unless I summon her. I love her dearly, as I love you, darling Rosalie, and the others; but no money, no friendship. Or if she still craves my love, she'll have to work for it.'

'Perhaps she has found a young man,' ventured Rosalie, smiling mischievously at her friend. 'It does happen, you know! Saying she has no money may be just an excuse to …'

'A young man? Not she! I know how she feels – of course I do – who else can know more about that girl's desires and pre-dilections than I? No, there's no young man.'

Rosalie looked at the camera, and then at her friend.

'It'd be a pity, you know, to lose her,' she said. 'In all these months since she joined us, I've not managed to take a single picture of her for our albums!'

'I know, and that's a great pity. A great – frustration. Once we're all photographed, we become even closer to each other than we are. There's nothing to hide, then, is there? I *don't* want to lose her, I must admit, and I'd love to have photographs of her to – to contemplate. The kind of photographs *you* take, I mean. In any case, I have her letters. She must know that I wouldn't scruple to use them, if I had to, to make her see sense and find the money. So we'll wait a while, and see what happens.'

She undid the girdle of her dress, and laid it carefully across a chair.

'Lady Kennedy will be here in an hour,' she said. 'She must see the new burgundy felts from the Paris summer collections. Meanwhile, my young friend, it's time for photography.'

Both women laughed, and while Ursula locked the door, her friend turned her attention to the camera.

Just after midnight on the same day, a young, flush-faced man of twenty or so managed a delighted chortle as he gathered in his winnings across the baccarat table with both arms. The upper room at Mr Paulet's gaming-rooms in North Audley Street was dim with tobacco smoke. A servant in a white alpaca jacket had begun to extinguish the table lamps by blowing across their glass chimneys. Various more or less tipsy men in evening dress congratulated the winner, who bowed mockingly at a man in his thirties who was slouched back in his chair.

'Never mind, Fowler,' he said, 'you can't win every time. Are you calling in tomorrow night? Maybe you'll win it all back. There's two hundred here, more or less. What about the rest? Are you going to write me a cheque?'

'Go to the devil, Castlemain,' said the man called Fowler. 'Clear out, won't you, and leave me alone. I'll send a cheque round to your place first thing tomorrow morning.'

Castlemain looked dubiously at the man in the chair, and shook his head as though more in sorrow than in anger.

'When a fellow comes to spend an evening at the tables,' he said, 'it's a good idea if he brings his cheque book with him. *I* do.'

'Confound your impertinence, Castlemain!' cried Fowler. 'You'll get your money tomorrow. Can't some of you fellows persuade him to go?'

Somebody whispered to Castlemain, and the young man followed the coterie of men in evening dress from the gaming room. A man in his fifties emerged from another room, and came to stand by the man who had lost at baccarat. Like the others, he wore evening dress, but his face was the face of an assassin.

'How much did Lord Castlemain take from you tonight?' he asked.

'Six-hundred-and-forty pounds.'

'You're losing too often, Fowler. This is *baccarat chemin-de-fer*, a game where skill is involved. You're losing your touch. Castlemain's only a lad, but he beat you hands down tonight. Last week, you lost a thousand to that squalid little City syndicate. One of them came here this morning, saying that you'd not honoured your note of hand.'

Mr Paulet, owner of the gaming rooms, looked at Fowler, who sat drooping mournfully in his chair at the green baize table, which was still covered with playing cards, scattered beside the wooden pallet used to deal them to the players. Fowler, he knew, was senior partner in a brokerage firm in Lombard Street, a firm that had conducted business there since 1750. He was a pleasant enough fellow, no bully, like some of his clients, but weak, easily roused to recklessness at the tables when challenged by a determined young fellow like Castlemain.

'Can you pay those debts, John Fowler?' asked Paulet bluntly. 'And can you pay the promissory notes I'm holding for you to the extent of £4,378? My patience is not inexhaustible.'

John Fowler rose from his chair, his face pale and contorted with impotent rage.

'Of course I can pay! Do you think that a man in my position will default on his debts?'

Mr Paulet laughed.

'I don't know. But while you are mired in debt, I rise above you as a gentleman, and I rise above you as a moralist. And if you do – default on me, I mean – then I will be entitled to let it be known immediately in the City. You cannot be held responsible at law for debts of honour, but a statement from me will bring your brokerage house crashing down in ruins. I won't say I'd do it, but I have the power to do so.'

Mr Paulet walked towards the door.

'I'm a reasonable man, Mr Fowler,' he said, 'and I'll give you until the middle of June to settle your debts both with me and with the other members here. There's Lord Castlemain, Lord Thomas Everett, Mr Weekes, Mr Price, and Mr Vane Tempest – in all you owe those gentlemen over £2,000. And £4,378 to me. That's £6,378 in all, and you must find it before the middle of June. After that – well, you know how these things pan out.'

John Fowler rose to his feet. The man in the white jacket helped him into his greatcoat and handed him his tall silk hat. Fowler gave him a shilling.

The man preceded him down the stairs to the ground floor, and opened the front door.

'Sir,' he said, 'some men were asking for you at the door earlier tonight. Ugly customers they seemed to me. I told them you weren't here, but they just laughed. Are you going along to the cab rank? Take care, sir. They may still be around.'

The man watched Fowler as he stepped out into the chill night air of North Audley Street. Poor Mr Fowler! He was such a nice gentleman, well set up, and modest in his way. He'd said as much one day to Mr Paulet. 'Jones,' he'd said, 'don't judge people by appearances. Mr Fowler is an inveterate gambler – he never knows when to stop, and one day, he'll ruin himself and his firm by reneging on his debts. Did you know he has a wife and children? He should think more of them, and less of the tables. I've no patience with him.'

Well, no doubt Mr Paulet was right. But it was a crying shame.

It was raining when John Fowler turned out of North Audley Street on his way to the cab rank in Grosvenor Square. As he did so, a brawny arm suddenly encircled his throat, and pulled him back against a wall. Two other men appeared out of the shadows: one of them, a fierce black man, wielding what looked like an open razor; the other a knock-kneed weasel of a man brandishing an iron bar.

The man with the brawny arm spun him round and began to choke him until he gasped in fear and pain.

'Listen, Fowler,' said the man, an Irishman with huge scarred fists and a vicious mouth, 'you can guess who sent us, can't you? Captain Macdonald's getting impatient for his money, and he wants it now. You've borrowed two-thousand pounds from him, and haven't paid him back a penny.'

The man fumbled among John Fowler's clothes and he felt him yank his gold watch and chain from his waistcoat.

'This will do on account,' said the Irishman. 'It'll buy you a few days' time. But if you don't pay the Captain all that you owe him, me and my friends here will come and find you, and we'll fix you for the summer. Just bear what I say in mind.'

The black man suddenly lunged at him, and he heard the fabric of his evening jacket tear open as the razor slashed him almost to his chest. In a moment, his tormentors had disappeared into the rain. Clutching his torn garments close to his body, he made his way to the cab rank. Once inside one of the musty vehicles, he sighed, not with relief, but with something approaching despair.

'They're all "captains" or "majors", these loan-sharks,' he muttered to himself, his heart racing. 'Oh, Father, if only you were.... All that money, and none of it for your children. All squandered on useless projects, colleges, libraries, obscure scholarships.... Don't we mean anything to you? Me, your eldest, and Timothy, and your daughter Frances? What am I to do? These debts, and that massive investment in our firm that Frobisher made – an investment that I can't repay? He's turning ugly, but I haven't the money to pay him. Oh, Father, if only you were dead!'

Ursula Forrest sat in a tapestry-covered chair beside her bed, and gave herself up to thought. What time was it? After one, and a rattling wind was blowing outside in Old Bond Street. By the light of a lamp on the bedside table she reread the letter from the girl whom she called 'the ring-dove.'

Dearest Swan,

You know that I love you, and wish to be with you as often as possible. And because I love you, I beg that you will give me time to make my monthly payment. As for the other, I hope that you will have sufficient compassion to wait until I have amassed enough to make you a significant return. I am in desperate straits at the moment, with creditors pressing upon me. Have mercy, and do not forbid me to come to you, as you did to our mistle thrush. I do not think that I could bear it.

With all my love, I remain

Your ring-dove

Beneath the message were the scrawled lines from Keats.

Ursula brought her little writing-desk over to the bedside, and composed a reply.

My little one,

Perhaps I will give you a little more time to get the money together. But you must repay my forbearance by coming more often to London, and pleasing me in ways that you have so far demurred to practise. I admire your strength of character, but you must not distance yourself from the ways of our little sisterhood. Dear Rosalie was here today, and she mentioned that you have always refused to let her take photographs of you for our albums. This must stop. You yourself have always enjoyed looking at the albums, and you must be willing to share your charms with me, and with the others.

As for our mistle thrush, she was a weak and foolish

girl, who needlessly threw herself in front of a train. I would have taken her back eventually, I expect. We still have our memories of her, and those pictures of her that we have all enjoyed.

I will remind you, dear one, that you owe me a large sum of money, and that you must make it a priority to discharge that debt as soon as possible. Otherwise, I may call upon you to repay the whole sum immediately.

With fond love,

Your Swan

That, thought Ursula, should bring the little fool back into the fold. I do not need the money, but I will use it to secure her as my *petite amie*. I love her dearly, but I love myself more; so she had better watch out.

1

AWAITING THE GRIM REAPER

GAUNT AND RAVAGED, Sir Montague Fowler lay in his great brass bed, propped up with pillows, his nerveless hands lying placidly on the plum-coloured counterpane. His face, rubicund in health, was now a sullen yellow, and the keen eyes that had been accustomed to miss nothing, seemed to be out of focus. The atmosphere in the room was close, and the tang of carbolic could not quite disguise the distressing smells of a vile, wasting illness.

Outside, in Sparrow Lane, they had laid down straw on the cobbles so that the iron tyres of cabs and carriages would not disturb the Warden's last days.

There were eight people in the room, apart from the dying man. Five of them had come to pay their last respects; the other three, two physicians and a nurse, were there to supervise the passing of Sir Montague Fowler, and, when the moment came, to confirm the cause of death.

Joseph Steadman, the Bursar, stood in a shady recess on the far side of the bed, looking at his old friend. Beside him stood the Vice-Warden, William Podmore, quiet and watchful. To Steadman, the Vice-Warden's presence in that room was an affront to decency. Podmore cared not a jot whether Monty lived or died.

Standing silently at the foot of the bed were the Warden's three children – two sons, one a businessman, the other a clergyman, and a daughter, headmistress of a school for girls. Steadman noted their presence; but all his attention was focused that afternoon on his dying friend.

What had brought the Warden to this appalling state? Monty had been a strong, lively man, a man with a loud, persuasive – but not hectoring – voice, a tall, hook-nosed man with flaming red hair and a beard to match. Whenever he had come into a room, he had filled it with an air of expectancy, as though he was the bearer of great news. The smallest detail of his professional life seemed to have the quality of an event.

And now he lay inert, his eyes open but clearly seeing nothing. Someone – presumably the nurse – had combed his beard so that it lay neat and tamed on the sheet. By this stage in his illness, his faculties had been deliberately numbed with morphia.

Fowler would not be the first Warden of St Michael's to have died in the Lodgings. Thomas Woolnoth, who had built the college library, had died there in 1690, of what had been described as a 'bloody flux'. The great Dr Nehemiah Maddern had expired gently there, in the same room, but not the same bed, in 1801, at the great age of ninety-four, having been Warden for fifty years.

Today was Friday, the first day of June, 1894. The physicians had told the family and the Senior College that Sir Montague would die on the coming Sunday.

Joseph Steadman and Montague Fowler had been friends since boyhood, survivors of the same public school, and former scholars of Lincoln College, though they had never met there. Monty was four years Steadman's senior, and had left Lincoln before Steadman had come up. Fowler had held two very successful lectureships in different colleges, and then had been appointed Principal of St Barnabas' College, which he had transformed from one of Oxford's ailing backwaters into a vibrant and much sought after place for young gentlemen of some learning and much prowess at sport, particularly rowing.

Monty had always pipped him to the post when preferment was offered, just as he had done at school; but Steadman didn't mind too much. Oh, yes, there had been jealous pangs, but they had soon passed. He had been in the running for the Warden's post when old Sir Benjamin Green had retired; but such was Monty's reputation in the university as an administrator, and such was his friendly, irenic nature, that his election as Warden of St Michael's College had been virtually inevitable. Oh, well, it hadn't mattered. Life was not designed to be a bed of roses.

Steadman had come to St Michael's in 1869, when Sir Benjamin Green was still Warden. Podmore, the man standing beside him, was an old alumnus of St Michael's, and had been a member of the Senior Common Room since 1865. When Sir Benjamin retired, Steadman found that he had a little cartel of supporters, as had Podmore. But the Crown had evidently decided that a new broom was needed, and Montague Fowler had been lured away from St Barnabas' College as the most eligible 'outsider.'

Well, it was time now for those with high ambitions to exert themselves, and when it came to ambition, William Podmore, the man standing beside him, had more than enough for the whole college.

Look at him! Or rather, don't look at him. If you do, he'll think you're admiring him. He was looking unusually gaunt and pale, but maybe that was because his lantern jaws were as innocent of hirsute adornment as those of a newborn baby. Some of the undergraduates declared that William Podmore had never shaved, and that he had not developed physically in other directions. Perhaps they were right.

The nurse approached the bed, and wiped Sir Montague

Fowler's forehead with a swab of linen. She glanced at the two doctors, who were standing in the shade of the bed-curtains, and Steadman saw them both shake their heads. Podmore uttered a little sigh, but his cold, incurious eyes remained fixed on the dying man in the bed.

Podmore was Vice-Warden, Tutor in Mathematics, and Consultant Statistician to the Exchequer. He claimed to be a tee-totaller, forever bleating about the virtues of pure spring water, but Haynes, the scout on his staircase, had been seen removing empty gin bottles from his room.

Steadman had never liked Billy Podmore, the stiff and stilted sipper of mineral water. Podmore had beaten him in securing the coveted post of Vice-Warden, which Steadman had always secretly thought should have been his, a sort of con-solation prize for having been passed over for the Wardenship. Steadman believed that Podmore's success had come about through undue influence brought to bear by some faceless people in Whitehall.

Now, no doubt, a few more strings would be pulled, and Billy Podmore would become Warden, as soon as Monty was consigned decently to the grave and forgotten. That was why Podmore was here in the sickroom. He had come to wait for poor Monty to die, and was, no doubt, already making plans for the initial months of his coming Wardenship.

It was time to go. He glanced at Podmore, and the two men quietly left the room. Outside, on the matted landing, two other dons were waiting their turn to pay their last respects. Stanley Fitzmaurice, the Senior Tutor, looked suitably grave. Young Gerald Templar, Junior Dean, bearded in the fashion affected by young men, and wearing a gown that was too large for his slender frame, seemed to Steadman to be mastering a kind of tremor of fearful expectation. What on earth was he expecting to see?

*

In the ancient hall of St Michael's College, the few dons who had elected to dine that June night in 1894 dallied with their port at the high table, where, according to custom, the cloths had been drawn and the decanters set out on their silver tray. All six men contrived not to look at the great carved chair set beneath the portrait of the Marquess of Dorset, the founder of the college, because the chair was empty, and had been so for the past ten anxious days. So powerful had the Warden's personality been that his absence seemed to reduce them all to a rather pathetic collection of individuals rather than part of the coherent body of scholars who constituted the Senior College.

So Dr Joseph Steadman thought, as he sipped his port, and automatically nodded his approbation. They still kept a good cellar at St Michael's, despite Billy Podmore's bleatings about the virtues of pure spring-water. Occasionally, the Warden would treat them to one of the bottles of rare vintages that he had amassed in his own spacious cellar beneath the Lodgings.

They had had clear soup, which, in the way of such things, was stronger on clarity than flavour. The cutlets had been tolerable, though the cook had never mastered the art of boiling potatoes. No amount of parsley sprinkled promiscuously like confetti could atone for potatoes with hearts of stone.

Steadman had made a point of recalling the dinner menus for the last three weeks. The cook had rung his usual changes on their standard fare of beef, lamb and pork, roast, braised or boiled; two curries had signalled to them that some joints of meat were about to go on the turn. Could it have been one of those curries? They had had curried beef on the night before the Warden had left for a visit to friends in the country.

He could recall the very day. It was a Friday, the eighteenth of May, a lovely early summer day: warm, but with a light breeze seeking its way through the main gate of the college from Swallow Lane. He, Podmore and the Warden had stood talking for a while in the coffered vestibule of the lodge, waiting for the cab that would take Sir Montague to the station.

'It's just for a few days, gentlemen,' the Warden had said. 'As you know, it's the time of year when I like to hide myself away in the country for a little while, staying with some old friends from earlier days. Podmore, will you receive the land-agent on Monday? And Steadman, when you send the battels bills out, will you enclose a note suggesting prompt payment? Our young gentlemen are getting rather lax over paying their way!'

Monty had been dressed for the country in a rather racy tweed suit, and with one of the new soft felt hats sitting atop his mane of red hair. His eyes had held a twinkling anticipation of pleasures to come. How well he had looked! His booming voice – he'd never been able to whisper – had brought one of the porter's out of the lodge to see if anything was amiss.

And then he had gone, clambering delicately through the wicket gate and on to the pavement in Swallow Lane where his cab had drawn up. It was like contemplating a vanished world.

It had been one of Monty's little foibles that he would never tell them what friends he was going to visit. He would smile, and wag an admonitory finger, usually adding words to the effect that if he told them, they'd bother him with telegrams bidding him return to put something right that they were more than capable of fixing themselves!

When they saw him next, he was like an animated corpse, pale and gaunt, and scarcely able to speak. It was distressingly clear that he could not possibly survive the week.

How Steadman loved this place! He was a bachelor, so that he lived in college in his own set of rooms in a corner of the second quad, conveniently adjacent to the Senior Common Room. He was part of the fabric of St Michael's. At 58, he knew that no further promotion could be his, and was more than content with his lot.

He glanced around the hall, and as always was thrilled with

its antique beauty. It dated from 1480, one year after Thomas Grey, Marquess of Dorset, stepson of Edward IV, had established the college as 'a place of abode for twelve poor scholars, learned in Latin, and in the mathematical arts'. It was panelled throughout in ancient oak, upon which hung numerous portraits, and was lighted by a fine window, full of writhing Gothic mullion-work, its leaded glass adorned with the dim shields and achievements of long-extinct noble families who had provided the college's early benefactors.

Above the high table, and the long oak tables running the length of the hall, at which the undergraduates were dining off rougher fare than their elders, the magnificent hammer-beam roof could be dimly discerned in what light reached it from the flickering candles set in silver candelabra on the tables.

'You seem unusually pensive tonight, Bursar,' said Podmore. 'Won't you share your thoughts with the rest of us?' Evidently Billy had broken the gloomy silence because it was becoming intolerable. Well, thought Steadman, better play the game.

'I was musing on the folly of this sort of life,' said Joseph Steadman, mendaciously. 'I am fifty-eight years old, and have sat at this table for twenty-five years. Not like you, Fitzmaurice, who used to be a dashing soldier, serving the Queen "in lands afar remote". Did I make that up, or is it a quotation?'

'It's from Henry IV,' observed Gerald Templar, from his seat at the end of the table.

'Oh, is it? How did you know that? You're a chemist.'

'We did it at school, Bursar,' said the Junior Dean. 'They were rather keen on Shakespeare at St Paul's. Fortunately for me, they were rather keen on chemistry, too!'

'You may not know this,' said Steadman, 'but I myself was very tempted to pursue a military career in my youth. Someone told me the other day that I'd have been a major-general by now if I hadn't abandoned the idea, and holed myself up here with poor Monty in this benighted backwater.'

Steadman saw his audience shift uncomfortably at this unexpected familiarity, and he hastily corrected himself.

'"Monty" was my name for the Warden when we were boys. I meant no disrespect to Sir Montague Fowler, when I spoke of him by that name. Well, he went far, and I went nowhere....'

'Hardly nowhere, Bursar,' said the Vice-Warden. 'As well as Bursar, you're Reader in Hebrew, Aramaic and Coptic, and author of that book on the decipherment of Akkadian ...'

'Yes, yes, Vice-Warden, but don't you see that it was all an intellectual waste! No one will ever read my book, or my academic papers. I've had no undergraduates for years, for no self-respecting young fellow would waste his time on what I offer. You see, in reality I'm the college plumber and gardener – no, don't laugh, gentlemen, because it's true! I'm commended by all for making the flowerbeds in the quadrangles my special remit.'

'Very well, I'll grant you gardener. But plumber?'

'If a washer comes off a tap in the night, I'll find myself summoned to a frightful overflow by a quaking undergraduate. That's one of the penalties of being a bachelor, and living in college. Those young men know that they can rely on "old Joe", as they call me, to put things right. Gardener and plumber.'

'"Old Joe?" Surely they are not so disrespectful?' said the Vice-Warden. He had refused the port decanter, and was sipping from a glass of spring-water.

Dr Joseph Steadman threw back his head and laughed, and the sound of his restored sense of humour banished the tension that had been building up during dinner.

'Anyway, Bursar,' said Stanley Fitzmaurice, 'I for one deny all this talk of gardening and plumbing. Everyone in the university regards you as a supreme master in your field. But if a washer fails on my sink, I'll know where to come!'

Good old Stanley! He was a man Steadman could talk to without feeling like a blithering old fool. Captain Stanley

Fitzmaurice – alert, bright-eyed, and just turned forty – was Senior Tutor, college lecturer in Russian, and University Professor of Slavonic Languages. A normal, no nonsense, utterly decent and fiendishly learned man.

'Time to adjourn to the common-room, gentlemen,' said Dr William Podmore, the Vice-Warden. He banged on the table with a small gavel, and there came a scraping of boots as the undergraduate body rose untidily to hear the recessional grace.

2

ANOTHER DEATH IN THE LODGINGS

When they left the hall, Stanley Fitzmaurice walked through the second quadrangle in company with the Junior Dean. Ever since the young chemist had arrived at St Michael's, just over a year earlier, Fitzmaurice had appointed himself a kind of unofficial mentor to the younger man.

What a wild fellow he looked! He wore one of the new artfully untidy beards that many modern young men favoured, and regarded the world warily through glittering gold pincenez. His evening clothes were baggy and a bit threadbare, and his academic gown, green and rusty, and too large, was quite obviously second-hand.

Templar's gait, he saw, was ever so slightly unsteady: no doubt he was grateful for the cool breeze of the June night, which would rapidly banish the fumes of vintage port from his befuddled head. Templar had evidently not yet grown accustomed to the extravagant libations of wine and spirits that accompanied every college dinner.

The two men could hear the desultory conversation of the other dons, who had preceded them, their boots crunching on the shale paths. As they rounded the corner that would take them to the Senior Common Room, several rather mournful sets of chimes from various quarters of the town announced that it was nine o'clock.

'You're very quiet this evening, Templar,' said Captain Fitzmaurice, glancing at his young friend. 'Is anything the matter?'

'No … no,' the younger man replied. 'But my mind's full of that harrowing visit we made to the Lodgings this afternoon. I fancy myself as an observer of men – and women, too – and I studied the faces of the family and the physicians as they stood around the bed, looking down at that – that ruin of a once-great man….'

'Ah! I thought it might be that. Give the Common Room a miss tonight, Templar, and come and smoke a cigar in my rooms. I've a little spirit stove there, and I'll warm up some coffee. Then you can tell me what you saw in those faces.'

A low fire was still burning in the grate of Fitzmaurice's sitting room, and the two men made themselves comfortable in well-used leather armchairs flanking the ancient stone fireplace. Fitzmaurice lit the candles, and then busied himself for a while preparing coffee. Presently, he and his guest were smoking the thin cheroots that Fitzmaurice favoured.

'So you studied the faces of the family and the physicians, Templar,' Fitzmaurice said, sipping his coffee. 'What did you read there?'

'I looked at the elder of the two sons, first – at least, I assume he was the elder: a well set up, pleasant-looking man in his thirties. He was dressed very formally, but didn't look a formal sort of man, if you understand me. He looked worried. More worried than sad.'

'That was indeed the elder son, John Fowler. He's a business-man, a commodity broker in the City. I think he's a partner in an old-established firm. Doing very well, by all accounts.'

'Well,' Templar continued, 'Mr John Fowler seemed to be genuinely distressed, unable even to glance at that awful bed. And yet the only time I saw him do so, his face showed not sorrow but vexation – not anger, you know, just vexation about something. And twice he slipped his watch from his pocket, as though he was anxious for the whole business to end. Nothing sinister there, you understand, but odd. Yes, decidedly odd....'

'And what did you see in Timothy's face – he's the younger son, the clergyman.'

'He seemed very calm to me, very accepting of the situation, which I suppose you'd expect from a man of the cloth.'

'He's a nice chap by all accounts,' said Fitzmaurice. 'He's curate to a decrepit old buffer out in the country somewhere. He married a girl of eighteen, just before he was ordained. Timothy, I mean, not the old buffer. John's married, too. He and his wife have two young children.'

'And then I looked at the daughter....'

'Ah, yes, the interesting Frances. And what did you see in *her* countenance? She's still in her twenties, and very attractive, as you no doubt saw. Nobody likes her, by all accounts. The ice-maiden, they call her.' Fitzmaurice laughed.

'I thought she was a commanding, haughty young woman,' said Gerald Templar. 'Very elegant, but rather forbidding. I had a few words with the sons, but I never ventured to speak to her. What does she do?'

'She's a headmistress, believe it or not! She graduated from London University, where she went with her father's permission, and at the tender age of twenty-three, just two years ago, she founded a school for young ladies with pretentions, out near Port Meadow, somewhere.'

'A girls' school? That's a brave thing for a young woman to do. What's it called?'

'Makin House. Apparently, Makin was some kind of

bluestocking who lived in the seventeenth century. So that's Frances for you. She's not married, of course.'

'Why "of course"?'

'Well, those women have to choose between domesticity or academe. It seems that they can't do both. Rather like nuns, I suppose. The Warden's very keen on her marrying some eligible young man, as a means of curing her of her desire to be a schoolmarm. He's trailed a few hopeful fellows past her, and gave her a rather splendid coming-out dance in London, when she was still at the university, but he's had no success so far. And what did you read in the fair Fanny's face?'

'Anger', said Templar. 'Pent-up anger and resentment. She looked as though she'd like to have murdered poor Sir Montague, and was vexed that nature or Providence was about to deny her that dubious pleasure. I saw…. Well, never mind what I saw.'

'Whatever it was, it won't go beyond these four walls. Come on, man, what did you see?'

'I was watching the nurse, who was doing something with bottles at the bedside. She chanced to look up from her work, and I saw her eyes widen with some kind of shock. She was looking at someone in the room, and when I glanced round, I realized that she had caught a dreadful expression of despair on Frances's face. It was gone almost immediately, but both the nurse and I saw it.'

'What do you think it meant?'

'It was nothing to do with her father, of that I'm convinced. It was some private thing – some memory or recollection. I've never seen despair so forcefully caught by a woman's expression. It was as though she had just had a glimpse of Hell.'

Captain Stanley Fitzmaurice looked thoughtfully at his friend.

'You haven't fallen for her, have you, Templar? Are you going to chance your arm with her?'

Templar seemed not to have heard his friend's half-bantering remarks.

'That look of despair shocked me,' he said, 'but it was the first expression, the anger, that I didn't like. There was some festering resentment there that was out of place at what is, in fact, a death-bed. That's why I fell to studying the faces of those two physicians. The older one had obviously accepted the situation at face value, and was preparing for the last ministrations. The younger man – the stout little fellow – seemed uneasy to me. It made me wonder....'

Fitzmaurice's face grew suddenly grave, and he put down his coffee cup on the floor beside his chair. Templar watched him. Were his words going to have the effect that he had desired?

'It made you wonder, did it?' said Fitzmaurice. 'Well, to tell you the truth, my own thoughts have wandered along the same sinister path. I'm not a scientist, and I know nothing of poisons and suchlike, but you are, and you will know what mischief can be wrought with the tools of your trade. But it's only a professional interest on your part, Templar. Don't let your imagination run away with you.'

'A little while after we'd all left the room,' said Templar, 'I went back, and managed to have a few words with that younger doctor. He seemed to think that I was a member of the family, and I didn't undeceive him. I asked him about the nature of Sir Montague's illness. He told me that he was suffering from severe gastroenteritis, with the expected diarrhoea, and bleeding from the stomach and bowels. They had applied white of eggs, as is customary, apparently, but with little beneficial effect. He told me that the Warden would succumb to fatal nephritis and circulatory collapse. Nothing more could be done.'

'You seem very *au fait* with the terminology.'

'I am. My father was a doctor.'

Templar looked at his friend, whose returning glance confirmed for him what had so far remained unspoken.

'So he is dying of a condition caused, probably, by eating meat which was on the turn, or rotten shellfish,' said Fitzmaurice, thoughtfully, 'or some other food that had become unfit to eat. He's suffering from gastroenteritis.'

'He is,' Templar replied. 'Or maybe someone has given him white arsenic, or even mercuric chloride. But as you say, this is a purely academic exercise on our part. Or is it? Do you know, I can't bear the thought of his leaving us.'

'I didn't think you cared much for him,' said Fitzmaurice. 'After all, he put paid to your dreams of a chemical laboratory here in college.'

'I care for him a great deal. He knew that I had neither money nor influence when I applied for the tutorship in chemistry – his foundation, incidentally. My mother died when I was a child, and my father perished in a cholera epidemic at Salford. I had no expectations, and the only references I could bring him were a letter of commendation from a vicar, and a report from the Headmaster of St Paul's – I was a scholarship boy there.'

'I didn't know that,' said Fitzmaurice. 'All honour to you that you proved the best candidate for the post. What happened about the proposed laboratory? You've never spoken about the matter since the project fell through.'

'As soon as I was appointed, and made Junior Dean, I looked around for somewhere to site a working laboratory for my undergraduates. As you know, the university has its own chemical laboratory, a sort of octagon behind the Natural History Museum in Parks Road, where Professor Oddling is based. But a teaching laboratory in a constituent college of the university would have been a first, and would have drawn attention to St Michael's as a college in the forefront of the development of science teaching here in Oxford.'

'And where would you have sited this laboratory? Really, Templar, I think I've caught some of your enthusiasm for the project! What did the Warden say?'

'You know that there are four empty storerooms on the first floor of staircase XVIII in the third quad? Well, that was the place I had in mind. The Warden and Podmore came up there to survey the rooms, and Sir Montague was quite enthusiastic. "It's an exciting thought, Templar," he said, "and I agree in principle. I'll need to consult the Bursar, and the Vice-Warden first, of course, but – yes, I'm excited at the idea."'

Gerard Templar banged his first on the arm of his chair. His face flushed with anger.

'And that was the end of it, Fitzmaurice! Joe – the Bursar, I mean – saw no impediment, but it was Podmore who scuppered the project. He's an obscurantist, one of those men who can't stand the idea of progress. The natural sciences were anathema to him. I'd already made contact with Marlborough and Wellington, hinting that within a year their brightest boys of a scientific bent could be properly accommodated here at St Michael's.

'And then Podmore vetoed the idea, and the Warden gave in to him. Podmore dislikes me, and the feeling's mutual. I lost credibility with the schools I'd approached, but more serious was the fact that Podmore went out to Parks Road and told Professor Oddling about it. I gathered later, from what Oddling hinted, that Podmore had suggested the idea for a college laboratory had come from the Warden, and that it was I who had blown cold on the project. I've no proof that that was so, but I'd put nothing past Podmore. I could tell you something else very nasty about our revered Vice-Warden....'

'It's getting late,' said Fitzmaurice, abruptly. 'Finish your coffee, and get away to your bed. Perhaps the light of day will banish these morbid thoughts, and these lingering resentments of yours. And in any case, the Warden's not dead yet!'

*

Sir Montague Fowler died in the Lodgings at seven minutes to eleven on the morning of Sunday, 3 June, 1894. His passing was accompanied by the cacophony of chapel bells summoning the members of St Michael's and adjacent colleges to morning prayer. The chaplain, the Reverend and Honourable Theodore Waynefleet, had been consulted about what to do if the Warden did indeed expire on Sunday morning, and had asserted that the worship of God must come first. And so Sir Montague Fowler passed away to the sound of bells, but with no clergyman to speed him on his way to the next world.

The physicians had washed out the Warden's stomach with bicarbonate of soda as a last medical gesture two hours previously. The family had said their brief farewells, and had retired to the dim parlour on the ground floor. Of the Fellows of the College, Joseph Steadman, the Bursar, together with the Vice-Warden, Dr Podmore, had been present. When the two dons left the bedroom, Podmore plucked Steadman by the sleeve, and drew him into a window embrasure that looked out on to Sparrow Lane.

'By virtue of the college statutes,' Podmore said, 'I assume the office of Acting Warden immediately. I shall need you, Bursar, to act in tandem with me to govern the college until a new Warden is appointed.'

'I knew Monty since we were little boys at school,' Steadman replied, his eyes brimming with unheeded tears. 'I can't believe that he's gone. Where did he catch that vile infection? He was only sixty-two.'

'I know, I know,' said Podmore, looking away in embarrassment. 'We're all diminished by his passing. Come to me in my room, will you, in half an hour's time. There's a lot for us to discuss.'

The Vice-Warden hurried down the stairs, and presently Joseph Steadman heard the front door of the Lodgings closed with a purposeful thud. I shouldn't be surprised, he thought, to find that Billy Podmore's completely unaffected by poor Monty's vile death. His mind's already preoccupied with his successor. And now, no doubt, with the help of his friends at the Exchequer, Podmore will become Warden.

It was at that moment, as he stood on the landing listening to the murmurs of the doctors behind the closed door of Sir Montague's bedroom, that Steadman's dislike of Podmore turned to something more sinister.

The nurse had composed the body, drawn the sheet up over the face, and left the room. Old Dr Hope and young Dr Chambers stood at a table on which an inkpot and a tray of steel-nibbed pens had been placed.

'We are agreed, I think,' said Dr Hope, 'that Sir Montague Fowler died from circulatory collapse consequent upon a fatal nephritis?' His words were couched in the form of a question, but had been composed in the formal wording required by the death certificate. He took up one of the pens, dipped it in ink, carefully signed the legal document lying on the table, and then handed the pen to his young colleague.

Dr Chambers seemed to hesitate. He glanced briefly at the bed, and then said in low tones: 'I have never seen so violent an attack of gastroenteritis. It can only have come from contaminated food, but no one else in the college has been affected. But there is a separate kitchen here, in the Lodgings....'

'You're not suggesting that he was poisoned, are you?' asked Dr Hope dryly. 'What do you think it was? Corrosive sublimate? Arsenious acid?'

Dr Chambers blushed at his colleague's dry mockery, stooped down, and rapidly added his signature to the death certificate.

'Of course not, Dr Hope,' he said. 'It's clear enough what caused Sir Montague's death. But it's been a tragic and horrible case, and the severity of the illness leaves me with an uneasy feeling…. Just a feeling, you know, nothing more.'

The old doctor sighed, and shook his head.

'I've seen things like this before, Chambers,' he said. 'Violent infections in the young; sudden collapses where no sinister lesions had ever been detected; an untreated scythe-wound in a man's foot that led to septic insanity – no two people are ever alike, which is why diagnosis is more a skill than a science….

'By the by, when are you leaving for Surinam? I must say that I admire your spirit of adventure – but rather you than me!'

The young man laughed.

'I leave this coming Wednesday, the sixth, on board the *Pacific Trader*, sailing out of Tilbury. Being a ship's doctor will be a welcome change from this kind of melancholy practice.' He nodded towards the bed. 'We call in at many South American ports before we dock in Dutch Guiana. Can't I persuade you to accompany me?'

The old physician smiled, but said nothing. He picked up his bag from the table, and turned towards the door.

'Disease is much the same anywhere,' he said, 'whether at land or on the sea. But I wish you well. As for me, I've handed my North Oxford practice over to Henshall. I'm well over seventy now, and I'm going to live with my widowed sister in Dorset. I'm glad there's to be no inquest in this case of Sir Montague Fowler. I'm leaving for Dorset on Friday. But come, Chambers, I'll celebrate my retirement by buying you dinner at the Mitre. Our work here is done. It is now the turn of the funeral furnishers.'

3

FAMILY AFFAIRS

A BRIGHT FIRE burning in the wide fireplace added some cheer to the dim ground-floor parlour of the Lodgings. The butler had brought in a tray on which reposed some wine glasses and a decanter of port, together with a plate of sweet biscuits.

'Well,' said John Fowler, warming his coat tails in front of the fire, 'it has been a terrible ordeal for us all, and we must be thankful that Father is now at peace. Yes, at peace after a trying affliction bravely borne.'

'Really, John,' said his sister Frances, 'you are a pompous ass! "Bravely borne", indeed! Father had no other option but to put up with it until his time came to shuffle off this mortal coil.' She turned her attention to the younger of her brothers. 'You're very quiet, Tim. Are you afraid of breaking out into clichés?'

'That's enough, Fanny,' said the Reverend Timothy Fowler, sharply. 'You've no right to speak to John like that. Father is in the hands of God, if I may say that without fear of being called trite.'

Frances Fowler felt herself blushing. She was accustomed to teasing her elder brother, who was quietly tolerant of her outbursts, but rebukes from Timothy always subdued her. He was only four years her senior, but he had been endowed since childhood with a gravitas and a quiet determination that had always left her in awe of him.

John was turning into a hypocrite. He had never been close to Father, and knew perfectly well what a blight he had been to all their hopes and ambitions. As far as she knew, John was a highly successful businessman, but when she had met him at Oxford Station, she had been startled at how gaunt and wild-eyed he had looked. Surely he could not have been so drastically affected by Father's illness? He seemed much better now, more his old self, unassuming, but quietly confident.

Now that Father was gone, maybe all three of them could throw off the shackles with which their parent had weighed them down all their lives. Tim knew all that, and prudently referred their father to the mercies of God.... What was John saying now?

'Father will be buried with Mother at Forest Park. We'll arrange a family service at St Mary's church. Margaret will come down with me for form's sake, and the children can stay with their grandmother till we return. Tim, will you take the service?'

'I will assist the vicar down there,' Timothy Fowler replied. 'I think that would be the right thing to do. But the committal is the vicar's prerogative. Kate will remain at home. She is too delicate to make the long train journey.'

'Good, good,' said John. 'I expect there'll be a memorial service for Father here in Oxford, and one or other of us can put in an appearance for form's sake. Fanny, as you're here on the spot, as it were....'

'It would look very bad, John, if you were not present,' said Frances. 'People might begin to talk.' She treated her brother to a rather unpleasant smile.

'Well, maybe so. Now, as to Father's Will – I had better ask Ballard where it is lodged. It's not with the family solicitors,

I know, so it will most likely be held by a legal man here in Oxford. It would be judicious to hear the Will read before the funeral. Are you content to let me take the matter in hand?'

Brother and sister nodded their agreement. Frances Fowler added a few words.

'Speaking of Ballard,' she said, 'where is he at this moment? I thought he might have wanted to join us, here.'

'Ballard is upstairs, paying his last respects to Father. I told him that it would be quite in order for him to do so.'

'Well,' said Francis, 'when he finally appears, John, make him tell you where Father's Will is lodged. If Father had any money left at all,' she observed, 'he has probably bequeathed it all to found yet another grandiose institute. You may be sure that his children will have been considered last of all. If only poor Mother had lived! She was the only person, apparently, who could restrain him.'

Her elder brother John, who was still standing in front of the fire, frowned, but it was not a frown of anger.

'I heard something in the City last week,' he said, 'something about a "very generous benefaction" for the establishment of some damned institute here. You're right, Fanny: there would have been precious little left for us if these latest schemes of his had been allowed to come to fruition.'

'It's providential, in a way,' said Sir Montague's daughter. 'It's almost as if....'

'That's enough, Fanny,' said her brother, the Reverend Timothy Fowler. 'You go too far in linking Providence with Father's death. "Thou shalt not take the name of the Lord thy God in vain."'

Frances blushed again. Really! It would be a blessing when the two of them had taken themselves off, and left her to her own devices. She managed a faint smile.

'Dear Timothy,' she said, 'you are so unworldly!'

'Perhaps that is a virtue in a clergyman, Fanny,' said

Timothy austerely. 'If you two will excuse me, I'll go up to Father again. He died with no clergyman present, and I intend to say some valedictory prayers.'

Later, after John and Fanny had quitted the parlour, the butler returned, and took away the untouched tray of port wine and sweet biscuits.

The premises of Vane, Paulet and Groom, solicitors and commissioners for oaths, lay in New Inn Hall Street, a quiet thoroughfare that could not make up its mind whether to throw in its lot with the ancient university city, or to hold itself aloof as the beginning of a suburb. Mr Arthur Groom, the junior partner, sat in a big winged chair behind his leather-topped desk, and scrutinized the offspring of the late Sir Montague Fowler as they entered the room. It was Tuesday, 5 June, two days after the passing of the Warden of St Michael's College.

John Fowler had arrived promptly, just as the clocks were striking eleven. Really, he looked a very pleasant man, his face, now set gravely for the business in hand, still revealing in the lines of humour about his eyes and mouth an inclination to smile whenever possible. Or was it weakness? A desire to ingratiate? Perhaps he had cultivated this as a way of disarming his clients. He was, so Arthur Groom had been given to understand, a prosperous discount broker, with offices in the City.

Ah! Here was the Reverend Timothy Fowler, just a minute beyond the appointed time. How old was he? It was hard to tell. Not much over thirty, but his severe clerical garb made him look older. A serious young man, who was reputed to be an excellent pastor, he still gave the impression that any opportunity for advancement would be seized immediately if it came his way. Groom had heard that Timothy Fowler, on the eve of his ordination, had married a very young but penniless lady; so in matters of the heart, the good parson had put love first. Or so it would seem.

Now, here came the spinster sister, Frances, who had been able to combine beauty with academic distinction, but at the cost of forming any kind of romantic attachment. Women of that sort never married.

Sir Montague Fowler's secretary, a self-effacing man called Henry Ballard, had called upon him earlier, and now joined the family from an adjacent room. All three bowed stiffly to him, and he returned the frigid compliment in kind. Arthur Groom cleared his throat, and began to address his now seated audience. How tense the offspring looked! He would enjoy tormenting them for a few minutes before relieving them of all anxiety in the matter of their late father's dispositions.

'Madam, and gentlemen,' said Groom, 'we have assembled here with the intention of hearing the terms of the Will of your late father, Sir Montague Fowler. I have here on the desk, a form of Will drawn up by me on his behalf on Monday, the twenty-second of October last, in which, after various small bequests to servants, and a legacy to his secretary, Mr Henry Ballard, he left the sum of £360,000 free of duty and imposts for the establishment of a School of Medical Jurisprudence in the University of Oxford, a project which had been close to his heart for a number of years. The residue of his estate was to be divided equally among his three children.'

John Fowler had turned pale, and seemed frozen with shock. Timothy remained inscrutable, but a nerve was throbbing in his temple. Frances, the blue-stocking daughter, had flushed with anger, and her eyes had filled with tears. She began to tremble, and Henry Ballard placed a diffident hand upon her arm.

'How – how much?' muttered John Fowler, the elder son.

'Well, after the minor bequests, you would each have received about forty-thousand pounds. Even in these times, that would be a very goodly sum....'

'It's nothing short of outrageous!' John Fowler had sprung up from his chair in agitation. 'Oh, God! What? I heard a rumour in the City that Father was going to squander our money on some damned useless institute or other. We shall contest this Will....'

'Oh, but that wasn't the Will, Mr Fowler! I never said it was, you know. It was merely a draft, and I urged Sir Montague to think very carefully before taking a step that he might have come to regret. This document was never signed, but it was important that you should have been aware of its contents.'

'Then you mean....'

'I mean that all is well as regards your respective legacies.' He held up a second document and showed it to them. What fun it had been! These Will readings were always like a gathering of vultures.

'In this Will, dated 11 February, 1890, after making the usual arrangements for servants, Sir Montague stated his major dispositions as follows:

'"To my faithful and, dare I say it, devoted, secretary, Henry Ballard, I leave the sum of ten thousand pounds free of duty." Yes, Mr Ballard, you may well exclaim! I have never before heard of such a generous bequest to one who is a servant at law. But let me continue. "The residue of my estate, that is to say, the monies lodged by me with Hodge's Bank, of 31a Queen Street, in the City of Oxford, and whatever sums are raised from the sale of my goods and chattels, together with my property in Woodstock Road, also in the City of Oxford, I leave to my three children, John, Timothy and Frances, to be divided equally among them. And I give and bequeath my house, Forest Park, at Lynham Hill, in the county of Wiltshire, to my son John, to enjoy absolutely, or dispose of as he thinks fit. And hereto I set my hand and seal," etcetera, etcetera.'

'How much?' asked John once again.

'Roughly £160,000 each.'

He could feel the elation of the three children like a tangible wave pouring into the room. During his reading of the draft

Will, they had all three sweated with fear, and the atmosphere had become close and stifling. What had those three siblings got to fear? They were all obviously badly in need of money. From their point of view, their father's death had been providential…. Had they…? No, such a thought was gratuitously wicked and uncalled for. John Fowler was saying something.

'We're all very grateful to you, Mr Groom, for dissuading Father from signing that appalling draft. I sometimes think that his brain was softening – but there, one mustn't speak ill of the dead. Please send me your bill as soon as you like. You have my London address.' The elder son turned to look with something like wonder at the self-effacing secretary, who was still sitting stunned in his chair.

'I must say, Ballard, that you were evidently a marvellous help to Father over the years. I congratulate you on a very opulent legacy.' There was no malice there, thought Arthur Groom. Now that John is a man of fortune, he can afford to be magnanimous.

'Well, sir,' Ballard replied. 'I must admit that I am overwhelmed, and deeply moved. I was indeed devoted to Sir Montague, but this … this….' His voice trailed away, and his eyes brimmed with tears. Standing up abruptly, he groped his way out of the room.

'Well,' said Frances Fowler as the brothers and their sister emerged from the solicitor's premises into New Inn Hall Street, 'Ballard may have been the ideal secretary, but ten thousand pounds was ridiculous. Maybe you were right, John. Father was entering his dotage. I'm sure you agree, don't you, Timothy?'

'What? Oh, very likely.'

Frances smiled to herself. Timothy had evidently relapsed into a brown study. Had he really heard what she'd said, he would have regaled her with one of his pious platitudes. Really, there was no earthly reason why a clergyman should be either overtly pious or tediously platitudinous.

They walked up New Inn Hall Street and into Queen Street,

and at Carfax they went their separate ways.

Timothy's elation at the news of his father's bequest had been overshadowed by something that came unbidden into his consciousness. It often came to plague him at moments of sudden happiness or success. It was a scene from his student days, a gently flowing river on a summer's day, a placid scene suddenly marred by a cry of distress and the frantic threshing of cramped limbs.... Shake it off! Banish it! *Sufficient unto the day is the evil thereof.*

'I was overcome, Mr Maxwell. Sir Montague left me what amounts to a fortune. He was always a generous employer, and I was able to put a bit aside during all the years that I worked as his secretary. But this! Ten thousand pounds!'

Henry Ballard sat in the dim, fire-lit bar parlour of the Manciple Tavern, which was to be found at the end of a cobbled alley lying in a tangle of old tenements behind the ancient church of St Peter in the East. He took a sip from his glass of port, and waited for his companion to frame a suitable answer. He liked thickset, belligerent Joe Maxwell, a police officer of the better sort, a detective sergeant no less, and a man who could keep his own counsel. Not very sharp, perhaps, but a good, respectable friend to have.

'Well, of course, Mr Ballard,' said Sergeant Maxwell, stroking his black walrus moustache, 'you and Sir Montague shared a natural affinity for each other, if that's the word I mean. Affinity. So I'm not surprised to hear that he left you a legacy. But I'd agree that ten thousand pounds is a hefty sum.' He drank deeply from a pewter tankard of mild ale.

'Did you – er – see the deceased after he was dead? Well, of course, he must have been dead if he was deceased. I just wondered whether the family had let you view him. I hope I'm not being indelicate.'

Henry Ballard did not reply immediately. His mind flew

back to the previous Sunday, when Mr John had sought him out in the Lodgings, and told him that he was welcome to view the body of his late employer. 'It's only right, Ballard,' he'd said. 'You were very close to my father, and he to you.' Mr John had always been a kind and courteous gentleman.

'I went into Sir Montague's bedroom,' said Ballard to his friend, 'and reverently turned down the sheet that was covering his face. As you may imagine, Mr Maxwell, his face was white and gaunt, and it still held the marks of prolonged suffering.'

Sergeant Joseph Maxwell saw his friend's eyes brim with tears. Yes, he mused, Henry had been very much attached to his employer, and he to him. Ten thousand pounds.... It made you think.

'His cheeks seemed to have collapsed inward,' Ballard continued, 'making him look far older than his years – he was only sixty-two – but that fine Roman nose was as intimidating as it had been in life. Not intimidating to me, you understand; but many people held him in awe because of his patrician appearance. He was always approachable, you know, but people knew from his general deportment that "Noli me tangere" applied very well to him.'

Sergeant Maxwell nodded his agreement, and drank some more of his ale. Henry was a good man, but at times it was impossible to know what he was talking about. 'Patrician', and that bit of Latin – what did it mean? He'd lose face if he asked him outright.

'You're quite right, Mr Ballard,' he said. 'I'm sure those words certainly applied to poor Sir Montague in life.'

'They did,' Ballard agreed, 'and despite the ravages of the last ten days, his mortal remains still retained an air of solemn dignity. I shall never forget him.'

'Food poisoning, wasn't it? You don't expect that in the winter, it's more of a summer malady, if I may put it like that. There was a family last summer out at Headington who consumed a tainted lobster one warm evening for their tea, and all died. Father, mother, and two children. Very sad, really.'

'Yes,' Henry Ballard continued, 'these things are really tragic. Sir Montague had left Oxford on a visit to a friend in the country on the eighteenth of May. He returned, looking pale and agonized, on the twenty-second. That same afternoon he took to his bed, and never left it. Severe gastroenteritis was diagnosed, and at first the physicians were cautiously confident that he might recover with time. Indeed, when they had induced Sir Montague to swallow white of eggs, there was a temporary rally. That was on the twenty-fifth; but on the Monday following, nephritis supervened, and the two doctors warned the family that the case was hopeless.'

Ballard's eyes once more filled with tears, which this time he angrily dashed away. He remembered how, in the chamber of death, his tears had fallen upon the Warden's dead face.

'Have you heard ...' Maxwell began, but Ballard stopped him abruptly by raising an admonitory hand.

'Yes, I have heard,' he replied. 'He's only been dead a few days, and already the rumours are going the rounds. People aren't content with the accidents of human life: they seek for sinister explanations. The Senior Common Room has been airing the lethal properties of various poisons, as though the death of the Warden was a mere intellectual problem. The Common Room butler told me that. I think it's all wicked nonsense.'

Later that day, Sergeant Maxwell encountered one of the Fellows of Magdalen College in the High. Maxwell had cleared up an incident of petty theft at the college, and had helped this particular don to avoid a scandal.

'Sir,' Maxwell asked, 'if I was to mention the word nephritis, would you oblige me by telling me what it means?'

'Why, certainly, Sergeant. It means inflammation of the kidneys.'

'And supervened, sir? What would you say that meant?'

'It means that something followed closely after something else.'

'Well, thank you, sir,' said Maxwell. 'I'm much obliged to you.'

As the college Fellow walked away, he thought to himself: Now, who has he been talking to? Evidently the police are taking notice of all this gossip about poor Fowler's death. It makes one wonder....

The Reverend Timothy Fowler was quietly satisfied with his wife's preparations to receive their distinguished neighbour Lord Stevenage at the curate's house. Dear Kate, she was now twenty-four, but had lost none of her endearing timidity and lack of self-confidence, so that even a quiet dinner for three presented her with a daunting challenge.

She had been assisted in the preparation of dinner by a rather clumsy but good natured village maiden whom they called the Slow Girl. Between them they had prepared oxtail soup, roast lamb with boiled potatoes, and a ginger pudding – all this in the minute kitchen with its old-fashioned rusted iron range.

'I suppose you could describe this little house as bijou, or conveniently compact,' observed Lord Stevenage, waving his fork in the general direction of his host, 'but others would say it was not only cramped, but riddled with dry rot. With all due respect, Fowler, it should be pulled down as soon as possible.'

Lord Stevenage, a white-haired, red-complexioned man in his mid-sixties, was the patron of the living of Clapton Parva, and owner of the advowson. He had a lot of respect for the curate of the parish, and had determined to do all that he could to liberate the young man from the genteel poverty in which he lived. He was also very fond of Kate Fowler, a very pretty, delicate and rather clinging type of girl who was the mistress of the mildewed house.

'On the other hand,' Lord Stevenage continued, 'the vicarage is a very fine house – a very fine house indeed. Poor old Canon Gossinge lives only in a couple of rooms on the ground floor.... I think the Bishop will have to move in the matter very soon. Gossinge has become senile, and he is quite unable now to carry out his clerical duties. He stood in for you, of course, on Sunday, and it was – well, it was embarrassing, to say the least. The burden of the whole parish is falling upon your shoulders – the services, the visiting, etcetera, all on a curate's stipend of seventy-eight pounds a year.'

Young Mrs Fowler was gazing at Stevenage as though he was the most fascinating man on earth. Her big violet eyes looked into his with what seemed to be awed devotion.

'So here's what I propose to do. Gossinge can't last the year out. I want you to have the parish, and I want you to achieve total security in the living. Gossinge is the incumbent, but I am the lay rector, as I think you understand. Twice during the last year I've offered to sell you the advowson for £1,000, and twice you told me that it was not possible. I will now offer you the advowson for £800. This will mean that, once you are appointed, the parish will be yours in perpetuity, together with the stipend from Queen Anne's Bounty of £180 per annum. Following the sad death of your father, and the reading of his will, I assume that you will now have expectations. This, by the way, will be my last offer in the matter.'

'You are very, very kind, Lord Stevenage,' said Timothy Fowler. 'And you are right in assuming that I have received a very substantial legacy. I hope that you will be able to wait just a day or two until the first cash payments of my inheritance have passed into my bank?'

'Of course, of course. You've done marvellous work here, and I want to see that work expanded, so that you and Mrs Fowler can live decently, as gentlefolk should. More claret? Thank you, my dear, I think I could enjoy another glass, and then I must bid you goodnight. Meanwhile, let's all rejoice at your well-deserved good fortune. What is it that Browning said? Or was it Matthew Arnold? "God's in his heaven, all's right with the world!"'

'Oh, Tim,' said young Mrs Fowler, after Lord Stevenage had departed, and the Slow Girl was washing up in the black slate sink, 'how kind he is! And you're quite sure that your papa has left you enough to buy the – whatever he called it?'

'The advowson? Oh, yes, my dear. There will be no difficulty about that, now. On those two previous occasions when I approached Father for help, he refused. He accused me of wanting to live in idle luxury, and said that he had other, more worthy, calls upon his purse. Well, all that is changed, now. Not only us, but John and Fanny have come into very decent inheritances. When we're alone tonight, my dear, I will give you the full details – I don't want to speak while the Slow Girl is in the house.'

'Oh, I'm so glad, Tim,' cried Tim's wife. 'If I'd had to live much longer in this damp ruin of a house I would have died!'

'Don't worry, little one. As Fanny rather unkindly observed, Father's death came just in time to save the whole family from ruin. You'll see: all will be well.'

He took one of her hands, and kissed it tenderly.

'You are content, aren't you, my love?' he said. 'You've no regrets about … about what might have been?'

'Oh, no, dear Tim,' said Timothy's wife, 'I've no regrets at all! Especially as we can leave this dreadful house now, and live somewhere really decent!'

Early the next morning, after breakfast, Timothy Fowler set off on his daily round of visiting. The sun had not yet risen, and the fields surrounding the little Hampshire village were clothed in low-lying mist, but Timothy felt an inward exhilaration that belied his sober clerical garb and wide-brimmed parson's hat.

He turned out of a side-lane and into the village street, his eyes turning automatically to the gracious, ivy-covered vicarage, the grounds of which faced the wide thoroughfare. Built in 1712, it was a fine example of the spacious and elegant architecture of that period. Very soon, if God so willed it, it would be his – his and Kate's.

A villager leading a horse from the livery stable greeted him deferentially, and he raised his hat it return. These poor folk had been suspicious of the new curate at first, but had soon warmed to his generosity and genuine concern for their spiritual and physical welfare. He had his own ambitions, but if he were appointed vicar of Clapton Parva he would be quite content to remain there for the rest of his life.

Both Kate and he loved the rolling fields and the gentle hills clothed with woodland that surrounded the village. They enjoyed the company of Lord Stevenage, who lived at Clapton Hall with his lady wife and three lively daughters. Yes, their life was about to take a decided turn for the better.

When Timothy reached the lively brook that flowed under a little bridge near the village inn, the sound of the water seemed to be interrupted for a brief moment by a strangled cry. *Help!* But of course there was no one there. He crossed the bridge, which led to a quiet lane, and in his mind's eye he saw the fresh and lively face of a young man, which still held the look of reproach that had seared him to the heart all those years ago. Death by water....

At his ordination to the priesthood, when the Bishop laid his hands on his head, he had seen the same censorious face in his mind's eye, and heard the reproaches from the lips of a man long dead.

Time to get on! What's done is done, as Lady Macbeth declared. The future, bright and hopeful, beckoned.

Kate Fowler was vexed. She had received a long letter from

her mother on the day of Lord Stevenage's visit, and had sat reading it in Tim's cramped little study. It was full of delicious gossip about various neighbours and their erring children, and amusing tales about her father, whom Mother always referred to as 'The Household Manager'. When the Slow Girl had arrived at the kitchen door, Kate had pushed the letter into her husband's desk.

And now, to her great annoyance, she realized that Tim had locked the desk before leaving that morning. Well, she wasn't going to sit doing nothing while the reading of Mama's letter remained unfinished. She knew where there was a second key!

Kate sat down at the now open desk, and unfolded the letter, but something in one of the pigeon-holes of the desk caught her eye. What could it be? She withdrew a blue paper packet, carefully sealed at each end with gummed wafers. A handwritten label told her what the packet contained. Kate's face was suddenly drained of blood, and her violet eyes opened wide in horror.

'Oh, Tim, Tim,' she whispered, 'what have you done? And what am I to do? Oh, Mama, Mama! How I wish you were here!'

Removing the letter, she locked the desk, and stumbled in tears from her husband's study.

4

A VISITOR TO MAKIN HOUSE

FRANCES FOWLER STOOD at the window of her study, and looked out at the wide expanse of common land known as Port Meadow. A few horses were grazing some fifty yards away from the rear wall of the house: freemen still had the right to graze their animals without cost there, a privilege granted to them in the tenth century. It was a very warm summer's day, with not the slightest hint of a breeze, and she could see people walking their dogs far away to the south, where the suburb of Jericho petered out, and the untamed sheep-nibbled grass of the common began.

She was waiting for the arrival of Mr Harkness, the landlord of the house and its two acres of gardens, and had ordered coffee to be brought as soon as he was announced. Harkness, a plump, balding man whose suits seemed almost comically tight, was a decent fellow enough, but he knew the value of money, and constantly asserted that 'times are hard, Miss.'

She agreed with him. The first quarter's rent had been due in March, and she had still not been able to pay him. In a couple of weeks' time, the second quarter would be due. Mr Harkness could not be expected to wait any longer, and had declared his intention of calling on her that Monday morning to ask what she proposed to do about the matter. Well, he would have his answer.

Frances Fowler had gone up to King's College, London University, in 1887, when she was eighteen. She had worked fiendishly hard, and had graduated with First Class Honours in Modern Languages in 1890. Then, when only twenty-three, she had founded Makin House School. Her father had reluctantly given her two hundred pounds to help her secure the tenancy of what had then been called Sevastopol Lodge, and she had opened her school. There were three other young women tutors, and together they covered all the entrance requirements for the University of Oxford.

Father had been quite unable to conceal his amusement at the whole venture, but had been content to let her have her way. She remembered calling at St Michael's to receive his cheque, and hearing him say to her brother Timothy, who had been visiting the Lodgings, 'I'm content to lose the money in this romantic venture, Tim, because it will give the girl time to realize how fatuous the whole idea is. When it fails, she'll see that her future lies with making a good marriage, and giving me some lusty grandchildren!'

Well, there would be no 'lusty grandchildren', and she would no longer have to endure the brief company of any more of Father's 'eligible young men' whom he had persisted in pro-curing for her. There had only ever been one young man in her life, a fellow student at King's, who had cynically used her for his own manly pleasure, and then abandoned her. Desperate, she had endured a secret pregnancy while pursuing her studies, and then had suffered a miscarriage, brought on by a fall in the street, which had freed her from her almost unen-durable torment. No one had ever known or even suspected what had happened to her, and when her father had thrown a coming-out dance for her in London, she had put up with the attentions of her chosen 'escort' for her father's sake. But she had sworn to herself that none of these predators would ever again seek to enslave her and diminish her integrity.

And her school had not failed. She had started with five girls from sympathetic families, and two of them had already secured places at Lady Margaret Hall and Somerville College respectively. Word of Makin House had come to the ears of other fathers of academically able daughters, and she now had twenty-three pupils.

It would soon be imperative to engage two more tutors, and contemplate building an extension to the old sandstone house, put up in the Gothic style in the forties, and full of quirky little staircases and closets. Everyone, tutors and pupils alike, loved the house, and its 'great hall', a long drawing-room with tables for four and a miniature high table for the tutors; it looked for all the world like one of the genteel cafés that you found in High Street or the Cornmarket.

A knock on the door heralded the arrival of Mr Harkness, preceded by Trixie, the maid, who brought in a tray containing a jug of coffee and some currant biscuits. The visitor lowered himself into a chair, cleared his throat, and began to speak.

'You must agree with me, Miss Fowler,' he said, 'that times are hard....'

'Oh, I do agree with you, Mr Harkness!' Frances replied. 'Will you have some coffee? That's right. How are you? And how are Mrs Harkness and the boys?'

'They're well, they're flourishing, Miss. But times are hard, and money is tight. So I very much regret that I have to ask you to pay me my due now. Otherwise, I shall have to – well, turn you out, Miss, that's the long and short of it.'

He managed a deprecating smile, but she could see from the hard glint in his eyes that he meant it. She sat down at her desk, and removed a slip of paper from under the blotter.

'There you are, Mr Harkness,' she said, her heart beating rapidly with a kind of triumphant joy, 'there's a cheque to cover the entire rent till the end of the year. It was very good of you to wait so long, and to be so forbearing.'

She saw him visibly relax, though his face still showed incredulity. Poor man! No doubt he had urgent creditors of his own badgering him for money.

'Well, Miss,' he said, carefully putting the cheque into his wallet, 'I'm very pleased that there's been no need for unpleasantness. This coffee is very good. Very good indeed.'

'Let me pour you some more, Mr Harkness,' said Frances. 'Now, I have a proposition to put to you. This is a very pleasant house, even though gas hasn't yet been laid on. A very pleasant house. What would you take for it?'

'Take for it? Why, Miss Fowler, whatever do you mean?'

'I mean, would you sell it to me, together with the two acres of ground? And the lease? What would you take?'

'Well, let me see.... I should want four hundred pound for the house, and two hundred and fifty for the two acres of land. As for the lease.... That's a very valuable commodity, and something that I'd be unwilling to part with. I couldn't let it go for under two hundred. So altogether, Miss, you'd have to part with four, and two-fifty, and two, that's eight hundred and fifty pounds. It's a lot of money. A fortune, really.'

'It is a fortune, I agree,' said Frances, 'but if you'll make it a round eight-hundred, I'll buy it immediately. You can see my solicitor, or send yours to him, or whatever it is you do, but yes, I'll buy it all.'

'Well, Miss, I'm overwhelmed. I don't know what to say. Eight hundred will be quite all right. And I hope it won't be out of order if I offer you my sympathy for the death of Sir Montague Fowler. A wonderful gentleman. And I, for one, Miss, don't believe a word of these rumours that are going around. No, indeed. So I'll bid you good morning, and God speed!'

When Harkness had gone, clearly delighted and profuse in his thanks, Frances sat down at her desk and thought. How money talked! If Father hadn't died when he did, she would have lost the house, lost the school, and entered the pathetic pool of young women in their mid-twenties looking for a man with sufficient money to keep them in some kind of genteel domesticity.

And she would have lost something else, something infinitely precious, a special friendship that was now to be hers again. She opened a drawer in her desk, and withdrew the letter that had come that very morning. The envelope was plain and businesslike, but the sheet of notepaper inside it was pale mauve and perfumed.

Dearest Child,

How wonderful it was to receive your cheque for the entire amount of the loan, and for your current subscription! How wonderful, too, to receive your assurances of undying love! I return that love, and ask your pardon for any brusqueness in previous letters to you. Come soon, and you will see how much my love for you has endured. Would that you would bind yourself more closely to us by yielding to Rosalie's desire to photograph you for the albums! That would be the perfection of trust on your part.

With all my love, I remain always
Your Swan.

She would visit the house in Old Bond Street as soon as was possible. And as for Rosalie's desire to take pictures of her – well, why not? It was the last leap that would take her into a world that she had already more than half entered. In any case, if she wished to build up a school that was to last and endure into the next century, she would have to remain single. She saw no difficulties about that.

Francis opened the glazed door of a bookcase and extracted

an ancient, scuffed volume bound in calf. The spine-label was missing, and the joints had sprung, but she handled the book with a special kind of reverence. Placing it carefully on her desk, she opened it at the title page.

An Essay to Revive the Antient Education of Gentlewomen
By Mrs Bathsua Makin
London: Privately Printed
1673

She had named her school Makin House, after this erudite, pioneering woman, who had lived from 1600 to 1676. Brought up in her father's school, she had produced a volume of Greek and Latin verse at the age of 16, and had later founded schools of her own for both boys and girls. In the 1640s she had been appointed tutor to Princess Elizabeth, the daughter of Charles I. A 'dutiful' wife, she had produced twelve children of her own. Who had even heard of her now?

Frances turned over the pages of the book, until she came to a passage that she had underlined in pencil. It was one of Bathsua's especially mordant comments, and a favourite with Frances.

'Had God intended Women only as a finer sort of Cattle, he would not have made them reasonable.... Monkeys (which the Indians use, to do many Offices) might have better fitted some men's Lust, Pride, and Pleasure.'

Smiling to herself, she closed the book and returned it to the bookcase. It would not do, she mused, to let her brother Timothy read the forthright views of Mrs Bathsua Makin.

Poor Timothy.... Did he know that his silly little wife Kate was incapable of keeping his secrets? Frances had that very morning received a hysterical letter from her sister-in-law, a letter containing information that she had been mad to commit to paper. Kate was a dear girl, very pretty, but dangerously immature, and totally dependent on Timothy in the sense that his views were hers, his opinions were hers; she no longer had any individual life of her own. Mrs Makin would not have approved.

Frances had written a reply, telling Kate to keep her own counsel and to show more trust in her husband. There was, she was quite sure, a simple explanation. It would be foolish to mention the matter to Timothy, and 'undutiful' to speak of it to anyone else. What a wealth of hypocrisy lay in that word!

Kate might well get her letter in the evening's post; if not, she would certainly receive it tomorrow. She would not be at Father's funeral, because Timothy deemed her to be too 'delicate' to attend. What a fool he was! And yet, she went in such awe of him that she had never been able to summon up sufficient courage to tell him that there was nothing wrong with Kate other than youth and inexperience. That particular delicate flower would, no doubt, survive all kinds of inclement weather, and outlive them all.

Frances left her study, and descended the main staircase. She could hear the subdued murmurs of staff and pupils coming from the various classrooms. Each room was different, carrying its own charm. In the days when it had been Sevastopol Lodge, the five classrooms had been two sitting rooms, a morning room, the owner's study, and a sewing room. In the hallway, she had caused a trophy case to be hung, and a long honours board, which already contained the names of those girls who had won entry to Lady Margaret Hall and Somerville.

The hall had been bathed in morning sunlight coming through the tall stained-glass window at the head of the stairs, but now a cloud passed over the sun, and the light fled down the passageway towards the kitchen quarters. Frances shuddered. She had nearly lost all this, because Father would never have come to her rescue. He would have sympathized, metaphorically patting her head, and urging her to come back home to the Lodgings until he had found her a suitable husband.

Now, his death had made her a wealthy woman, free to turn her many dreams into reality. Matrimony, however, was not one of those dreams. Her father had held her life and her future entirely in his hands. No other man, she swore, would be allowed to do that.

Frances Fowler and her brother John walked back from St Mary's church at Lynham Hill, and passed through the wicket-gate that opened into the gardens of Forest Park. It was a warm, sunny day, with one of those grey, leaden skies that betoken the coming of a hot night, possibly culminating in surly thunder and the flickering of distant lightning.

The service in the church had been brief: the vicar had presided, and Timothy had read a lesson from Scripture. John had delivered a brief address, and the committal at the family tomb had soon been over. The vicar had declined their invitation to take refreshments with them, pleading a prior engagement.

Frances had experienced a brief pang of nostalgia on seeing the neat Regency mansion again, the house where she had spent her happy childhood. She and her brothers had been devoted to their mother, who ruled them – and their father – with firm good humour and common sense. She had always been successful in curbing Father's airy ambitions to expand the house, or to invest his capital in the latest financial craze. It was Mother who had brought Forest Park to the marriage: she came from a family of gentlefolk. Father was of what biographers liked to call 'obscure origin.' His father had been a country schoolmaster in Essex.

'Will you keep the house, John?' Frances asked her brother as they walked side by side on the path that ran diagonally across the lawn.

'No, Fanny, I don't think so. I've lived in London so long that this particularly obscure corner of Wiltshire holds no appeal for me any longer. I'll put it up for sale.'

'We had some good times here,' said Frances. 'When we were children, I mean.'

'Yes, we did, but that was mainly while Mother was alive. Things became rather tenuous after we lost her. Incidentally, what's happened to Timothy? I thought he was following us from the churchyard.'

'He was, but he saw old Dr Hooper in the congregation, and stayed to have a word with him. Dr Hooper! He must be over eighty by now.'

They went together into the house, where two elderly servants from the old days had come out of retirement to wait upon them. In the faded drawing-room, the traditional seed cake and port wine had been laid out. Frances and John sat down by the fireplace, where a cheerful fire was burning. They still retained their outer clothing, because they both felt that they were strangers now in Forest Park. It held some part of their past, but nothing of their future.

'Fanny,' said John Fowler to his sister, 'I didn't want to mention it while Timothy was here, but Father's legacy came just in time to save me from disaster. All's well, now, and will be in the future; but it was a near thing.'

'What did you do?'

'I borrowed a large sum of money to secure our firm's exclusive right to broker a massive discount on the paper of one of the railway cartels. It was perfectly legal, you understand, but perhaps not entirely ethical....'

'A bribe.' Really! She was quite fond of John, but he *was* a hypocrite.

'Be that as it may, Fanny, the man I borrowed it from suddenly wanted it back, and became very nasty when I demurred. He'd found himself in a hole, too. And I had gambling debts, and was being threatened in the streets by the loan-shark's thugs. So when Father's legacy was confirmed, I was able to pay the man back. We're the best of friends, now.'

'How much did you borrow from this man?'

'Twenty-six thousand pounds, at six per cent.'

Frances was silent for a while. John crossed to the table, and brought her a glass of port and a piece of seed cake. Helping himself, he resumed his seat by the fire. Really, thought Frances, what a weak fool he was! His amiable manner masked a shifty and dishonest dealer, and as for his gambling, he would never cure himself of that. How long would his new fortune last?

His wife, Margaret, had cried off at the last moment, and had joined her children at her mother's London house. Perhaps it was fitting that just the three children of Sir Montague Fowler had come to see him join their mother in the family vault.

'I met a man in town yesterday,' said John, 'who told me that tongues were beginning to wag about Father's death. I didn't like it, but I couldn't ignore what he was saying.'

'What kind of a man was he?'

'He was an analytical chemist, who has a practice in a lane near Lincoln's Inn. Not a pharmacist, you know, but a man who analyzes samples of various goods for lawyers preparing cases of malpractice. I asked him what he meant, and he told me that he'd been at a meeting earlier this week at Apothecaries' Hall, and had met a man from St Michael's who told him about the rumours going round.'

Frances thought of her sister-in-law's hysterical letter, and felt a sudden coldness clutch at her heart. What had Kate written?

Oh, dear Fanny, I have found a packet of poison in Tim's desk, and I am frantic with worry. It had mercuric chloride written upon it. Surely that is a poison? Oh, dear Fanny, what am I to do?

'This man from St Michael's. Did your chemist give him a name?'

'Yes, he did. Now, what was it? Templar. Yes, that's right. Perhaps, when you go back to Oxford tomorrow, Fanny, you could find out something about him.'

'There are rumours circulating already in Oxford,' said Frances. 'Only yesterday, I had a visit from my landlord, who told me that he for one didn't believe all the rumours going round about Sir Montague Fowler's death. He said that partly because I'd just paid him the large debt that I owed him. I said nothing, but I noted what he said.'

John, she saw, had gone suddenly grave. He was not a naturally sombre man, and his knitted brow, and nervous wringing of his hands made him look like a different person from her normally sanguine brother.

'I don't like it, Fanny,' he said. 'You and I have been saved from disaster by Father's legacy, and I've no doubt that Tim will find his path smoothed by his inheritance. He can buy the freehold or whatever they call it of that parish of his, after the old buffer's retired. If people are hinting at murder – there, I've said the word aloud – we three will be the immediate suspects. Not only that, but if it's thought that we gained our legacies through murder, then our new fortunes will be forfeit to the Crown. I'll try to find out more, and you can make some discreet enquiries at Oxford.'

'Well,' said Frances, dryly, 'I didn't murder Father.'

'I'm sure you didn't. Neither did I.'

'I should think not. And I'm sure Tim….'

'Let's leave Tim to speak for himself, shall we?' said John. 'In any case, I don't suppose he had any debts to pay off. That fortune just fell into his lap. It would have been better if Father had left Tim to the bounty of God, and divided his portion between you and me.'

He rose from his chair, came across to her, and kissed her on the cheek.

'Dear Fanny,' he said, with a tenderness that surprised his

sister, 'nothing must be allowed to destroy our good fortune. Father died of gastroenteritis. I'll fight all rumours to the contrary with all the power at my command. I know you think I'm a pompous hypocrite, and a rogue, too, I expect, but I'll not stand by, and see all our bright futures ruined by evil rumours.'

The Reverend Timothy Fowler sat in the dim parlour of a cottage near St Mary's church, listening to old Dr Hooper talking about deathbeds. This was the man who had attended their mother in her last illness, many, many years ago, and who had attended all three of them for a multitude of childhood ailments. Timothy knew that the old physician had had a lifelong interest in the subject of poisons. He wore a faded frock coat, with a black mourning-band on the sleeve.

'Sometimes, Timothy,' said Dr Hooper, 'there can be no doubt of the cause of death – no ambiguities, you know. Your dear mother died of consumption of the lungs, a condition that had become fatally advanced before she sought medical treatment. Your father was often away, securing his position at Oxford, and your mother was placed almost entirely in the charge of nurses – well, of course, you remember all that, I'm sure.'

Timothy Fowler let his mind go back in time to the year 1871, when Mother had died. John was twelve years old, he, Tim, was eight, and Fanny a tiny girl of four. Father had insisted on the three of them paying their last respects to Mother as she lay in her coffin. It had been a harrowing experience. John, white-faced, had put a reassuring arm round him, so that both of them had survived the ordeal. Little Frances had been terrified. She had screamed and screamed until one of their female relatives had picked her up and taken her away.

'So that was what happened with your mother. I knew her before her marriage – oh yes, didn't you know? Victoria Mary Hallett. She was a lovely girl, and married your father when she was twenty-one, here, at St Mary's. She left him a great fortune, you know, but....'

Yes, thought Timothy, that 'but' speaks volumes. Mother's private fortune, entailed to her during her lifetime, had passed to Father on her death. It was an open secret that Father was planning to make a massive gift to the university, an endowment of some sort. At the reading of the Will, Groom the lawyer had revealed that it was to have been a School of Medical Jurisprudence. No doubt Mother's legacy, and a great deal more besides, would have been swallowed up in that airy project.

Some weeks before Father's death, on a visit to Reading, Timothy had met the Archdeacon of Berkshire, a former Lincoln College man, who had told him in confidence that Father was using this gift in order to secure a peerage. Moreover, the rumoured foundation of the School of Medical Jurisprudence would have put him in the front running for the Vice-Chancellorship of Oxford University, an office that was soon to fall vacant.

Father's cavalier attitude to his family didn't bear thinking of. Well, he had gone now to wherever Providence had deemed fit to send him.

The old doctor fixed Timothy Fowler with a pale but very intelligent eye. It was as though he was reading the young clergyman's thoughts.

'What has put this idea of mercuric chloride into your mind? The very fact that you come to me with your query – a doctor with an interest in such things – tell me what's in your thoughts.'

'I ... I heard about it, you know,' said Timothy. 'Somebody told me that if it were used as a poison, its symptoms would be very like those of gastroenteritis.'

'Hmm.... Be very careful, Timothy, before you come to any tentative conclusions that you may regret later. You tell me that

Sir Montague died of gastroenteritis, certified as such by the attendant physicians. Why not leave it at that?'

'This mercuric chloride,' Timothy persisted, 'I'm not a chemist or a medical man, but surely I am right in thinking that this is a noxious substance?'

'It is. It's sometimes called salts of white mercury, or corrosive sublimate. It's a particularly cruel poison, which destroys the entire body system by absorption, similar in its effects to arsenic and antimony.'

'Does it have any medical application?'

'It does. It can be prescribed for the treatment of certain diseases consequent upon a life of vice. In some cases, it has killed the wretched patient. It would have had nothing to do with your poor father's medical regime.'

After a few civilities, Timothy left Dr Hooper's cottage, and made his way back to Forest Park. The old doctor watched him from the window. Now what, he thought, was all that about? Timothy Fowler knows something, or is concealing something. I wonder what that 'something' is?

5

'ENTER RUMOUR, PAINTED FULL OF TONGUES'

INSPECTOR JAMES ANTROBUS followed the young nurse down the stone steps leading to the basement of the London Chest Hospital in Bonner Road, Victoria Park. This would be his last creosote treatment, as he was to be discharged at noon that day. They entered a chilly tiled room, where Antrobus sat in a chair, flinching as the nurse placed a light mask impregnated with creosote over his nose and mouth, securing it in place with elastic straps.

'Half an hour will do today, Mr Antrobus,' said the nurse. Her cheerful voice went well with her general air of crisply starched liveliness. 'This is your tenth session, so you know what you have to do.'

Yes, he knew what to do. Breathe in through both nose and mouth, hold your breath for four seconds, and then exhale. Do this without a break for thirty minutes. Keep your eye on the second-hand of the large clock fixed to the wall in front of you. Try not to cough until the half-hour was over.

Anne Stuart – that was the nurse's name – had retreated to the next room, where he could see her observing him through the special window let into the wall. Breathe in, hold, breathe out. He closed his eyes, and for a few moments imagined that he was weather-proofing a garden fence with the pungent tarry paint. Tar and milk – these were the defining smells of the basement, which also housed the kitchen and its annexes – the larders, some storerooms, and the milk pasteurization parlour.

He had suffered from consumption of the lungs for over five years. After an alarming haemorrhage earlier in the year, the Chief Constable, no less, had arranged for him to become an in-patient for three weeks at this renowned London hospital. He had been assigned to one of the open wards, little more than wide balconies, where his damaged lungs could breathe what passed for 'fresh air' in smoky London day and night. Tomorrow, he would be back in his beloved Oxford.

Anne Stuart came back into the room, and deftly removed the stifling mask. Almost immediately the tickling began in Antrobus's throat. In a few moments, the coughing would start, heralding the grim and painful clearing of his lungs. Without speaking, he nodded his thanks to the young nurse, and walked swiftly into the adjacent coughing-room.

At eleven o'clock, dressed in the smart black suit that he favoured, James Antrobus was shown into the consulting-room of Dr Jelke, the hospital superintendent.

'You will find your condition much improved, Inspector Antrobus,' said Dr Jelke. 'Continue to take the medicines I have prescribed, and be sure to visit your own physician at least once a month. I wish you well. We have ordered a cab, which is standing at the Bonner Road entrance, to convey you to Paddington Station.'

Some minutes later, Antrobus stepped into the cab, and was waved on his way by Dr Jelke and Nurse Stuart.

'What do you think, Dr Jelke?' asked the nurse.

'He could live for many years yet, Nurse, if he takes care of himself. But his lungs are very badly damaged, and he'll never be free from sudden haemorrhages. His right lung is virtually useless, and will have to be removed at some time in the future. The creosote treatment will have been of enormous benefit to him, so I have hopes for his future. Yes, I have hopes for him.'

Captain Stanley Fitzmaurice, the Senior Tutor, looked up from his work as the door opened and his scout, Hammond, came into the room. It was a hot summer's day, and the perfume of the great wisteria covering that side of the hall which gave on to the second quad wafted through the open window.

'Yes, Hammond, what is it?'

The scout, a tall, balding man in his fifties, was wearing a canvas apron over his dark suit, and there were smears of soot on his hands. Evidently he had started the blackleading of the grates. It was 20 June, and the undergraduates had gone down five days earlier when Trinity Term ended.

'Captain Fitzmaurice, sir,' said Hammond, 'I've been plucking up courage to speak to you for some days now, but as I've been working here on staircase VI this morning, and knowing that you were here, sir, I've taken the liberty of knocking.'

Fitzmaurice laid aside the letter that he was reading and gave the man his full attention.

'And what is the matter, Hammond? How can I help you?'

'Sir, there are rumours going round – rumours about the late Warden. Not just here, in St Michael's, but in other places, too, places where you gentlemen wouldn't go to, or know about. Alehouses, and the like. So I've come to you, sir.'

Years ago, Hammond and Fitzmaurice had served in the same regiment, Fitzmaurice as officer commanding 'C' Company, and Hammond one of the two corporals in the senior platoon. Their experiences in the field had forged a bond between them. Fitzmaurice motioned to a chair.

'You'd better sit down, Hammond. See that the oak's sported first, so that we'll not be disturbed. Now, tell me about these rumours.'

The scout sat down gingerly on the chair, and cleared his throat nervously.

'Captain Fitzmaurice, sir,' he began, 'the Warden died in the Lodgings on the third, and his death was brought in as stomach trouble. Now, sir, I have a daughter, Lucy, and when the wife died, I sent her to live in the country with her aunt, my wife's sister. It was the Warden, God rest him, who got her a place with his son, the Reverend Timothy Fowler, in a place called Clapton Parva. It's a little village in Hampshire.'

Fitzmaurice leaned back in his chair. Evidently, Hammond was going to take his time.

'Well, sir, Lucy's not the brightest of girls, I must admit, but she's got more sense than people give her credit for. Begging pardon, sir, but gentlefolk talk among themselves as though their servants were deaf, and Lucy knows that the reverend gentleman and his good wife call her "the Slow Girl". But it works both ways.'

'What does?'

'Hearing what people say, sir. A few days after the Warden had died, Lucy was in the scullery, washing up, when she heard the mistress cry out in alarm. She rushed out into the passage and heard Mrs Fowler say: "Oh, Tim, what have you done? What am I to do?" And then she began crying for her mother. She's twenty-four, so Lucy tells me, but acts more like a girl of eighteen. Not lacking, exactly, sir, but immature.'

'This is all very interesting, Hammond,' said Fitzmaurice, 'but where's it all leading?'

'I'm coming to that, sir, now. Later that day, Lucy used her mistress's key to open the desk in Mr Fowler's study. She knew where Mrs Fowler hid things, you see. And in the desk she found – well, let me show you the letter that she wrote me.'

Hammond produced the letter from the pocket in his apron, and handed it to Fitzmaurice. It had been written on a sheet of printed note paper, headed 'The Curate's House, Clapton Parva, via Beaulieu, Hants.' For a servant girl who was supposedly 'slow', it was surprisingly well written. One paragraph stood out from the rest because it had been written in capital letters.

OH PA, I SAW A PACKET OF SOME STUFF, AND IT WAS THIS THAT HAD MADE THE MISTRESS CRY OUT. I SAW IT IN HER HAND BEFORE SHE PUT IT BACK. I HAVE WRITTEN OUT EXACTLY WHAT IT SAID ON THE PACKET. IT SAID IT WAS POISON. HERE IT IS.

Beneath these words Lucy Hammond had reproduced exactly what had been written on the label:

POISON! Mercuric Chloride. POISON!
To be administered only by a physician.
William Hart, Chemist. Winery Lane,
Kingston upon Thames, Surrey.

Fitzmaurice stirred uneasily. His mind flew back to his conversation with Gerald Templar, the Junior Dean, who had hinted at poison while the Warden was still alive. And this substance – this mercuric chloride – surely Templar had mentioned it as a means of doing away with people? He looked at Hammond the scout, still sitting uncomfortably on his chair. Servants hated being told to sit in the presence of their master or mistress.

'Will you leave the matter with me, Hammond? I promise you that I'll look into it. I will copy out your daughter's letter now, and return the original to you. Is there anything else you wish to tell me?'

'Only that rumours are still going round here, in Oxford, sir. Mr Ballard, the Warden's secretary – he's got his suspicions. And that nurse – I shouldn't wonder if she hasn't a tale to tell. Will that be all, sir?'

'I think so. You've set my mind racing, Hammond. When

I've discovered anything tangible, I'll let you know. Meanwhile, there's no need for your daughter's name to be mentioned in all this. Let us try to keep her out of it all.'

Hammond rose from his chair. He looked both pleased and relieved.

'Thank you, sir,' he said. 'It's very hot today. I'll bring you up a glass of iced barley water presently.'

'An excellent idea. Are you doing the grates?'

'I am, sir. Now the young gentlemen have gone down, there's plenty to be done!'

Obviously grateful for the change of subject from possible murder to something more mundane, the scout thrust his daughter's letter back into his apron pocket, and left the room. He returned in a few minutes with the promised barley water, and then went about his duties.

It was half past eleven. Where would Gerald Templar be, now? With no undergraduates to tutor or discipline, he would have gone about his own business. It was Wednesday, the day when Templar left the college to earn himself a welcome additional stipend in the service of the city authorities.

On the eastern side of St Aldate's, and within sight of Christchurch Meadow, was to be found a little street called Floyd's Row, part of the slate-grey suburb of St Ebbe's. Here was situated the Oxford City Mortuary. Stanley Fitzmaurice mounted the steps from the road and entered the gloomy building. He was assailed immediately by the smell of formalin, which mingled with the cleansing scent of carbolic.

Doors to left and right, doors with frosted windows, led, he knew, into the silent chambers where corpses lay beneath their white sheets. Thankfully, he had no business there.

He found Gerald Templar in a long room at the rear of the building, sitting at a bench covered with chemical apparatus. Racks against the walls held numerous glass jars, the screw caps of which were sealed with red wax. Each jar had affixed to it a label, which held details of what the liquids inside them contained, and from whose body they had been taken. Other jars, decently obscured with crepe paper, held the organs of bodies that had required a fuller version of the standard autopsy.

Templar looked up from the microscope through which he had been peering, and smiled a greeting. He looks for all the world like one of those Russian anarchists with which the newspapers delight in frightening us, thought Fitzmaurice. The ill-disciplined beard, the glittering pince-nez, the slightly threadbare suit contrived to make him look older than his years. He was only twenty-five.

'Fitzmaurice! What brings you here? Or needn't I ask?'

Templar removed a glass slide from the microscope, and set it carefully aside.

'I've been examining specimens of lung tissue this morning,' he said. 'They all confirm that the late owners of the tissue had died from emphysema, despite some busybody policeman suggesting that they had been poisoned. Poison has been in the air over the last ten years. Remember George Lamson and his deadly aconite, in '81? And Pritchard, with his antimony? But what brings you here?'

Fitzmaurice told his friend the story that the scout Hammond had recounted. While he was speaking, he saw that the young man was becoming more and more excited. When he had finished, Templar burst into speech.

'I felt all along that the Warden had been poisoned,' he said. 'In fact, I more or less told you my own suspicions. I've done a lot of mortuary work here over the past two years, and have learnt much about the effects of poison, and how easily they can be mistaken for the concluding stages of fatal illnesses. And now Hammond brings us this story....'

Fitzmaurice produced the copy that he had made of the label that Lucy Hammond had seen on the packet of poison, and

70

handed it to the young chemist.

'There, what did I say?' cried Templar. 'Mercuric chloride. That doesn't surprise me in the least. But surely the Warden's own son didn't poison him? Timothy Fowler, I mean. I don't believe it. But he needs to be questioned….'

'Steady!' Fitzmaurice replied. 'What authority have we to question anyone? We may find ourselves relishing the role of amateur detective, Templar, but it won't do. If you ask a fellow whether he murdered his father, he's going to say no. But it does set the mind racing. Who would have had a motive for doing away with Sir Montague Fowler?'

'I can think of a number of people,' said Templar, 'Miss Fowler, for one. I've heard from certain people I know that her precious school was facing ruin, and that Sir Montague's legacy came just in time. And what about John, the London business-man? Who knows how near Queer Street he may have been? But there are others….'

'Yes, there are,' said Fitzmaurice. 'People who have no con-nection with the family. Joe Steadman, for one. Joe's an amiable fellow, but he has spent his life seeing others promoted over him. Sir Montague was brought in from outside when Joe was the strongest internal candidate. Not that Joe minded – or so he always says; but it may have rankled over the years.'

'Well, I for one refuse to countenance the idea of Joe doing away with the Warden,' said Templar, hotly. 'He's clearly heart-broken at losing so old a friend. No, if we must look to college personalities, I should think that our revered Vice-Warden, Dr William Podmore, is a likely candidate. He never liked Sir Montague, and felt diminished by every triumph that came the Warden's way. Or so I've been told. And everyone – himself included – knows that he'll be appointed the next Warden. What if he'd decided to sweep his path clear beforehand? Billy Podmore's a hypocrite, with his spring-water and his prim admonitions. I've heard – well, never mind that. Rumours have been going the rounds for the last ten days.'

'So what's to be done?' asked Stanley Fitzmaurice. His question was partly rhetorical, but it seemed that Templar had already prepared an answer.

'I suggest that I lay all this tale before the Chief Anatomist here, Dr Armitage. He is, ex officio, a coroner's officer. Let me do that, Fitzmaurice. If Armitage convinces the coroner that there are grounds for investigation, then he will contact the police.'

'It's a cowardly thing to do, Templar, to set a deadly rumour afoot, and then leave it to others to investigate. I don't like being a sneak.'

'No more do I. But if the Warden was murdered – yes, murdered! – then I for one will risk being considered a sneak.'

Gerald Templar glanced around the grim room, and pointed to the jars lining the racks.

'You remember how foully the Warden suffered,' he said. 'If that suffering was the result of someone administering mercuric chloride, a vicious and evil thing to do, are you content to let the matter drop?'

'You're right, of course,' said Fitzmaurice. 'And I withdraw that word "sneak", at least, as it may have applied to you. In fact, what you intend to do is a brave act, and one motivated by a scientist's desire to seek out the truth.'

'You make me sound very noble,' laughed Templar. 'The Chief Anatomist will be calling in later this morning. I'll talk to him then. Can you come back here at one o'clock? Dr Armstrong should be here at half past twelve, and I'll have told him the whole story by the time you arrive. If he concludes that this business is a matter for the police, you could go with him. Someone from the college should be present.'

An insignificant lane at the side of 130 High Street gave access to the headquarters of the Oxford City Police. It was an undistinguished building, acquired in 1870, when the force had moved from its cramped premises at the conjunction of Queen Street and St Aldate's.

Dr Armitage and Stanley Fitzmaurice entered a small office looking out on to a flagged yard, where they found an elderly police sergeant, sweltering in his heavy serge uniform, writing in a ledger. Armitage told the man that Inspector Antrobus was expecting them.

'He is, gents,' said the sergeant, putting his pen back into the inkwell. 'Step this way, if you please.' He led them across the yard and into the inspector's office. James Antrobus, busy at his desk, rose to greet the two men. He was well known to Dr Armitage, but Stanley Fitzmaurice had never seen him before.

He saw a tall, gaunt man clad in a black morning suit. His face was pale, and his eyes hollow. His shoulders were bent in a premature stoop. Fitzmaurice thought: this man, surely, is emerging from some devastating illness from which he has been very lucky to recover.

Despite his almost cadaverous appearance, the inspector's voice was both firm and friendly. He wore a light beard and moustache, which looked as though they had been grown simply because the business of shaving had become too much of a chore.

'Now, gentlemen,' he said, 'in what way can I serve you?'

'I have come to see you, Antrobus, because I have information to lay before you. And Captain Fitzmaurice has an important document to show you. You'll gather that we are talking about the death of Sir Montague Fowler.'

Inspector Antrobus listened while the Chief Anatomist gave him an account of Gerald Templar's suspicions of foul play in connection with the recent death of the Warden of St Michael's.

'I wouldn't have approached you, Antrobus,' said Dr Armitage, 'unless I had already been partly persuaded by the rumours that have been going about. They started as gossip among college servants, which could have meant anything or nothing. But this young man who works with me, Gerald Templar, is a fellow of St Michael's and Junior Dean, a man to be listened to with respect. That's so, isn't it, Fitzmaurice?'

'It is. Mr Templar is a chemist of the first rank. He is Tutor in Chemistry.'

'Well,' Dr Armstrong continued, 'what he told me was very disturbing. I thought you should know about it, though I'm conscious of the fact that I am regaling you with stories that are coming to you at second and third hand.'

'I've heard a few of these rumours myself,' said Antrobus, 'and so have some of our constables. "Enter Rumour, painted full of tongues." Opinions are divided in the alehouses. Some say that Sir Montague Fowler was murdered by his own family. Others think it was one of the dons at St Michael's. We'll have to see.'

Fitzmaurice handed the inspector the copy of Lucy Hammond's letter that he had made. The inspector read it without revealing any reaction to its contents, but when he had finished he folded it neatly, and put it in a drawer.

'Do you think there's sufficient reason to move in the matter?' asked Fitzmaurice.

'Exhumation, you mean? Yes, I do. The contents of that girl's letter clinch the matter, as far as I am concerned. It's beginning to sound decidedly sinister. Mercuric chloride.... I'll have to speak to the superintendent first, and then directly to the coroner. Is the deceased buried here in Oxford, Captain Fitzmaurice?'

'Oh, no. He's been put in a family vault somewhere in the Home Counties. Now, what was the place called? Yes, I remember. He was taken down on the railway to a little country place called Lynham Hill, in Wiltshire. His family home was there, a house called Forest Park. Poor Sir Montague would sometimes reminisce about it.'

'As he was buried away from here,' said the inspector, 'there will be some minor inconveniences to overcome. But if he was the victim of foul play, then the investigation itself belongs here, with the City Police. So that will mean that you, Dr Armitage, or someone deputed by you – in either case you will be acting in your capacity as coroner's officers – will need to go down to this place where he's been laid, conduct the autopsy there, and bring whatever specimens you think necessary back here to Oxford.'

Antrobus spoke with the pleasant accents of a native Oxfordshire man, but his choice of words, thought Fitzmaurice, showed that he had received a sound education in his youth. And he was a man who quoted Shakespeare. Really, a very interesting person. It was obvious that Armitage held him in high regard.

'Captain Fitzmaurice,' Antrobus said. 'I'll have to hear the account of that scout – what was his name? Hammond – first hand. Perhaps you could arrange for him to call in here tomorrow? Just for a chat, you know. There's no need to alarm the man. It'll take some time to apply for permission to exhume, but if we find that Sir Montague Fowler was indeed poisoned, then you may be sure, gentlemen, that I'll ferret out the truth, without favour and without fear.'

6

THE BOETHIAN APICES

THE BURSARY AT St Michael's College occupied a suite of interconnecting rooms at the top of Staircase III in the first quadrangle. It was a cosy, secluded kind of place, an oasis of peace and calm, with low, carved plaster ceilings, ancient panelling, and walls covered with Ackerman prints and fading photographs of former dons.

Here, Joseph Steadman reigned supreme. The finances of the college, the drawing up of each term's battels bills for dons and undergraduates alike, together with the investment portfolio, for over a century administered by Hoare's Bank in London, but ultimately in his hands, fell to the bursar's lot. In a cupboard near the door of the outer room was a stout straw bag containing the tools necessary for basic plumbing. If something went wrong with a tap or a flush in the night, the young men knew that the thing to do was to send for 'Old Joe'.

'We are, of course, very sorry for the family, but with the death of Sir Montague Fowler, they are no longer an immediate concern of the college. After the memorial service in St Mary the Virgin, which will be on 6 July, we can put the whole matter behind us.'

Dr William Podmore, the acting Warden, had invited

himself up to the Bursary to show Steadman how he intended to put the world to rights. Podmore looked more self-righteous than ever, and there was a kind of smirk forming around his lips that he was trying to suppress. But his voice was thick and not quite under his control; at such times, Steadman knew, Podmore would say more about his affairs than was judicious. What was he up to? He looked very smart, pristine, like a coin newly minted, but there was a tremor in his right arm that he was doing his best to suppress. Steadman had seen that tremor before, and knew what it portended.

'Do you think the matter can be dismissed as lightly as that, Podmore?' said Steadman. 'There's rather more to the business than laying Monty's ghost. There are sinister rumours going around....'

'Yes, yes, I know, and that's all they are: rumours.' The Acting Warden looked personally affronted. 'He was always a man to hog the limelight, and he's now doing so even after he's dead. There is one statute of this college, Steadman, that should be repealed and replaced, and that is the one that allows a Warden to stay in office for life.'

'You weren't very impressed by Sir Montague, then?'

Podmore blushed at the Bursar's barbed understatement.

'He did little or nothing for the college in the last ten years of his tenure. The place was stagnating! Come, now, you know that I'm right. It was "no" to anything practical, and "yes" to anything flighty and ill thought out....'

'You mean Templar's proposed laboratory in the third quad.'

'I do. There's a crying need for three new classics scholarships here, funded by us, and linked with some of the northern public schools. That was something I suggested to Fowler, but he couldn't see the wisdom of it. Yet he waxed enthusiastic about Templar's scheme until I blew cold about it. He'd have paid for those scholarships out of his own pocket, you know. I told him that the College could find the money by making economies; I knew that would have made him open his own personal cheque book!

'But Templar's laboratory…. Where did the fellow come from? Some provincial university, wasn't it? He's an intruder here, not our kind of man at all. What was I talking about? Oh, yes. That laboratory would have involved a major reordering of the whole range of buildings facing Northgate Lane, at a cost of £11,000. Fowler neither knew, nor cared, where the money was coming from! But I soon put paid to that, as you know. Templar went into a prolonged sulk for several weeks, and then decided to behave sensibly.'

'It was University College, Liverpool.'

'What was?'

'Where Templar studied. He won a scholarship there, and was an outstanding student. As for the cost, speaking as Bursar, I think we could have found the money.'

'Perhaps so. But there are many priorities for St Michael's, Steadman, and providing Templar with a place where he can play with his chemicals is not one of them. That space in the Northgate Lane buildings will be used to create ten extra rooms for undergraduates.'

The acting Warden had been standing near the empty fireplace, fingering the silver trophies that lined the mantelpiece. Now he sat down opposite Steadman at the Bursar's great leather-covered desk. He took an envelope from his inside pocket and handed it to Steadman.

'This is what I really came up here to see you about, Steadman,' he said. His pink, hairless face suddenly flushed with pleasure. 'I know you will be the first to congratulate me.'

Alone of all Oxford college headships, the Wardenship of St Michael's was in the gift of the Crown, and was awarded for life. The letter informed Podmore that the Queen had been graciously pleased to appoint him Warden of St Michael's College with immediate effect.

'Well done, Podmore – Warden, I should call you now. You can rely on me to support you in every way, that is, if you still wish me to continue as Bursar. You are at liberty now to make your own appointments.'

'Oh, not at all. Not at all. Let me leave the financial affairs of the college in your capable hands – if, that is, you wish to continue as Bursar.'

'I do. When will you tell the others?'

'I thought that I'd do so tonight, at dinner. Most of the Fellows are still up, so it would be a practical thing to do. And over the next fortnight, I'll move into the Lodgings. I'll write to Mr John Fowler, and ask him to collect Sir Montague's things.'

Podmore suddenly laughed.

'I usually get my own way where college business is concerned. Do you remember when old Earnshaw wanted to get G.F. Bodley in here to restore the chapel? That was in your time, wasn't it? Sir Benjamin Green was still Warden. It was an appalling idea, and would have wrecked the whole interior, which is fifteenth century, and with the original pews. Well, Earnshaw was recovering from a bad bout of pneumonia that year – yes, it was 1872. His specialism was Celtic poetry, and he'd written a couple of monographs on the subject.'

'Earnshaw? Oh, yes. I'd just about forgotten him entirely. So what happened?'

'It was a very cold winter, with snow on the ground, and I told him that a cache of ancient Celtic manuscripts, including hitherto unknown poems, had been discovered at Craigarvon Castle, in Fife. Lord Craigarvon was rumoured to be about to sell them to an American institution. Would he like to go up to Scotland there and then, and examine them? So he went, and it was so cold that he caught pneumonia again, and when he got to the castle, they'd no idea, of course, what he was talking about. They put him up, naturally, but he died at Craigarvon, and was buried in the kirk-yard there. Rather vexing, for a staunch Anglican. And so the college chapel was saved. I can always find ways to get rid of a trouble-maker.'

'Why didn't they know what old Earnshaw was talking about?'

'Well, of course, there were no ancient manuscripts there! I just made that up to lure him as far away from Oxford as possible. You might say that his death was a kind of bonus!'

'How very droll, Warden! Thank you for telling me that. I used to wonder what had become of the old fellow.'

When Podmore left the Bursary, Steadman sat for a while in thought. Podmore had come with the sole intention of gloating over his appointment as Warden, and making it quite certain that he intended to be a new broom. He set no store by Podmore's assurance that he could remain Bursar forever.

Podmore had also come to enjoy his discomfiture, knowing that the glittering prize of Warden had slipped once more from Steadman's grasp. Well, he had not given him the satisfaction of seeing how much he, Steadman, smarted under Podmore's hypocrisy, and how humiliated he now felt: he and his colleagues were to be the underlings of a man whom most of them secretly despised.

So he had sent an old, ailing man – Earnshaw, Reader in Celtic Languages, had been well over eighty – to snow-bound Scotland in the depth of winter, hoping that his pneumonia would break out again, and kill him. Wicked, wicked! It made one wonder whether he hadn't helped poor Monty out of this world to achieve his own ends.... No, that kind of speculation was wicked, too.

Podmore, the enemy of 'ardent spirits', had left the reek of gin behind him in the Bursary. It was gin that loosened his tongue, and made his hand tremble. As far as Steadman was aware, there were only two men in the college who knew for certain that Podmore was a secret drinker. One was himself; the other was Haynes, Podmore's scout, a buttoned-up, surly fellow whom Podmore evidently paid handsomely to remove all traces of his secret vice from his rooms. They were to have an alcoholic Warden. An alcoholic hypocrite.

And perhaps something more. There were few crimes in academe more heinous than forgery.

Steadman rose from his seat, and began to examine the old photographs adorning the walls of the Bursary. Among them was a faded image of an elderly gentleman, his eyes wide and gentle, his face lined and creased as a result of much physical suffering. He wore a frock coat over a low-cut, lapelled waist-coat, and a patterned silk tie arranged below a raised collar in the form of a loose bow. An inscription on the frame read:

Georg Joachim Bosch (1794 – 1873)
Dean of Degrees and Tutor in Mathematics

Older dons, themselves long gone, had spoken affection-ately of the old mathematician, who had come from Germany in his mid-thirties, having achieved the highest honours at the University of Heidelberg. He had proved to be a most able and popular tutor, and a true college man. He had still occupied the post of Tutor in Mathematics when Billy Podmore came up from Rugby in 1862. It seemed that Podmore had been an apt and proficient student, and a favourite with the old German don.

It was in the early sixties that Herr Doctor Bosch had begun to betray the signs of dementia, allied to the onset of the shaking palsy. In the way of Oxford colleges, it was agreed that he should keep to his rooms – he lived in the college – until such times as his removal to an asylum proved necessary. His students, including Podmore, were 'farmed out' to mathematics tutors at other colleges.

Steadman could just remember Herr Doctor Bosch, as he was always called. He had retired to his rooms the year before he had been appointed Tutor in Semitic Languages, but would occasionally emerge to be walked round the second quad by the common room butler, or the senior scout. A smiling, gentle man, he was an academic researcher more than a tutor; but he had been universally esteemed, and when he died, quite insane, in 1873, he had been widely mourned.

It seemed to be a day for recollections. Steadman recalled his own career. He had come up to Lincoln College in 1862, from Harrow, to study Biblical languages, having been introduced to them at a very tender age by his father, a learned clergyman of the old school, who left most of his clerical duties to a series of curates, while he immersed himself in study. He had been an eager pupil, and proved to be an outstanding student at Lincoln College. In 1857, the year of his graduation, he had won the University Prize for Hebrew, and the Archbishop of Canterbury's Award for Coptic Studies.

He had been immediately offered a fellowship in Semitic Languages at St John's College, and had stayed there for nine happy years. It was while he was at St John's that he published his book on the decipherment of Akkadian, an extinct Semitic language spoken in ancient Mesopotamia.

And then, in 1869, at the age of 33, he had come to St Michael's, and there he had stayed, growing more and more cynical as the years advanced and further promotions eluded him. He was now 'Old Joe', the well-liked college plumber....

He looked again at the photograph of Georg Joachim Bosch, and recalled one winter's night in 1870, when he had seen the old man in earnest conversation with William Podmore, his assistant tutor, then a young man of twenty-six or so. The two men had adjourned to the Herr Doctor's rooms, and had been closeted together for what seemed like hours.

Steadman had been standing at the window of his sitting-room in the second quad when he had seen Podmore emerge from Bosch's staircase, clutching a thick cardboard folder, which he was contriving to hide under the folds of his academic gown. It had been raining, and he had probably been trying to prevent the folder from getting wet. But there had been other possibilities.

In 1870, when still only twenty-six years of age, Podmore had published the book that had secured his reputation as a mathematician. It was a dense, profoundly learned tome, which had been brought out by the Oxford University Press to great acclaim. It was entitled: *The Boethian Apices: The Application of the Hindu-Arabic Numeration System to Computation in 10th Century Spain.* Few would read it, and fewer still would understand a word of it. But word of Podmore's ability as a mathematician spread abroad, and it was this publication that ultimately led to his being appointed Consultant Statistician to the Exchequer, and his being awarded the degree of DCL, *honoris causa*.

Steadman had always wondered about that book. He had taken great pains to read all 480 pages, and had been left with a sense of profound unease. The bibliography had contained over two hundred entries, many referring to authors who had flourished in the 1830s. Herr Bosch had come to St Michael's as maths tutor in 1829. Surely it had taken at least a decade to research those two hundred sources? Many of them were in German. It had seemed to Steadman that *The Boethian Apices* could only have been the work of an older man.

He could still recall seeing Podmore emerging from Bosch's staircase, clutching that bulky folder beneath the folds of his gown, as though to hide it. Had the old German scholar, realizing that his faculties were failing, entrusted his own precious manuscript to his favourite pupil, asking him to see it through the press?

He had allowed that question to remain unanswered for a quarter of a century.

A sudden surge of anger almost overwhelmed him. Podmore had come that morning to gloat over his failures, and to flaunt his own triumph! Well, pride came before a fall. The hypocrite had rejoiced over his old enemy once too often.

The third room in the Bursary, known as 'the archive', was a windowless chamber, containing shelves full of old-fashioned deed boxes and leather cylinders in which the founding documents of St Michael's were kept. There were, too, a row of wooden filing cabinets.

Lighting the single gas-jet near the door, Joseph Steadman rummaged through the files in the furthest cabinet until he found a cardboard folder containing a single sheet of paper. It was a handwritten record, dated in August, 1832, of the home addresses of fellows who owned property outside the college. Apparently there had been an attempt to compile a register of such properties, but some of the fellows had objected, and the idea had come to nothing, but the few pieces of paper remaining had been carefully filed in the Bursary, and forgotten.

Joseph Steadman, however, was an avid reader of old records, and he had known about the documents filed away out of sight and memory in the 1830s. This particular sheet gave him the address of a property that Herr Doctor Georg Joachim Bosch had bought for his sister, Fräulein Helga Bosch: Church Lane Cottage, Hampton Stonor, Warwickshire.

He remembered someone telling him, in 1880 or thereabouts, that Herr Doctor Bosch's sister had died. The College chaplain, the Reverend and Honourable Theodore Waynefleet, had attended the funeral, and had told him that he had met the sister's companion, a civil sort of person called Mrs Langrish. Did she, perhaps, still live there, in Hampton Stonor? It was a very obscure kind of place, a couple of miles east of Long Marston. It would do no harm at all to go out there and ask a few questions.

The following day, Joseph Steadman hired a cab to take him out to the little Oxfordshire village of Hampton Stonor, which nestled unobtrusively under the shadow of a long wooded ridge. A row of cottages lined one side of an unmade street facing ploughed fields. There was an old church rising from its own graveyard, and nearby, in a neat garden, stood Church Lane Cottage. Fortune had evidently smiled on him, for Mrs Langrish was not only still alive, but welcoming. He was ushered into a dim little sitting-room, tastefully furnished, and bade to make himself comfortable on the settee while his hostess prepared some refreshment.

Some minutes later, Steadman, sipping his tea, looked at the frail old lady sitting opposite him. She was dressed in the style of the 1870s, with a black bombazine dress adorned with a jet necklace. She wore a lace cap over her grey hair, secured beneath her chin by tapes tied in a neat bow. She regarded her visitor through gold-rimmed spectacles.

'It's over twenty years ago,' said Mrs Langrish, 'since old Dr Bosch died. This cottage belonged to his sister, Fräulein Helga Bosch, who came with him from Germany to be his house-keeper, though in fact the old doctor preferred to live in rooms in his college. She was a lovely, gentle person, and a fine piano player. I still have some of her music, and her bound copy of Schumann's piano pieces.

'After Dr Bosch died – it was in 1873, I think – I came to live with Helga. I had been lately widowed, and she and I had been friends for many years. We had a marvellous time together, Dr Steadman! We lived quietly enough, but we made forays to London, and to the Continent occasionally. We went to stay with her relatives, once, in Nuremberg.'

'And Fräulein Bosch….'

'Helga died in 1880,' said Mrs Langrish, anticipating Steadman's question. 'It was a bad winter here, and she caught a chill which turned to pneumonia. She lies at rest with her brother in the churchyard here. Would you like some more tea? That walnut cake is really very nice, you know.'

Steadman settled down on the sofa and abandoned himself to tea and cake, listening to his hostess's reminiscences, and asking the occasional question. Mrs Langrish told him that poor dear Helga had left her the cottage in her Will, which had been a very kind and thoughtful thing to do.

No, she had felt no desire to move away from Hampton Stonor. It was a quiet rural backwater, suited to her temperament. For many years now she had done parish visiting, and flower arranging in the church. Her garden gave her much pleasure, though she could not do a lot now without assistance.

Papers? Well, a lot of Dr Bosch's books and papers had been stored in the attic after his death. Yes, they were still there, or so she supposed. She'd no interest in abstruse subjects, preferring to read edifying novels, those of Mr Trollope in particular. He was a more straightforward writer than Thackeray, didn't he think?

'I don't suppose, Mrs Langrish,' said Steadman, 'that you'd let me look through those old papers? Although it's a quarter of a century since the good doctor died, we are still interested in his work at St Michael's College.'

'You're most welcome to look at them,' said his hostess, with a little silvery laugh. 'You'll have to make your way through the cobwebs and the spiders to find them. They're in an old suitcase up there somewhere. Or maybe it was a paper parcel. One of these days I'll bundle them all up and send them back to Oxford. What do you call the man in charge there?'

'The Vice-Chancellor. But....'

'Ah! Here's little Florence walking up the path. She's come to help me with the housework. Go up the stairs, and you'll see a little door to the right of the landing. Behind it are the steps going up to the attic.'

Mrs Langrish rose to open the door to a young girl, presumably Florence. Steadman mounted the stairs, and some moments later found himself in the attic of Church Lane Cottage.

The place was not as cobwebby as Mrs Langrish had suggested, but it was very dusty, and the little window under the eaves, which looked out over the rear garden, was dim with grime. The suitcase lay on the floor behind a couple of trunks, and an old sideboard minus its drawers. It was clear the suitcase had not been opened or examined since it was placed there, a quarter of a century earlier.

When Steadman picked it up, the case flew open, and its contents cascaded to the floor with a crash and a cloud of choking dust. He hastily picked up the various items, and placed them on the sideboard.

It was at that moment that he felt the presence of someone in the attic with him. He turned round with a start, but there was no one there. No one, at least, that he could see. At the same time, he knew that something or someone wanted him to examine the old books and papers: instead of being an intruder – a desecrator, even – he was certain that he had been made welcome, and with that realization the sense of someone else present in the attic abruptly left him. He peered through the little grimy window, and saw that he was looking beyond the cottage garden and into the ancient churchyard.

There were two books, both backed in faded brown paper. One was a German-English Dictionary, very dirty and scuffed; at one time it had been nibbled by mice. The other was a copy of Scott's *The Heart of Midlothian*, with many underlinings, and translations into German scrawled in the margins. There was a packet of letters, still loosely fastened by faded pink tape. They proved to be correspondence from his relatives in Germany, some dating back to the 1830s. There were also several books of logarithmic tables.

There was a single page of an ancient manuscript, written in Arabic, and pasted to a square of cardboard. And a diary, a simple cloth-bound affair of the type that one could buy at any stationer's.

*

Joseph Steadman stood with the diary, which Bosch had written in English, open in his hands. This dim, dusty attic was not the place to give full attention to the old German scholar's words. But a cursory glance showed him that in stumbling upon this diary, he had acquired the means of delivering his enemy into his hands.

When he descended the stairs, Steadman found that mistress and maid were undergoing a small domestic crisis in the kitchen. The stone sink was near overflowing, its murky waters brown with tealeaves. The tea-things stood inverted on the drain-board.

'Mrs Langrish,' said Steadman, 'I should very much like to make a copy of some of the entries in this diary, if you're agreeable. Thank you. Now, please fetch me a knitting needle, or a length of curtain wire.'

While the astonished womenfolk stood by in amazement, Old Joe the college plumber removed the blockage from their sink, and flushed away the unwanted detritus with a bucket of fresh water from the yard pump. Then he sat down at the tea table, and copied one particular and damning entry that Dr Bosch had made in his diary on Thursday, 17 November 1870.

7

AN EVENING RECEPTION

THE BURSAR STEELED himself to wait until after dinner in hall to examine more closely the entry that he had copied from old Dr Bosch's diary. The great carved-chair was now occupied by the new Warden, Dr William Podmore, who seemed rather subdued that evening. He was evidently quite sober, and may have begun to regret some of the confidences that he had shared with Steadman.

Nevertheless, a certain feeling that normality had returned to St Michael's was in the air that night. How long would it last? Steadman would readily admit that he had never liked Podmore; but what he had learned that day at Hampton Stonor told him that the man was unfit to hold any office in the University of Oxford.

It was dusk when Steadman climbed the little winding stair to the Bursary. The lamps were still lit, and he made his way directly to the archive, lit the gas-jet by the door, and opened the safe. From it he took his copy of the diary entry, and laid it on a desk. It was time to read it more carefully, and at leisure.

Thursday, 17 November 1870. My faculties are failing. So, I fear, is my strength. Today, I summoned my young friend William Podmore to my rooms, and handed him the manuscript of my book, The Boethian Apices. I urged him to revise and present the text for publication, and then to offer it to the Oxford University Press. I have toiled over it for the last five years, and I fear that, when published, it will serve as my epitaph. Podmore promised most solemnly to see the work through the press. I have consequently left him the sum of £100 in my will as a thanks offering. Am I a vain man? I can see in my mind's eye, the title page of the book when it finally appears:

The Boethian Apices: The Application of the Hindu-Arabic Numeration System to Computation in 10th Century Spain
By Georg Joachim Bosch,
Sometime Fellow of St Michael's College, Oxford

What was it that the preacher said? All is vanity!

Plagiarism! The unforgivable sin of academe. What should he do? To have this knowledge, and not speak out, made him an accessory after Podmore's cursed fact of cheating and chicanery. It was not his book. He held his doctorate under false pretences. What....

There came a knock on the door, and in a moment Gerald Templar had joined him in the archive. As usual, he looked rather unkempt, his evening clothes crumpled, as though he habitually kept them in a trunk instead of a wardrobe. His eyes shifted uneasily behind the little round gold pince-nez that he was wearing.

'Look here, Bursar,' he said, 'you're sending out the battels bills for the Senior College this week, aren't you? Would you think it awful cheek if I asked you to tell me now what I owe? I want to be prepared, you see, as money is tight this month.'

Steadman rose from his chair and went back into the far

room, which was his office. He spent some time looking through one of the filing cabinets until he found young Templar's bill. It was hardly a fortune, he thought, but then, these things were relative. He took the bill with him to the archive, and handed it to the nervous young man.

'Hmm…. Twelve pounds, fourteen and eleven. Not as much as I'd feared. Thank you, Bursar. It was very civil of you to let me see it.'

'Look here, Templar,' said Joe Steadman, 'are you in financial difficulties? If so, you can confide in me, you know. I can give you all kinds of advice about managing money, if you're not too proud to accept it!'

'That's very good of you, Bursar, and I'll bear it in mind.'

Templar seemed enormously relieved, and his anxiety had given place to a kind of secret exultation. His eyes blazed with excitement. Well, thought Steadman, it was a change from his habitual moroseness. He seemed to linger at the door, as though making up his mind to say something.

'I remember mentioning in hall one night,' he said, 'that my father was a doctor. That was true, but he died two years ago, leaving my sister and me in very straitened circumstances. Mother died when I was sixteen, and Grace – my sister – only twelve. I shared the stipend that went with my scholarship with my sister, until such times as she could find employment, which she did when she turned sixteen. It was at a typing bureau, and she's still employed there. Of course, I'm finding my feet, now, but it will be a long haul yet until various out-standing debts are paid. That's what brought me here tonight. I'll bear in mind what you said about financial advice. Good night, Bursar, and thank you.'

Steadman watched the young man as he left the Bursary, head held high, and listened as he clattered confidently down the little staircase to the first quad. He returned his copy of the diary entry to the safe, and extinguished the gas-jet at the door.

*

On Thursday, 28 June, two days following Steadman's visit to Mrs Langrish, Dr William Podmore, MA, DCL, gave an evening reception in the Senior Common Room to celebrate his elevation to the Wardenship of St Michael's College. There were twenty-five Fellows on the Foundation, and all of them had flocked to dinner in hall, and then had trooped across the Fellows' lawn and into the Senior Common Room. They knew that Billy Podmore's eyes would scan them all, looking for defaulters.

College servants, retained for the evening at the Warden's expense, circulated among the assembled dons, offering glasses of champagne arrayed on silver trays. On a buffet at one side of the room, canapés and sweetmeats had been set out enticingly, and near them, open boxes of cigars, for the pleasure of those who desired a postprandial smoke.

Glass of spring-water in hand, the Warden surveyed his guests. This was the most triumphant moment in his life. The governance of the college, which he had first entered as an undergraduate thirty-two years ago, was now his. No major actions affecting St Michael's could be taken without his consent.

He was now free to set his sights on the greater prizes, such as that of Vice-Chancellor, an office that would fall vacant within the year. He had mentioned the possibility in early February, at a meeting with the Chief Secretary to the Treasury, who had told him that a knighthood for him had already been considered; if he were to become Vice-Chancellor, then the accolade would most assuredly be his.

What was Steadman doing? There he was, contriving to look happy, and deep in conversation with Stanley Fitzmaurice. Those two had always been friends. It was time to wean Fitzmaurice away from the Bursar: he had other plans for the Senior Tutor.

Poor Steadman belonged to the world of Sir Montague Fowler, now dead and gone, and good riddance! Steadman had flaunted his intimacy with Fowler for years, and his own appointment as Vice-Warden had been obtained only after a very pointed intervention from the college Visitor, the Earl of Caernarvon. But the Wardenship was in the gift of the Crown, and Sir William Vernon Harcourt, the Chancellor of the Exchequer, had made sure that no college skulduggery could prevent his expected promotion.

He would leave Steadman at the Bursary for another year or so, and then replace him. He would have to be content with remaining as Reader in Hebrew and – what was it he called himself? – college plumber. Fitzmaurice would make an admirable replacement.

What should he do about Gerald Templar? He had been one of Fowler's last appointments, a sop to the science faculty. He did not like the man, and when his fellowship came up for renewal in '96, he would get rid of him. He was a clever chemist, of that there was no doubt, but he was a misfit, with the appearance of an anarchist and the crude ambitions of the worse type of 22-year-old *nouvel-arrivé*. He had attached himself to Fitzmaurice; there was another relationship that it would be wise to sever. Well, it was time for him to address his fellows, who tonight were his guests.

'Gentlemen,' he began, when the assembly had been called to order, 'I asked you all here tonight as my guests, to thank you for all your kind remarks on my being appointed Warden of St Michael's College. We all mourn the loss of my distinguished predecessor, but I think I speak for you all when I say that, as a college, we must turn our eyes firmly to the future. (Hear, hear!)

'I don't intend to weary you with a long speech, but I must make public acknowledgement tonight of the great support and friendship that I have received over the years from our Bursar,

Dr Joseph Steadman. It was he whom I first informed of my elevation to the Wardenship, and my news was received with what I can only describe as joyful enthusiasm. My thanks to him.'

Everybody clapped, and then the Bursar himself called for silence as he rose to speak.

'Gentlemen,' he said, 'the Warden has been very generous in singling me out for praise this evening. But if praise must be bestowed upon anyone, here, it should be upon him. His distinguished career, his notable book, *The Boethian Apices*, and his devotion to this college over the course of more than thirty years, richly deserved to be crowned with this well-merited appointment as Warden. So let us all spare him further embarrassment, gentlemen, by raising our glasses in a toast. I give you, the Warden.'

'The Warden!' they cried, and then turned their attention to the remaining glasses of champagne.

William Podmore threw off his gown, and tossed in on to the settee in his rooms in the first quad. He all but collapsed in his armchair, drunk with praise, and overheated with the triumph of success. They had been splendid, all of them, especially Joe Steadman. Had he really meant all those kind things that he'd said? Well, of course, he had himself praised the Bursar to the skies, so that he was virtually obliged to reply in kind.

Next week, he'd move into the Lodgings. John Fowler would send a pantechnicon to collect his father's effects, and the old house, built into the fabric of the college, was his. He would follow Fowler's practice of inviting one or two undergraduates at a time for a glass of sherry or Madeira in the morning, questioning them in such a way as to get to know them better. Fowler had been able to do that: he knew the name and former school of every young man in residence. Well, he would do the same.

Time to retire. He went into his small bedroom, and lit

the candles. He removed his watch from the fob of his dress waistcoat, and laid it carefully on the strip of baize designed to receive it. Someone, he noticed, had placed an envelope under one of the glass candlesticks. He tore it open, and removed a single sheet of paper.

The cry that he uttered was the cry of a man who knew that he was suddenly standing on the threshold of utter ruin. He tried to burn the paper in the candle-flame, but singed the fine hairs on his wrist. He groped inside a dim cupboard beside the wash-stand and withdrew a bottle. He ignored the need for a glass, and drank the neat gin in gulps, until he became unconscious, falling across his bed. The bottle fell to the floor, and the candles burnt until they guttered, and went out. He remained in that state of blind despair until the surly scout Haynes found him in the morning, and tidied away the evidence of his Warden's debauchery. He glanced at the sheet of paper lying beside the candlestick, and slipped it unread into Podmore's trousers pocket.

Later that day, Haynes found an envelope waiting for him in the porter's lodge. There was no letter inside. All it contained was five gold sovereigns.

Inspector Antrobus sat in the corner of one of the second-class carriages of the London train, and gave himself up to thought. Opposite him, a young mother with two little boys had got on the train at Reading, and had spent all her time trying to amuse and pacify her mutinous offspring. She had had little success, so the realm of recollection was Antrobus's only refuge.

The new Warden of St Michael's College had summoned him to explain himself. Dr Podmore had found the idea of exhumation scarcely credible – those had been his own words. It was not only a disgrace, he had told him, but a calumny. Everybody had loved Sir Montague Fowler. No one at St Michael's could possibly have done him harm.

And then Podmore had tried to lead him gently away from his precious college and its occupants by a little subtle calumny of his own. If a post-mortem did indeed reveal anything sinister, would he interview Sir Montague's children? If it was murder, who would gain from the murdered man's death? The Warden had concluded his remarks with a final attempt to teach the inspector his job. 'Motive, Inspector,' he'd said, 'that's what you will need to investigate. Sir Montague Fowler left a vast fortune.... But I'll say no more.'

One of the little boys banged the other's head against the window, and he began to cry. Mother lost her temper, and began to smack the first little boy's legs. Antrobus glanced out of the window, and saw that they were passing through the drab purlieus of Paddington. Another few minutes, and he would be rid of the little boys. Their mother would not be so lucky.

Podmore, of course, had been right. It would be imperative to interview Sir Montague Fowler's children, but he would do that now, before the exhumation took place. He wanted to meet these newly-rich inheritors of their father's wealth in order to make provisional judgements of his own.

Today, he would visit the elder son. Then, when occasion offered, he'd pay a call on Miss Frances Fowler at her school for girls in Oxford. The clergyman son, the man who had hidden a packet of mercuric chloride in his desk drawer, he would leave to the last. He'd take Sergeant Maxwell with him when he called on the Reverend Timothy, and while he interviewed the brother, Joe Maxwell could have a few words with that man Hammond's daughter – the lass whose employer dismissed her as 'the Slow Girl.' Not so slow, when all was said and done.

Mr John Fowler lived in an opulent town mansion in a secluded square near Clarence Gate. He received Inspector Antrobus in a room that was part office and part study, where he had been working on a number of account books set out on a great mahogany desk.

'I felt it was a courtesy, sir,' said Antrobus, 'to advise you, as head of the family, that the Home Office has authorized us to conduct an exhumation of the body of your late father, and to perform an autopsy.'

They were simply words, nothing more, but they gave him time to judge the elder son's reaction to the news. The man had turned deadly pale, and had sat down suddenly at his desk, as though his legs had failed him. Perhaps he had never even considered that his father's death had been anything other than natural. Or was his pallor the pallor of guilt?

'I can't believe it,' said John Fowler, his voice quavering with shock. 'Murder? Everyone respected my father. He was universally loved. You will find that Father died of natural causes, Inspector. Nevertheless, do what has to be done, and then leave him to rest in peace.'

Fowler had regained some of his normal colour, but it was clear that he was profoundly shocked. Antrobus had been quietly studying him, and had almost concluded that the man's demeanour expressed shock and disbelief, but not guilt.

'Have you – will you visit my brother and sister?' he asked.

'I will indeed, sir,' said Antrobus, 'though you are quite at liberty to communicate with them independently. Nothing positive can be done until the results of the autopsy are known. I shall visit Miss Frances Fowler after I've returned to Oxford, and then call upon the Reverend Timothy Fowler at Clapton Parva.'

John Fowler looked at him. This police officer seemed frail and ill, but there was an unusual intelligence in his eyes. It would be best to tell him now how they had all benefited financially from their father's death.

'The alternative to a natural death would be murder, wouldn't it? Well, all three of us inherited great sums of money from Father, and I'll tell you frankly now, Inspector, that my portion came just in time to stave off a financial disaster. Things had come to a pretty pass. I found that I was unable to pay back a large sum that had been placed in my hands, because the investor concerned had dishonoured his pledge to see the term out. And I had debts to moneylenders, and other – er – obligations that I could not meet. So, yes, Inspector, Father's legacy came just in time to save me from ruin. But I did not murder him – God forbid! I had contemplated throwing myself on his mercy if the worst came to the worst, and I think then he would have heeded my pleas.'

'You've spoken very frankly to me, sir,' said Antrobus, 'and I will bear that in mind. I understand how perilous it can be for a businessman to make such a confession of near insolvency. What you've told me today, sir, will be a secret between the two of us.'

'Thank you, Inspector. I can't – won't – speak for my brother and sister, but it's inevitable that all three of us are going to fall under suspicion if anything sinister is found. So yes, Mr Antrobus, I shall write to them both immediately, telling them how the land lies.'

Antrobus left John Fowler's house wondering whether the man was sincere in what he had said, or if he was, in fact, an accomplished liar. Full and frank confessions of that type were often a mask for something more sinister. He would postpone any decision about John Fowler until after the autopsy.

8

TAKEN FROM THE TOMB

FRANCES FOWLER STOOD in front of the cheval glass in her small bedroom in the attics of Makin House, critically appraising her newly-fitted mourning dress. She had been right to wait for it to be tailored by Jay's of Regent Street, rather than have chosen something ready-made from the catalogue of the mourning-warehouse. It fitted perfectly, and had been contrived in such a way as to have an air of fashionable youthfulness about it. White lace cuffs and collar contrasted well with the black parramatta silk of the dress. It was trimmed with dreary crepe, but she would remove that as soon as decency demanded, probably in September. She would go into grey before Christmas.

Trixie, the maid, had given it her full approval.

'Oh, mum,' she'd said, 'that's the nicest dress you've ever had! It makes you look even younger than you are.' Well, that had been the idea.

She left the room, and descended the narrow staircase, glancing out through a landing window at the sunlit Port Meadow stretching away beyond the house. She could see some children flying kites, and a man walking his two dogs on long leads.

John had written to tell her the appalling news of the impending exhumation of Father's remains. It had filled her with an almost paralyzing fear, for she recalled Kate's indiscreet letter, in which she'd babbled about deadly poison hidden in Timothy's desk. Timothy! Did the silly little fool seriously imagine that her husband, an ordained clergyman, had done away with his own father?

In a few minutes' time, at eleven o'clock, she was to receive a visit from Detective Inspector Antrobus, who had written her a letter from the police station in High Street. It was, he said, to be a courtesy call, and he apologized for obliging her to receive him on a Saturday.

Earlier in the morning, she had been accosted by one of the mistresses, Olivia Graves, who had asked her whether it was ever permissible to gloss over historical matter that was not suitable for the ears of young ladies. She was referring to Charles II's powerful mistresses: Louise de Keroualle, and the Duchess of Cleveland.

'Miss Graves,' she had replied, 'intellectual integrity is of paramount importance in a school like this. You cannot give an estimate of Charles's true character without bringing in those women, and explaining to the girls what kind of women they were. They wielded immense power, and you must not gloss over the means that they employed to achieve that power. I leave it to you to manage how you do this, but do it you must. There can be no true scholarship where facts are suppressed for whatever reason.'

What she had said was true and binding. Suppressing evidence, cheating with facts, was deeply subversive. Her girls – 'young ladies' as Olivia liked to call them – had to be equipped to take their place in a man's world. One day, she was convinced, that world would have to be shared with women.

When she reached her study, she found that Inspector Antrobus was waiting for her. He stood with hands behind his back, peering at a watercolour by Edmund Warren fixed to the wall near her desk. He looked pale, almost cadaverous, and his close black beard and moustache accentuated that pallor. Rather than give the little bow expected of her, she held out her hand, which he shook without hesitation. She saw that he was grateful to be asked to sit down.

'Inspector,' she said, 'I have already heard from my brother that Father is to be exhumed. I am naturally distressed, but of course I must conform to the law.'

'That's very civil of you, miss. Your brother, Mr John Fowler, was very frank with me. He told me that his father's death had extricated him from a very parlous financial situation.'

He left the implications of this statement hanging in the air, and waited to see what effect it would have. He did not have to wait long.

'I think we all benefited from poor Father's death,' said Frances. 'I, too, was facing the loss of this school, and received notification of my legacy just in time to stave off disaster. So there, Mr Antrobus, I, too, am a suspect!'

'Your candour does you credit, Miss Fowler. But for the moment, there can be no question of anyone being "suspect". The autopsy has not taken place, so in law no crime has been committed. Nevertheless, I am bound to ask you whether you have any information that could throw light on the manner of your father's death.'

Frances turned towards the window to hide her sudden spasm of fear. This was a clever man. He clearly knew something, something about Timothy, perhaps, and he was waiting for her to enlighten him. Who could have told him about that packet of poison?

Only that morning she had lectured Olivia on the necessity for academic integrity. She herself would have to abide by the same rule, or lose credibility. She crossed the room to a writing desk, and opened it with a key taken from her reticule.

She removed a letter from a pigeon-hole, and handed it to Antrobus. She stood by the window and watched him as he read it. When he had finished, he folded the letter and handed it back to her.

'In that letter, miss,' he said, 'your sister-in-law, Mrs Timothy Fowler, states that she found a packet of mercuric chloride, a lethal poison, in her husband's desk. It's a rather incoherent letter, but its contents are clear enough. Did you not tell anyone what the letter contained? Your doctor, perhaps, or a trusted friend?'

He means a lawyer, thought Frances. What was she to say?

'For all I know, it may have been rat poison.'

Inspector Antrobus smiled, and shook his head.

'For all you knew, miss,' he said, 'it was nothing of the sort! But thank you for showing me this. I already knew from another source about this packet of poison, but it was brave of you to confirm it in this way – brave, and wise.'

She watched as Inspector Antrobus glanced around the study. He was clearly interested in what he saw: the glazed bookcases, the globe, and framed star-map, and the carefully selected watercolours adorning the walls. He suddenly turned aside, and coughed delicately into a handkerchief. As he returned it to his pocket, she saw that it was smeared with blood.

'It must be a great adventure, miss,' he said, 'to establish a school such as this, where young ladies can be prepared for life at the university.'

'It is, Inspector. This place is my creation, though I had some initial help from the Headmistress of Cheltenham Ladies' College, and a small financial contribution from my father. Does education interest you?'

'I have a daughter, miss, who's a pupil-teacher at an elementary school in Battersea. While she teaches letters and ciphering to the little ones, she receives a secondary education from the teachers there.'

He smiled ruefully, and seemed to relax as his conversation turned from crime to the education of girls.

'I had some trouble getting her placed, miss,' he said, 'because the original scheme – it was brought in by a gentleman called Sir James Kay-Shuttleworth – applied only to what they called "youths". Girls didn't qualify. So I told them that the term "youth" could apply equally to a girl, and they saw the point. And there she is, miss, training to be a fully-blown teacher.'

Frances rang the bell beside the fireplace, and in a moment Trixie appeared.

'You will take a cup of tea with me, Inspector? I think it would benefit both of us.'

'"The cups that cheer, but not inebriate." Thank you, miss, I'd enjoy that.'

'You have not been well, I think?' asked Frances delicately.

'I was very near death three months ago, having suffered for a number of years from consumption of the lungs. It is only by miracle that the severity of the disease abated to some degree, and I live to tell the tale. How very kind of you, miss, to ask me.'

'I'm no stranger to illness, Mr Antrobus. I was a constant visitor to my father in his last days. Do you still take medicine, as a preventative, I mean?'

'Yes, I have some prescribed medicines, and from time to time I still feel the need to use a lavender shovel. I find smoking greatly helps my breathing, and the doctor approves. I have only recently been subjected to the creosote treatment at the London Chest Hospital.'

Tea was brought in, and they occupied themselves for a while in quiet and unthreatening conversation. Frances asked after the welfare of his wife.

'I lost my wife some years ago, miss, while I was still a uniformed sergeant. I live in a nice boarding house down at Botley, which is very comfortable, and easily affordable on my present wages.'

'You speak well, Inspector, and you quoted Cowper just now. You evidently received a good education.'

Again, she saw the rueful smile.

'I attended a grammar school until the age of fourteen, Miss Fowler, and lapped up everything that they could teach me there, including French, and a good dose of English literature. My father was a grocer, but he became trade-fallen, and I had to leave school. I got work on a farm for a while, but when I was twenty, I applied for the City Police here in Oxford, and was accepted. And I've been here ever since. Yes, I set great store by education, for people of all classes.'

'Well, Inspector,' said Frances, 'that's something that we certainly have in common. Now, after this dreadful business of poor Father's exhumation, what do you propose to do next?'

'As for that, Miss Fowler, I will do nothing until the results of the autopsy are known. If those results indicate foul play, then I shall visit your brother, the Reverend Timothy Fowler, and ask him about that packet of poison. No doubt he will have a complete explanation for how it came to be in his possession. I'm sure I needn't ask you not to mention the matter of the poison to your brother, or to his young wife.'

Frances had felt an affinity for this ailing man from the moment that he had entered her study. It would have been impossible for her to explain why, even to herself. But her liking for him would not blind her to the fact that he was investigating the possibility that either she, or either of her brothers, or all three of them, had contrived to murder their father for gain.

'You won't forget, will you, Inspector,' she said, 'that Father was Warden of St Michael's College, and that he actually lived there – and died there? I hope that you'll be questioning his colleagues.' Before she could stop herself, she blurted out: 'You know what tensions and jealousies can mount up in a closed society made up of old maids!'

Inspector Antrobus laughed. It was the only response possible to her bold condemnation of the Senior College. He stood up, and extended his hand to his hostess.

'I'll leave you now, miss,' he said. 'As for your late father's colleagues, you may be sure that I will not leave any of them unquestioned. Thanks for the tea. I look forward to our next meeting.'

Frances accompanied him to the front door of Makin House, which gave on to Occam's Lane, a pleasant tree-lined thoroughfare that led to the village of Binsey. At the end of the lane, she saw him accosted by a short, heavy man in a black overcoat, who raised his bowler hat before engaging the inspector in what looked like animated conversation. Another policeman? A sergeant, perhaps?

It was as she turned back into the house that Frances Fowler realized that she was slowly becoming convinced that her father had indeed been murdered. It was now both foolish and unrealistic to believe otherwise. Could it have been Timothy? Surely not. Being in Holy Orders would certainly have restrained him from doing such a heinous deed. Besides, though too prim and proper for his age, he had a kindly heart: she had heard of many good deeds of charity that he had performed for those less fortunate than himself.

John? She could see John quite easily as a parricide. He was weak, and weak men did desperate things when cornered. John had made apparently full and frank confessions as a kind of effective defence. Admitting readily to lesser crimes, like financial skulduggery, was an effective way of masking something infinitely more sinister. And yet, she had to admit, it was Timothy who had hidden away the packet of poison in his house. She would think no more of the business until the autopsy was over.

*

The coffin of Sir Montague Fowler was taken from the family vault in St Mary's churchyard at four o'clock in the morning of Wednesday, 4 July. It was early enough to be both cold and forbidding as the assembled officials followed the grim procession across the churchyard, guided by the light of lanterns, until they came to a brick-built stable, where a trestle table had been prepared for the reception of the coffin. It was a grim place, lit by flickering candles and oil lamps.

Dr Armstrong, who was to perform the autopsy, was assisted by Gerald Templar, and the proceedings were overseen by two officials from the Home Office. Two other doctors were also present. After all was completed, they left the stable, carrying a number of sealed jars containing the stomach, part of the liver, the kidneys and other viscera of the dead man. As the sun came up behind the trees, the remains of Sir Montague Fowler, duly returned to the coffin, were carried back to the family tomb.

The results of the autopsy were conveyed to Inspector Antrobus on the Friday following. He had been summoned to the City Mortuary in Floyd's Row, where he found Dr Armitage waiting to receive him. The doctor told him the results of the post-mortem without preamble.

'It was murder, right enough, Mr Antrobus. Murder most foul and malignant, and the means of committing this murder was the administration of a substance known as mercuric chloride, or corrosive sublimate.'

'And you found traces of this in Sir Montague Fowler's body?'

'Hardly traces. Massive quantities. Embalming had had no significant effect on the organs which Templar and I selected for special attention. The stomach had been washed out during the final stages of Sir Montague's illness, and was consequently empty of contents, but crystalline deposits deeply adhering to the stomach lining proved to be lethal quantities of mercuric chloride. The liver, and the kidneys also contained large deposits of this deadly substance.'

'When you examined the organs today, did you do so alone, or were you assisted by Dr Templar of St Michael's?'

'Templar had helped me to remove the organs from the body at the post-mortem on Wednesday, but today I examined the organs alone – well, not alone, because my surgical assistant, Mr Highgrove, was in attendance. Wheeler was not there.'

'Was there anything else in the organs? Any other poison?'

'No. The standard tests that I carried out yielded the reactions characteristic of mercuric salts, and of chlorides – what on earth is that noise?'

'That noise, Doctor, is being made by a little knot of reporters clamouring at the mortuary gates. As you might expect, word's got out already.'

'I shan't tell them a damned thing, the scoundrels!'

'Neither shall I. But we'll need to concoct a statement of some sort for release later today. It will only affirm what they've already guessed.'

When Antrobus left the mortuary, he found his way barred by six or seven reporters, including one from *Jackson's*, the local Oxford newspaper. Others, he judged to be from much further afield: from among the clamouring voices he discerned a Birmingham whine, and a cockney accent.

He was about to speak to them when they were shouldered aside by a thickset little man in a bowler hat and a drab overcoat. In a voice so loud and commanding that all the reporters to a man stopped speaking, the newcomer bellowed:

'Inspector Antrobus has nothing to say at this juncture, but a statement will be issued later. No, there's nothing to say, so disperse, if you please. At once.'

Muttering disconsolately, the little throng melted away into the streets of St Ebbe's.

'As always, Sergeant Maxwell,' said Antrobus, 'you turn up in the nick of time to rescue me. Let's walk back into town. Those fellows won't dare come near me, now.'

He gazed fondly at his sergeant. He looked like a bookie's runner, or like one of those dangerous ruffians employed by clubs and theatres to eject unruly members. Five years ago, he had been invalided out of the army, where he had been a corporal drill instructor in the Oxfordshire Light Infantry. He had joined the county constabulary as a uniformed constable, and had soon progressed to the detective branch. He had transferred to the City of Oxford Police in '92, and had proved an invaluable help to Antrobus.

'I'm thinking of last Saturday, sir,' said Sergeant Maxwell, 'when I met you at the end of Occam's Lane. You'd been to visit Miss Frances Fowler, at her school for young ladies. I was eager to tell you all about how I arrested Twister Thompson in the market that morning, so I'd no time to ask you how you got on with the young lady.'

'I found her an interesting and sympathetic person, Sergeant, frank and fearless, you know. We'll investigate her, of course, but I left that school almost – *almost* – convinced of her innocence.'

'Well you would, wouldn't you? You always fall for the wiles and deceits of young women. They flutter their eyelashes at you, or pretend to faint, and then you go all soft. In the army, we used to call that "the tender trap". You watch her, sir. She may be out to pull the wool over your eyes.'

'You have a delicate, respectful air, Sergeant, that I find very endearing. But the time has now come for you to button your lip. When we get back to the office, we'll start drafting a release for the gentlemen of the press.'

'Are you free tomorrow night, sir?'

'I may be,' said Antrobus cautiously. 'What have you in mind?'

'Mildred and I would like you to come to dinner again. We've got a very nice leg of mutton, and she's made one of those ginger puddings that you like. She's also allowed me to have a bottle of whisky on show – normally, she won't allow it, because it "lowers the tone". That's what she says. The wife's very partial to a glass of milk stout, sir, when the occasion offers, but she don't like spirits.'

'Well, that's very kind of you both, Sergeant, and much appreciated, but….'

'A friend of mine, Mr Henry Ballard, will be there, too.'

'Ballard? The man who was secretary to the late Sir Montague Fowler? How come that he's a friend of yours?'

'Why shouldn't he be, sir? I've known him for years. I can vouch for him, Inspector. He's not violent or demented, you know. Besides, I know that he wants to talk to you private-like, but is too proud to be seen stepping into our premises in the High Street.'

'Ah! Then I accept. It's very kind of you. So I'll look forward to meeting your wife again, and your friend Mr Ballard, tomorrow night. Now, let's get back to the office and draft that statement.'

9

LOUIS DE NEVILLE'S STORY

'ALL THIS GOSSIP's not very nice for you, is it, Mr Ballard, now that it's murder? You having been Sir Montague's secretary, and very well thought of by the family. It's in all the newspapers, now, all kinds of speculations. Mr Antrobus, will you have another couple of slices of mutton?'

Inspector Antrobus accepted Mrs Maxwell's offer. It was very cosy and relaxing in the back parlour of his sergeant's neat house in Cowley Road. The Maxwells evidently believed in comfortable chairs and yielding sofas, and they contrived to keep a good table. The back parlour doubled as their dining room. He looked at Henry Ballard, the secretary who had come into money. A handsome, well-dressed man, who carried with him the diffidence born of years of service. This man has something that he wants to tell me, he thought. Maybe after we've finished dinner, he'll contrive to let me know what it is.

'Well, of course, Mrs Maxwell,' said Ballard, 'it's not at all nice for any of us, particularly the family.' He turned his gaze upon Antrobus, who could see the mute pleading in his eyes. Ballard was desperate to talk to him alone.

'Sergeant Maxwell tells me that you are looking into the case, Mr Antrobus,' he said.

'Yes, that's right, Mr Ballard. It's early days yet, of course, but Sergeant Maxwell and I are already making progress. Ginger pudding? Thanks very much, Mrs Maxwell. And plenty of custard, please.'

When dinner was over, Sergeant Maxwell helped his wife to clear the table, and then retired with her to the little scullery behind the kitchen, leaving Inspector Antrobus and Henry Ballard alone together.

'Now, Mr Ballard,' he said, 'I can see that you have something of a confidential nature to discuss with me. We are quite alone here at the moment, and no one can overhear us. So let me hear your story.'

'It's something that I observed on that fatal Sunday, 3 June,' Ballard began. 'Soon after Sir Montague died, Mr John sought me out, and said that I could pay my respects to the body. I did so, turning down the sheet so that I could take a last farewell of my employer.'

His tones are those of an educated gentleman, thought Antrobus, but he speaks of Sir Montague's elder son as 'Mr John.' Many folk would call him a gentleman, but the Fellows of St Michael's probably wouldn't.

'The family had said their brief farewells,' Ballard continued, 'and had retired to the downstairs parlour. I didn't stay long, but as I was leaving, Mr Timothy – the Reverend Timothy Fowler – came into the room. "Ballard", he said, "Mr John wishes to see you downstairs." Then he added: "I have come to say some prayers over Father's body, as there was no clergyman present when he died."'

Ballard stopped speaking, and glanced speculatively at the inspector.

'I wondered …' he began, but Antrobus replied before he could frame a sentence.

'You wondered why Mr Timothy felt it necessary to excuse himself. He had no need to explain his actions to you.'

'Exactly, Mr Antrobus. And that's why I lingered in the passage after I'd left the room. I'm not the kind of man who sneaks on others, but I was much moved by Sir Montague's death, and not really myself. I looked back into the room, having left the door open just a crack.'

'And what did you see? Come now, Mr Ballard, you must tell me!'

'I saw Mr Timothy kneel down for a moment, and search with his hand under the bed. He retrieved a blue paper packet, the type of packet one receives from pharmacists, with white gummed wafers at either end, and slipped it into his pocket.'

'And what did you think it was?'

'I – I thought at first that it might have been bicarbonate of soda, or some such preparation, but then I asked myself the question: What concern of Mr Timothy's was the nursing of Sir Montague? No, it was something that he had hidden there, and was now retrieving. I was very disturbed. There had already been rumours of poison going the rounds during the thirteen days of Sir Montague's illness. Dons, you know, excel at gossip, much of it ill-natured.'

'And did Mr Timothy Fowler actually say any prayers?'

'He did. He knelt beside the bed, and I could hear him reading parts of the burial service from *The Book of Common Prayer*. After that, he pulled the sheet back over Sir Montague's face. It was the right moment for me to make a judicious retreat.'

Inspector Antrobus sat in silence for a while, thinking over what the secretary had told him. Ballard was a decent, faithful man; it was unlikely that he held any kind of grudge against his late employer's younger son. Nevertheless, one or two questions would not be out of order.

'Where were you educated, Mr Ballard? And when did you come into the employment of Sir Montague Fowler? There's no need to look so startled: I need to know something of your background for purposes of elimination.'

'Elimination?' cried Ballard, his normally placid face flushing with anger. 'Are you suggesting....'

'I'm suggesting nothing, Mr Ballard. Please answer my questions.' He contrived to add a steely edge to his voice, which had the desired effect. Ballard relapsed into his habitual air of deference and respect. He seemed to atone for his outburst by giving the inspector a complete résumé of his life and career.

'I was born in 1860, and orphaned as a small child,' he began. 'I was adopted by a very respectable couple, a well-to-do but childless market gardener and his wife. Their name was Winterbourne, but I retained my own surname of Ballard. We lived in a little village a few miles out from Cheltenham. I went to the dame school there as a little boy, but when I was ten, I was sent as a boarder to Cheltenham Boys' Academy, where I received an excellent education. It was a wonderful place to be.

'I left the Academy in '78, and worked as an elementary school teacher for a couple of years. Then, in 1881, when I reached my majority, I received the offer of the post as secretary to Sir Montague Fowler. It came out of the blue, and I was astounded to be chosen in this way. I believe that it was secured for me by the headmaster of Cheltenham Boys' Academy, though I never enquired into the matter.'

Ballard's eyes filled with tears.

'Do you know that Sir Montague left me a legacy of ten thousand pounds? It's a fortune, Mr Antrobus. I never expected for one moment such generosity. But I must finish telling you my story.

'Sir Montague and I "hit it off", as they say, as soon as we met. I said my farewells to the Winterbournes, and attached myself completely to my employer. There began the happiest and most fulfilling thirteen years of my life. I always maintained a distant regard for the family, as became my position, but now that we know Sir Montague was cruelly poisoned, I have no scruple in telling you what I saw. You'll draw your own conclusions as to what it may have signified.'

'Do you like the Reverend Timothy Fowler?'

'I respect him, but he has always been a rather distant, censorious man. I neither like nor dislike him.'

'And the others? Mr John, and Miss Frances?'

'Mr John is an open-hearted, kindly man; I have always liked him. Miss Frances is very clever, with her own laudable ambitions. She cultivates a hard and cynical exterior, but I have always found it impossible not to like her.'

Antrobus was satisfied. Henry Ballard had spoken frankly and fearlessly, and seemed to have no personal axe to grind – why should he, when he had received a legacy of £10,000?

It was time to investigate the Reverend Timothy Fowler. Ballard clearly had no idea that the blue packet had contained mercuric chloride. Why had Timothy Fowler hidden it beneath his father's bed, and why had he slipped it into his pocket in order to carry it away?

He would seek answers to those questions that week, but not until Sergeant Maxwell had returned from the Radcliffe Infirmary. He had sent him there to interview the nurse who had attended Sir Montague in his last illness. It would be interesting to hear what she had to say.

Nurse Townley, a sprightly woman in her fifties, agreed to talk to Sergeant Maxwell during a break from her duties on the wards at Oxford's Radcliffe Infirmary. Opened in 1770, it looked more like the grand country-seat of a duke or earl than a hospital. Nurse Townley led the sergeant into a small office near the entrance, and bade him sit down.

'I've heard all about the post-mortem, Sergeant,' she said, 'and the finding of mercuric chloride in the viscera of the deceased. I can see how your mind must be working, so I've brought my case notes to consult. I always keep a running log of the progress or otherwise of private patients. So what is it you want to know?'

'I want to know, Nurse, how often Sir Montague Fowler's children visited their dying father, and whether they would have had access to the medicines present in the sick-room. By access, I mean were they allowed to administer any of the medicines to their father?'

'No, Sergeant, that would have been quite improper. All medicines were prescribed by the doctors called in to the case, Dr Chambers and Dr Hope, and administered either by them, or by myself.'

Nurse Townley had produced a cardboard file, from which she took a number of sheets of paper filled with neat, small writing. She consulted these pages for a while before continuing.

'Sir Montague took to his bed on 22 May, the day on which he had returned from a visit to friends. Dr Hope was called in, and immediately diagnosed gastroenteritis. Dr Chambers, brought in the next day, concurred. I arrived with him at St Michael's, and could see immediately that their joint diagnoses were correct.'

Sergeant Maxwell looked at the woman who was talking to him. She was wearing the crisp linen dress and starched cuffs and collar that belonged to her profession, and her greying hair was crowned by a stiff cap. A small silver watch hung from a chain round her neck. There was something about her that suggested a knowledge and competence born of years of experience.

'Sir Montague never left his bed for thirteen days, at the end of which period he died. The two doctors called daily. I myself was in constant attendance, and I was sometimes assisted by a pupil nurse. We, and we alone, administered medicines to the patient. Obviously, procedures such as gastric lavage – necessary in such cases – were carried out by us, the medical staff.'

'And as to visitors....'

'Yes, I'm coming to that, Sergeant. I just wished to make clear to you that the administering of poison by introducing it into medicine-bottles, would have been impossible.'

'How about introducing it into food? I expect the Warden's meals came up from his own kitchen in the Lodgings.'

'Food?' For a moment Nurse Townley seemed taken aback. 'Well, I suppose that could have been possible. The poison would have to have been introduced in the kitchen, or on the way upstairs, but – oh! It seems most unlikely, Mr Maxwell.'

'But not impossible?'

'No. But Sir Montague ate very little solid food, because of his condition. Brand's Essence, and calf's-foot jelly were the staple, and these were supplied by us – the medical staff. Now, here's my log of family visitors. Miss Fowler, who lives in Oxford, called in almost daily, usually in the afternoon. She never stayed long, until Friday, 1 June, when it became evident that Sir Montague would not survive. She was almost constantly present for the last three days of Sir Montague's life.

'Mr John Fowler made four visits from London, on Thursday, 24 May, Monday, the 28th, Wednesday, the 30th, and Friday, 1st June. He, too, stayed in Oxford for the last three days. He spent most of his visits talking to the doctors, when they were present, though occasionally he would sit on the bed and chat to his father. I got the impression that Mr John Fowler expected his father to recover from his illness, though both doctors and myself knew that there was no possibility of this.'

'And the Reverend Mr Timothy Fowler?'

'Well, Sergeant, he was very assiduous, you know, very concerned. Although he lived a very long way off, in Hampshire, he came up to Oxford on five occasions, and stayed all day. He contrived to alternate his visits with those of his brother. He came on Wednesday, the 23 May, and then on the Friday and Saturday, staying at the Mitre. He came again on Tuesday, the 29th, and then on Thursday, the 31st. On that occasion, he stayed at the Mitre again, remaining there until after his father had died.'

Sergeant Maxwell had been writing rapidly in his notebook.

He now closed it, and stood up.

'Thank you very much, Nurse Townley,' he said. 'You've been a very great help. Before I go, can I ask you, in confidence, for your own views on the death of Sir Montague Fowler?'

'Mr Maxwell, I've been a nurse for over thirty years. In my view, Sir Montague Fowler died of gastroenteritis, and all this talk of poison is a mare's nest. And yet – the results of the autopsy showed conclusively that mercuric chloride was present in the organs of the deceased. So it's a mystery, something that you and your colleagues are better able to solve than I.'

When Maxwell returned to 130 High Street, he found Inspector Antrobus reading a letter, which he put aside until the sergeant had finished his account of the meeting with Nurse Townley.

'Most assiduous, was he, our Reverend Timothy? A devoted son, rushing up from Hampshire to visit his father, despite the distance and the inconvenience. Well, Sergeant, I received this letter by the noon post. It's from a Mr de Neville, a gentleman living at Abbotsmead Manor, a mile or so out of Wolvercote. Read what he has to say.'

Dear Inspector Antrobus,

The newspapers have made mention recently of the suspicious death of Sir Montague Fowler, and there has been avid speculation about the role played in that tragedy by members of Sir Montague's family and colleagues. If you will come to visit me, at a time that can be mutually arranged, I will tell you something about one member of that family that has been a close secret for many years. Murder has been committed, and if justice is to prevail, there are hidden facts which must now be brought into the light of day.

Sincerely yours,
Louis de Neville

'One member of the family – do you think he means the Reverend Timothy, sir?'

'He may well do, Sergeant; I really can't see Miss Frances Fowler as the repository of close secrets, and Mr John Fowler, the elder brother, had no qualms in confessing to me how near he had come to ruin before he received his inheritance. So I'll leave you here in High Street to hold the fort for a day or two while I seek out this Mr de Neville and hear what he has to say. Perhaps you could keep a benevolent eye on Miss Fowler while I'm away. See what she gets up to, if anything. And then, Sergeant, you and I will go down to Hampshire and beard the Reverend Timothy Fowler in his den.'

'Why should this Mr de Neville write to you? We don't know, him, do we? I've not heard that name crop up among the people who knew Sir Montague.'

'Well, I'll find out, won't I, when I meet him. Maybe he's impelled by a sense of public duty. Duty, "stern Daughter of the Voice of God". Or maybe he's holding an ancient grudge against the family, and wants to cause trouble. We'll see.'

Abbotsmead Manor, the residence of Mr Louis de Neville, lay four miles to the north of Oxford, some way beyond the village of Wolvercote. It was a redbrick Tudor edifice of two storeys, and it still retained at its east end the gaunt, ivy-clad ruin of the monastery that had once occupied the site.

Inspector Antrobus was received by a butler, a slight, greying man wearing a black tailcoat. He led him into a long, dim library, where the morning sunlight filtered through a range of leaded windows. Sitting in a wheeled chair near one of the window embrasures was the owner of Abbotsmead Manor. The way he sat, as though he had become part of the chair that supported him, told Antrobus that Mr de Neville must have lost the use of his legs many years ago.

'Sanders,' said de Neville after Antrobus had been formally

announced, 'bring us coffee, will you? Antrobus, come and sit down here beside me.' De Neville waited until the butler had left the room before he spoke again.

'I have been in this condition, Inspector Antrobus,' he said, 'since I was a boy of thirteen. What is called infantile paralysis deprived me of the use of my legs, and I have been confined to a wheeled chair ever since.'

'I am very sorry, sir.'

The man in the wheeled chair held up a hand as though to fend off the inspector's commiseration.

'I mention the fact not to elicit your sympathy, Mr Antrobus, but because my condition is an important part of the story that I am going to tell you.'

De Neville paused, and seemed for a moment to be absorbed in his own thoughts. How old was he? Surely no more than forty, but his face, creased and lined by years of frustration, made him look far older. His legs were covered by a plaid blanket, but even with that discreet disguise, Antrobus could see that they were wasted. His shoulders, though, and his chest, were those of a man born to be strong and vigorous. Nature's cruel trick, that had robbed him of so much in his life, must have left Louis de Neville with a permanent sense of injustice.

'I have read all the accounts of Sir Montague Fowler's death that have appeared in the popular prints,' said the crippled man, 'and during the last couple of weeks I have noticed a lot of sinister speculation concerning Sir Montague's son, the Reverend Timothy Fowler. There has been talk of poison, and this talk has been linked more or less directly to Timothy. It was that particular thread of gossip that determined me to send for you. I gather from the newspapers that you are the officer investigating the case?'

'I am, sir.'

'Well, I want you to listen to what I have to say concerning Timothy Fowler. I am going to impart to you a secret that I have kept hidden in my heart since the year 1887. I feel that it is my duty to share that secret with you now.

'I am the younger son of the fourteenth Earl of Haddington, and I lived until comparatively recently at the family seat, Haddington Castle, in Buckinghamshire. You will understand that my condition precluded marriage, and I had no desire in those days to live away from our ancestral estates.

'Well, in the castle grounds there stands what was once a dower house, a substantial dwelling, built in the late seventeenth century, and this house has long been used as a residence for retired colonial bishops. For many years it had been the home of the Right Reverend Colin Bates, a former Bishop of Gondwanaland, and a celebrated tutor for young gentlemen who had decided to read for Orders.'

Mr de Neville paused again, and seemed to lose sight of Antrobus. He was leading up to something, and it would be a mistake to let him wander away into withdrawal from the present moment.

'And this Bishop Bates....'

'What? Yes, he was a very learned man – Latin, Greek, Hebrew, all that kind of thing. Well, Timothy Fowler graduated from Oriel College in 1884 – he'd have been twenty-one – and immediately came down to Haddington to read for Orders with Bishop Bates. There was another young man there, an attractive, athletic fellow called Adrian Fortescue, and the two of them became friends. Fowler was a renowned swimmer, and a celebrated cricketer, who had played for the varsity.

'I was not as reclusive then as I am now, and I was often in the company of the two ordinands, who would come over to the castle to swim in the river that flowed through the estate. They dined with us, too. Father was not a very devout man, but he liked Fowler and Fortesque, because they were both examples of "muscular Christianity", much given to physical pursuits.'

De Neville's mouth twisted in a sudden spasm of what

seemed like silent rage. So there had been envy as well as admiration, thought Antrobus. That was understandable, but if ever this gentleman came to the point, he would be on his guard against unconscious bias.

'Now, in Haddington village there dwelt a physician called Doctor Edward Grace, a man very well regarded, and blessed with a wife and a beautiful young daughter, called Kate. She was only seventeen, and very inexperienced in the ways of the world, and was rather taken aback when both young men fell in love with her. They *did*, you know: it wasn't just a case of flirtation. They fell for her, and as time went by it looked as though Adrian Fortesque would carry off the prize. This vexed Timothy Fowler, who knew that, in order to gain advancement in the Church, a fellow had to be married.'

There's the envy, thought Antrobus. That cynical remark arose from this man's physical incapacity. Who knows, he may have been in love with Kate himself.

'Kate's father was very fond of Timothy, but little Kate seemed to have a special affection for Adrian, and I remember my father saying that when all the reading was over, Adrian Fortescue would leave Haddington with Kate Grace on his arm.'

'But he didn't, sir, did he? So I assume something happened to prevent him.'

'It did. In the summer of 1887, when both young men were twenty-four, they came to Haddington Castle to spend the day swimming in the river. I vividly recall that day: it was very hot, with not a breath of air stirring. It was a Friday, 29 July, just days before they were to finish their studies. One of the footmen wheeled me out into a grove of trees from which I could look down at the river bank. I recall that I took with me Mary Braddon's *Cut by the County*, which had appeared the previous year.

'From time to time, I glimpsed the two of them as they ran along the bank towards a little diving-station, and I'd heard the splashing and good-humoured shouting as they vied with each other to swim to the further bank. As I have said, they were both powerful swimmers, and from time to time, I'd look up from my book, watching them idly, and appreciating their skill.

'After about an hour, they began to swim towards the bank. Fowler had just stepped up on to the wooden platform when Adrian Fortescue cried out that he was in difficulties. I was near enough to see the fear and distress in his eyes.'

The man in the wheeled chair treated Antrobus to a bitter smile.

'I was in the same condition then as I am now, Inspector. There was nothing that I could do. But Fowler – he just stood there on the platform, his arms folded, watching his companion drown. Fortesque struggled for a while, and then disappeared from sight. It was only then that Fowler swam out to the spot where Fortesque had disappeared. True, he dived twice, and was down for what seemed like an age on both occasions. But there was no doubt in my mind that he left Fortescue to drown. It was deliberate.'

'What happened next?'

'I stayed where I was, hidden from sight, hoping that my servant did not come for me while Fowler was there. I was terrified, you see. I was a witness to his moral dereliction, and had he seen me, he could easily have wheeled me to the margin, and tipped me into the river. In the end, he went away, and a quarter of an hour later my servant came to take me back to the house.'

The invalid writhed in his chair – it was a movement of impotent rage rather than pain.

'He left him to drown! And he did that because he wanted to marry Kate Grace. Murder by omission. And now it is being said that he might have poisoned his own father, again in the pursuit of gain. Well, this time, Mr Antrobus, I'll risk my life to make sure he is punished. I am at your service as a witness to that earlier crime – for crime it was.'

The invalid was lost in thought for a while. Then he spoke again.

'Timothy Fowler was – is – a very talented man, with all the gifts that would advance a clergyman in his career. The following year, which was the year in which he was ordained deacon, Fowler married Kate, who had just turned eighteen, with her parents' blessing. He never came to Adrian Fortescue's funeral.'

Louis de Neville sat back in his chair with a sigh. It was as though he had relieved himself of a burden that had oppressed him for the last seven years.

'I often wondered why he sought out an obscure country parish, when more than one London church was after him. Maybe Fortescue's death was the reason. Obscurity can shield a man from the observation of those who know the dark side of character. That's why I came here, you know, to Abbotsmead Manor. I wanted to hide from the sight of men. But at times like this I have to force myself to return to the world for a while.'

Inspector Antrobus rose. It was time to go.

'Thank you for telling me this story, Mr de Neville,' he said. 'It would be as well to keep your own counsel until the whole matter has come to a conclusion. I'll bid you good day, sir.'

Monstrous! A monstrous, wicked crime! There was no reason not to believe de Neville's story. A man who could leave a friend to drown – deliberately stand still and watch him die – would surely not scruple to send a parent out of this world if it suited his convenience.

Mr de Neville had said that Timothy had been 'down for what seemed like an age' when he had dived into the water to locate Adrian Fortescue's body. Perhaps, when he was lost to sight beneath the water, he had made doubly sure that his rival was dead? No time should be lost in confronting the Reverend Timothy Fowler. He and Maxwell would go down to Clapton Parva the next day.

10

TIMOTHY FOWLER'S ORDEAL

Mrs Mary Trefusis turned to her friend, Lady Corrina Davenant, and said: 'I never go anywhere else for hats, these days. Miss Forrest has impeccable taste. Look at these straw boaters! Aren't they just the *dernier cri*?' Lady Corrina looked doubtful. 'They're very nice, dear, but don't you think they're a trifle too young for us? They'd look exactly right on your youngest girl, Julia, of course.'

Mary Trefusis smiled. Corrina was a dear soul, but there were times when she could be vexingly obtuse.

'I was thinking of Julia, not myself – or you, for that matter,' she replied. 'It's her birthday next week, and one of those boaters would go well with…. Ah! Here's Miss Forrest, now!'

Ursula Forrest, looking elegant in an emerald green morning dress, came out of her private room, closing the door carefully behind her. She smiled at her visitors.

'Lady Corrina, Mrs Trefusis, how delightful to see you both! Will you take coffee? It's just on eleven o'clock.'

Both ladies declined coffee, and began to admire the straw boaters, each of which was adorned with a silk ribbon. They were very smart, and clearly of the highest quality.

'I'm considering one of those hats for my daughter, Julia,'

said Mrs Trefusis. 'I'm trying to picture her wearing it with one of those leg-of-mutton blouses that girls like so much these days. What do you think, Miss Forrest?'

'An excellent choice, Mrs Trefusis. Now this one here, with the dark purple band – this would go so well with one of the new striped blouses from Jeanne Paquin, who's starting to take Paris by storm. As a matter of fact, I'm stocking a small selection of her better creations.'

Ursula opened a glazed press, and pulled out a shelf on which lay a beautiful silk blouse, cream in colour, and with vertical purple stripes. Both ladies exclaimed with delight.

'Oh! That would be ideal, Miss Forrest. I'll take that one. Let me see – yes, the size is just right. And two of the hats. Two, in case she loses one, you know.'

Ursula clapped her hands, and a young girl of fifteen or so appeared from a back room. She looked at her employer with a mixture of devotion and awe.

'Céline,' said Miss Forrest, 'pack up these items, and tell Robert to take them immediately to 14, Queen Adelaide Gate. Shall I debit them to your account, Mrs Forrest?'

'Yes, do. I'm so very pleased. Really, you have so many wonderful things here.'

'Thank you, madam. I've always believed that quality tells. Lady Corrina, can I interest you in anything this morning?'

'No thank you, Miss Forrest. I've just come to look around.'

Ursula gave all her attention to Mrs Trefusis, who seemed disinclined to leave the premises.

'Miss Julia, your daughter – I think you told me that she is approaching eighteen? Perhaps she is old enough to come to visit me unaccompanied – I mean just with her maid, of course. It's quite a thrill for a young lady to visit a fashion house on her own!'

'Well, she's at a boarding establishment in the country at the moment, but she will be home for her birthday, so perhaps I'll add a visit here as an extra treat!'

Ursula smiled, and excused herself. She went into the back room where the girl called Céline was busy packing Mrs Trefusis' purchases.

'Mary,' Lady Corrina whispered, 'don't insist on Julia coming here alone. I don't think it's quite nice, you know. I'm not one to gossip, but....'

At that moment the door of Miss Forrest's private room opened, and a young woman dressed in a rather risqué bloomer suit emerged. She was struggling with a mahogany camera mounted on a wooden tripod. She smiled at the two startled ladies, and made her way to a small hydraulic goods lift in one corner of the room.

Miss Forrest emerged from the back room, followed by a cheerful young boy, who was carrying the parcels that Céline had made up. He, too, made his way to the lift.

'Robert will be at your house in Queen Adelaide Gate within the hour, Mrs Trefusis,' she said. 'I very much look forward to seeing you again before the autumn.'

Once more, the door of her private room opened, and a beautiful young woman emerged. She looked flushed and excited. With scarce a glance at the two ladies, the young woman hurried through the swing doors that led to the stairs down to Old Bond Street.

'Goodness me!' said Mrs Trefusis. 'I could have sworn that that woman was Julia's headmistress in Oxford – Miss Frances Fowler. Oh, no, it couldn't be. Although the undergraduates have gone down, Miss Fowler's girls are still up till mid-August. She's quite a beauty, you know, just like that girl who's gone out.'

Miss Forrest made as though she had not heard what her customer had said. After a few more civilities, she bowed the two ladies out of her salon through the swing doors.

'Mary,' said Lady Corrina Davenant, 'don't let Julia come

here alone. I don't like that woman. I've heard things.... Do you remember little Rose Jacobs, who threw herself in front of a train? She was only nineteen. Well, she was involved in some way with Miss Forrest. I'll say no more, as some things should not be spoken of aloud in polite society. But you know what I mean. At least, I hope you do.'

Mrs Trefusis was very quiet as they emerged into Old Bond Street, and walked the short distance to the spot where Lady Corrina Davenant's carriage was waiting. She thought of her dear daughter, doing so well at Makin House, and speaking so highly of the young headmistress. To herself, she said: I'm as certain as anything that that was Miss Frances Fowler who came out of Miss Forrest's room. When Ernest comes home tonight from the City, I shall tell him all about it.

Frances Fowler's heart was beating so rapidly that she wondered whether she was about to suffer a seizure. She sat back carefully on the seat of the cab, and closed her eyes. She would not feel secure until she was on the 12.30 train from Paddington to Oxford.

The visit to Ursula and Rosalie had been one of the most thrilling events of her life. At last, having thrown convention aside, she was a fully-trusted member of the coterie. She had planned to return in a week to see the prints of Rosalie's photographs. It was a prospect that had sent her blood racing.

And then, as she left Ursula's private room, she had come face to face with the mother of one of her girls! She had been wise to hurry from the shop, relying on the very improbability of its being she who had apparently been closeted in private with the fashionable milliner. Pray God that Julia Trefusis' mother had soon convinced herself that she had been mistaken!

But what if she asked her outright? If she admitted that it had been she, she would have to elaborate a tissue of lies to explain her presence there. She could say that she had asked to see Miss

Forrest privately in order to question a bill that she had received. But the very fact of offering an explanation would in itself seem odd, a kind of justification for having done something as seemingly innocent as stepping into a milliner's private room. Well, there had been nothing innocent about it.

So much, then, for integrity. She had always stressed the necessity of truth to her girls – truth in their relationships with others, truth in the evaluation of theories and the interpretation of facts. But now, a vital part of her life had become a living lie. No one must know of her membership of the coterie. To outward seeming, she knew of no such group, and would deny any knowledge of it. To maintain this kind of lie required constant vigilance. Was it Quintilian who said: 'A liar should have a good memory'?

What would happen if those photographs were ever made public? The parents of all her pupils would withdraw their girls immediately. There could be no doubt whatever about that. It would be the end of her school, the end of her career, and the end of her standing in society. Had something like that happened to the girl who had thrown herself under a train?

And – oh, God! What if Timothy found out? Would he reject her? He had often spoken of God's wrath at the commission of unnatural acts, and had once given a sermon on the text of Romans 1, verse 26: it was a condemnation of those who abandoned God in order to pursue their own wicked desires.

'For this cause God gave them up unto vile affections: for even their women did change the natural use into that which is against nature.'

Timothy must never know. No one must ever know. Only God knew the disposition of her heart, and perhaps He would, in His infinite mercy, forgive her.

The village street of Clapton Parva was wide, but as yet unpaved, so that the two policemen's feet sent up little clouds of dust as they walked. The left side of the street was flanked with farm labourers' cottages, a few little shops, and a forge, but the right-hand side boasted a gracious, ivy-covered mansion, built in the early years of the eighteenth century. It was separated from the road by a low wall, with railings and gates, giving access to a well-kept lawn.

'That'll be the vicarage,' said Inspector Antrobus. 'Our Mr Timothy doesn't live there – at least, not for the moment. He's due to move in as soon as the ancient vicar is removed to pastures new.'

'How did you know that?' asked Sergeant Maxwell.

'It's my business to know things. Yours, too.'

Their arrival in the village had not gone unnoticed, though the majority of the menfolk were out in the fields. But women talking at their front doors stopped to look at them, and whispered behind their hands.

We're both in sober civilian garb, thought Antrobus, but I wager that all those ladies will know that we are policemen.

Confound this chest pain! It always came when his ravaged lungs were about to make him spit blood. Was there time to chew a pulmonic wafer? Yes. Doing that would give him relief for half an hour or so.

He took a folded paper from his pocket, removed the quick-dissolving wafer, and put it in his mouth. As always on such occasions, Sergeant Maxwell looked away, and began to hum a tune. It was usually *Rule, Britannia*; today, for some reason, it was the Prussian national anthem.

They turned off the main street into a lane, little more than a track, that led them through a coppice, and into a sort of clearing, in which stood the curate's house. It was small, and very old, sagging with the weariness of centuries. The roof slates had turned green with lichen, and the wooden palings defining the little patch of garden were for the most part either broken or missing.

'I'm not going to beat about the bush, Sergeant,' said Antrobus. 'A frontal attack will produce the best results. I know he's there, you see, but he doesn't know that I'm coming. The little wife should be there, too.'

They rang the bell, and after what seemed like an age, the front door was opened by a tearful young girl in cap and apron. She shrank back from them in evident fear. What ailed the girl?

'You're the police, aren't you? You'd better come in.'

She stood aside, and they entered the little hallway of the decrepit house. She made no attempt to take their hats or coats. Instead, she began to sob.

'It's all my fault,' she whispered. 'I shouldn't have told my dad what I saw....'

'You'll be Lucy Hammond, I expect,' said Antrobus. 'Well, Lucy, you've done nothing wrong. So take me to see your master, the Reverend Mr Timothy Fowler. And when you've done that, go into the kitchen and talk to Detective Sergeant Maxwell here. My name's Detective Inspector Antrobus. Come on, girl, take me to see your master!'

As the weeping maid-servant ushered him into the dark parlour of the curate's house, a clergyman dressed in a black frock coat, and wearing the Roman collar now coming into common use in the Church of England, rose from a chair, not so much as to greet him, Antrobus thought, as to confront him as a potential foe. He was a tall man, with fair hair, handsome and well made, but his eyes could not conceal his fear. The inspector handed him his warrant card, and the clergyman fumbled in his waistcoat pocket for a little pair of steel-rimmed reading glasses.

Antrobus glanced around the room. There were some good pieces of furniture, but the carpets were worn, and the place looked in dire need of redecoration. A glance at the ceiling told him that gas had not been laid on. Presumably, Fowler, now the possessor of a considerable fortune, was 'camping out' in this genteel hovel for reasons of his own.

The mantelpiece held a massive ebony clock, which had stopped, and beside the clock was a silver-framed photograph of a young woman. Presumably it was a likeness of Mrs Fowler. Antrobus had heard her described as 'pretty', but to his way of thinking that was an understatement. To judge from the photograph, Kate Fowler was beautiful. No wonder that her husband, seven years earlier, had stood by and watched his rival in love drown....

'Inspector Antrobus?' said the clergyman, handing back the warrant-card. 'We have not met before, I believe, though I have heard much about you. How can I be of service?'

He had managed to control his voice, but his eyes still held a look of fear. Perhaps he fully expected to be arrested.

'Mr Fowler, I'll not beat about the bush. As you are aware, I am the police officer investigating your father's murder, a murder motivated by the greed of gain. It was thought at first that he had died from circulatory collapse, consequent upon a fatal nephritis. But that was not so. He was poisoned most cruelly with a substance called mercuric chloride, and his murderer hoped that his death would be put down to gastroenteritis. Now, sir, how do you account for the fact that you were seen retrieving a packet of that poison from beneath your dead father's bed?'

Timothy Fowler jumped with fright, and sat down hastily on a sofa. He had gone deadly pale, and for a moment seemed quite unable to speak.

'Good heavens! What are you suggesting? I never....'

'You were seen retrieving that packet, sir, and concealing it about your person. You brought it back here, to this house, and locked it away in your desk. I know that you benefited from your father's death by inheriting a considerable fortune at a time when you most needed money. I tell you I know all these things, and it will be profitless to pretend that you did otherwise than I have stated.'

'Retrieved? That is not so. I had knelt down to say some prayers, and saw the packet lying beneath the bed. I was curious to know what it was. I picked it up.'

'Did you read the label? The label that said it was a packet of mercuric chloride?'

'Yes, I did. Of course I did! But....'

'And then, instead of informing the police immediately – you would have found us in our headquarters in Oxford High Street – you put it in your pocket, and when you got home here, to Hampshire, you locked it away in your desk. Why did you do that? What am I supposed to think? I am sure that you found it difficult to make ends meet on a curate's stipend of seventy-eight pounds a year. Your father's death relieved you of all financial worries.'

'This is outrageous! Are you accusing me of parricide? You have no right!'

'I have every right. I have seen the frantic letter that your wife wrote to her sister-in-law, telling her what she had seen in your desk. Why did you lock it away? And where is Mrs Fowler? I need to question her, too. Is she not here?'

The Reverend Timothy Fowler uttered a deep groan, and buried his head in his hands. He looked utterly forlorn. Instinctively, Antrobus realized that his wife had left him.

'My wife – I thought it judicious to send her to stay with her parents at Haddington, in Buckinghamshire, until this terrible business is over. But she knows nothing....'

'Knows nothing of what, sir? Does she know that you went up to Oxford on five occasions during your father's illness, and stayed all day? Plenty of time to make deadly use of the packet of mercuric chloride that you later locked away so secretively in your desk. You went there on Wednesday, 23 May, and then on the Friday and Saturday of the same week, staying at the Mitre. You went again on Tuesday, 29th, and then on Thursday, the 31st, when you stayed at the Mitre again, remaining there until after your father had died.'

'Do you really think that I, an ordained clergyman, could commit such an unnatural and heinous crime?'

'Why did you take the packet of poison away with you, and conceal it? Did you, perhaps, fear that your brother, or your sister, had done the deed? If you are not guilty, then perhaps you want to accuse either of them of parricide? And as for committing such a crime, it would not be the first time, Mr Fowler, that a man close to you had died.'

'What do you mean?'

'I am referring to a man called Adrian Fortescue, whom you deliberately left to drown, although you could have saved him. He, too, stood in your way, so you murdered him by default. Do not try to hide behind your Holy Orders in this matter, Mr Fowler. Be sure your sins will find you out.'

There came a cry of anguish from the man on the sofa, and Antrobus saw that he had fainted: his deliberately relentless barrage of accusations had had more than their desired effect. He sat still, waiting for the stricken man to recover from his faint. He wondered what Sergeant Maxwell had contrived to find out from Lucy Hammond, the weeping maid known in that house as 'the Slow Girl.'

'Missus was terrified,' said Lucy Hammond. 'The rumours were flying round that Master had poisoned his own father with that stuff that he'd hidden in his desk. She waited until he was out of the house on his round of visits one day, and told me that she was going to run away to her mother in Buckinghamshire.'

Having a policeman in the house had evidently given the young girl courage to speak freely. She sat with Sergeant Maxwell in the little cramped kitchen; where a stew was simmering in a pan placed on the old-fashioned oil-stove.

'"Have you not told Mr Fowler that you're going?" I asked her, and she said no, because if she'd told him, he'd have forbidden her to go. And so I helped her to pack, and she left in the post-chaise from the village. So Master's all alone here.'

'Why do you think she ran away?'

'She was afraid that … she never told me in so many words, Mr Maxwell, but I think she was afraid he'd poison her, too!'

The young girl's lip curled in ill-disguised contempt.

'What a terrible thing to imagine! He dotes on her, Mr Maxwell, and she should know that. She's not much use in a house, and depends on him for everything. He's in trouble, right enough, but she should have stuck by him, instead of running home to Mother.'

'Do you think she's left him for good? This is all between you and me, Lucy.'

'If things go bad for the Master, she'll stay away. But if it turns out well with him, then she'll be back, and he'll welcome her with open arms. She knows what side her bread's buttered on.'

'So you're looking after him all by yourself?'

'Yes. Somebody's got to see to him: he can't manage by himself. Father – he's a college servant in Oxford – wants me to come home to him, but I'm not leaving Mr Fowler to fend for himself. A gentleman doesn't know what to do.'

'How old are you, Lucy?'

'I'm fifteen. Sixteen this coming December.'

'And you're not afraid that Mr Fowler might poison you, as well?'

Lucy Hammond laughed.

'Poison me? Of course he won't poison me. And he won't poison Kate, either. Beg pardon, Mrs Fowler, I should say. He's too soft-hearted for that. As for what happened to his father, well, I don't know. Master's a shadow of the man he was only a few weeks ago. He's haunted by fears and fancies, and, of course, he won't confide in me. A gentleman doesn't unburden himself to a servant-girl.'

Sergeant Maxwell got to his feet.

'Well, Lucy,' he said, 'Mr Fowler's very lucky to have you on his side. You're a good girl, and one day you'll have a husband and house of your own. And when you do, share your troubles with your husband, and he'll share his with you. No locked drawers, hey? Goodbye, Lucy, I must go and see how my guvnor's getting on.'

Sergeant Maxwell entered the parlour just as the Reverend Timothy Fowler, pale and trembling, was rising to his feet. He did not seem to see Maxwell: his eyes were riveted on Inspector Antrobus.

'Are you going to arrest me?' he whispered.

'I am advising you to be prepared for that contingency,' said Antrobus. 'You must not leave this village without first informing me by telegram of your destination. My case is not yet complete, but when it is, I shall be calling on you.'

He bowed stiffly to the stricken man, and followed his sergeant out of the room.

The next morning, Timothy Fowler came downstairs to find his breakfast of egg, bacon and sausage waiting for him on the table. At the same moment, Lucy Hammond came in from the kitchen, carrying the teapot. She contrived to give him a cheerful 'good morning.'

Why had they laughed at her, dubbing her 'the Slow Girl'? As things stood, he would be utterly helpless without her. Kate.... Had she not realized that her flight – for such it was – would add further scandal to their situation? That man yesterday – relentless, remorseless, seeking his father's murderer, and raking up the horror of seven years ago, when he had stood by and let Adrian Fortescue drown. He was to stay here, in his parish, a virtual prisoner, until, one day, Antrobus returned with a warrant of arrest.

'Lucy,' he said, 'you have been so kind to me in my time of need. God will richly reward you for your good heart.'

The girl blushed with pleasure. It was the first time the Master had praised her. Well, she would stick by him. Maybe things would soon turn out for the better.

Half an hour after Lucy left to go home, the postman arrived, bringing him two letters. One of them bore the crest of Lord Stevenage. Its contents brought a new chill to the wretched clergyman's heart.

My dear Fowler,

Of recent days I have been gravely disturbed by the rumours circulating about your father's death. As you know, I have the highest regard for you, both as a man and a clergyman, but I cannot ignore the sinister imputations that are being made against you from different quarters. Of that, I shall say no more.

However, you will understand that I cannot now let you have the advowson of the parish until this whole matter is cleared up. Meanwhile, the present incumbent is clearly unfit to carry out his duties, and a replacement must be found soon. I have written to the Bishop telling him of my decision, and I have no doubt that he will soon communicate with you.

Please convey my compliments to your charming wife.

Stevenage

The second letter was little more than a note, but it was equally sinister in its implications. It was from the Right Reverend Anthony Thorold, Bishop of Winchester.

My dear Fowler,

In view of your present situation, I should appreciate

your coming to see me here at Wolvesley Castle as soon as possible. I can make time to see you on any day of your choice.

Yours sincerely,

✝ Anthony Winton.

Timothy Fowler went into his study and opened his desk, in order to write three letters. It would be judicious not to reply to Lord Stevenage's letter, but he was obliged to reply to the Bishop immediately. He would also have to let Antrobus know that he was travelling to Winchester. Finally, he would write to Fanny. When the Bishop had done with him, he would seek refuge with his sister at her school in North Oxford.

11

SOPHIA JEX-BLAKE

THE MEMORIAL SERVICE for Sir Montague Fowler was held in the University Church of St Mary the Virgin on the morning of Monday, 16 July. The little procession of dons from St Michael's College, resplendent in their gowns and hoods, walked out of Sparrow Lane, passed down Brasenose College Lane, and came into Radcliffe Square. A group of visitors, who had come to admire the Radcliffe Camera, stopped to look at them as they entered the great church.

The Warden, Dr William Podmore, found that he and Joe Steadman had been assigned seats next to each other to the left of the pulpit. For the last three weeks, he had contrived to show various favours to the Bursar, supporting him at meetings of the Senior College, and suggesting that he should move into a grander suite of rooms in the first quadrangle. Steadman had received that particular sop to Cerberus with due deference, but with a faint smile of amusement that had chilled Podmore to the bone.

The church was packed with representatives of the university and the town, together with delegations from the many charities and institutions that the late Warden had supported. The Chancellor of the University, the Marquess of Salisbury, sat with some senior clergy in the distant sanctuary. Up in the west gallery, a number of men stood with notebooks at the ready; the press were still interested in anything to do with the murdered man, his family, friends and colleagues.

Ah! Here was the outgoing Vice-Chancellor, the Reverend Henry Boyd, mounting the pulpit. He was an able speaker, but everyone knew that he'd feel obliged to talk about Fowler for longer than was decent. Well, best settle down and wait patiently for the encomium to end.

Podmore thought: had it been Steadman who had sent him that vile, anonymous letter? Could he have possibly known about his wretched, contemptible plagiarism of old Bosch's work? But Steadman had shown no signs of exulting in his torment. He seemed his usual cheerful self, content to regale them in the common room with tales of undergraduate folly based on incidents in his second persona of 'Old Joe', the college plumber.

Vice-Chancellor Boyd was getting into full stride.

'Many of us here today will remember Montague Fowler's work in establishing the research library that bears his name, a library which he most generously endowed, and which will help future generations of scholars, through the field scholarships attached to it, to throw fresh light on the origins of North African civilization....'

And a colossal waste of money *that* had been, thought Podmore. No wonder his children had become alarmed.

There were only two possible successors to Henry Boyd as Vice-Chancellor: himself, and John Magrath at Queen's. Well, it would remain to be seen who was the better man. But this – this cursed burden of the plagiarism: if the truth of it ever came out, he would be ruined. There would be no possibility of his being eligible for the coveted post, and there was more than a possibility that he would be dismissed as Warden of St Michael's.

Possibility? No: certainty. What was he to do? Was it really Steadman who had placed that terrible letter in his rooms?

There is someone who knows that you plagiarized and pillaged the work of Georg Joachim Bosch. That person has seen documentary proof of your cheating. The *Boethian Apices* is not your work. Perhaps one day your infamy will become known.

It had been produced on a typewriter, which gave it a terrible anonymity.

Podmore glanced at the man sitting beside him. Steadman seemed to be listening to Boyd with rapt attention. But then, he had been devoted to Fowler – 'Monty', he'd called him.

He had destroyed that hateful letter, but its words had been seared into his memory.

Dr Joseph Steadman contemplated slipping his watch out of his waistcoat pocket to see what time it was, but thought better of it. He had long ago mastered the art of seeming to be enraptured by something that was boring him silly. Would old Boyd never stop?

He glanced at the nearby Cranmer's pillar, where he could see the ledge that had been cut into the stonework to provide a support for the wooden stage that had been erected in 1556. There, Archbishop Cranmer had sat on the morning of Saturday, 21 March, to hear a sermon preached by Dr Henry Cole, Provost of Eton. It would not have been as interminable as Boyd's encomium, because all present on that occasion were anxious to see Cranmer burnt at the stake outside Balliol later that day.

Podmore was clearly not listening to Dr Boyd: his mind seemed to be elsewhere. Steadman had no desire whatsoever to expose the Warden publicly for the plagiarist that he was – there was a limit to one's dislike of the man. But it was inwardly satisfying to know that the fellow was a cheat and a fraud. Perhaps there was a suffering, guilty soul lurking behind that smug carapace of superiority? He doubted it. Men of Podmore's stamp, whatever their outward appearance, were as hard as nails.

'And now to God the Father, God the Son, and God the Holy Ghost....'

At last! The Vice-Chancellor had stopped. He left the pulpit, and they all rose to receive a blessing from Bishop Mackarness. The organ sounded, the Chancellor left in his own little procession, followed by the Mayor and Council. The congregation poured out thankfully into sunlit Radcliffe Square.

'If you are lucky enough to succeed Henry Boyd as Vice-Chancellor,' said Steadman, 'will you promise not to give such unconscionably long addresses?'

Podmore laughed.

'Well, I'm not in Holy Orders, Steadman,' he said, 'so I will have no clerical records to break in that respect! But come, let's get back to the reception in hall. You used the word "lucky" just now. I don't think luck will come in to it. I'm more than confident that the powers-that-be will see the wisdom of making me their choice. John Magrath will come a worthy second.'

Fanny Fowler left the church, and hurried to a private-hire hackney carriage drawn up in nearby Catte Street. It was still the period of full mourning, so that she was afforded a welcome anonymity by her long mourning veil. What an ordeal it had been! John had attended as a matter of form, but had contrived to leave the church early through a side door, in order to catch a train back to London, where business beckoned.

Timothy – poor Tim! He was in her house, now, skulking like a fugitive. She would tell him about the service, and how appallingly dry and formal it had been.

The carriage turned into Broad Street. It would be a long haul from there, down past the Ashmolean Museum, and then along the seemingly endless Walton Street and out to Port Meadow. She sat back on the cushions and thought about her brother.

He had written to her, telling her of Inspector Antrobus's visit, his terrible accusation, and his insistence that Tim should inform him by post or telegraph of his whereabouts at all times. Kate had left him to stay with her parents. Well, she could stay there, for all Fanny cared. Little fool!

At first, Timothy would tell her nothing. He had been summoned by the Bishop of Winchester to an interview. He had received the Bishop's letter last Thursday, and in a kind of fit of desperate rage and humiliation, he had dashed off a telegram to Inspector Antrobus and hurried down to Winchester by an early train on Friday. The Bishop had seen him immediately, but Tim would not tell her what he had said to him.

Lord Stevenage had withdrawn his offer of the advowson, but really, there was nothing else that he could have done.

Fanny sighed. Poor, foolish, ambitious Tim! She had always gone in awe of him, but now she felt only compassion and a desire to protect him, both from himself, and from a hostile world. Publicly, she would deny that her brother had had any part in his father's death, and yet she could fully understand Mr Antrobus's determination to think otherwise. Her brother's conduct in retaining the packet of poison had been more than suspicious: it could only be explained by assuming that he was guilty.

That very morning she had confronted him about the matter.

'You say that you saw that packet lying under Father's bed, and that you picked it up. Why did you put it in your pocket? Why did you take it back secretly with you to Hampshire, telling no one about it? Can you blame people for thinking that you are a guilty man? Do you care? Do you care what *I* think about you?'

Her vehemence had evoked a response of sorts.

'When I saw it, Fanny, I was horrified. I immediately jumped to the conclusion that either you or John had dropped it there. I thought that one or other of you could not wait for Father to die in the natural course of things. And so I hid it away. How it came to the light of day I don't know. Do you believe me?'

'It's not a very pleasant thing to hear you say that you thought your own brother and sister were capable of murder,' she'd replied. 'But yes, I do believe you. And you, Tim, should have had more faith in your own family. You should have taken that poison straight away to the police. As I once told Mr Antrobus, Father lived in St Michael's College. It was there, among that pack of dons, that he should be looking for his killer.'

It was then that he had told her about his interview with the Bishop of Winchester.

The Bishop had told him that the Church could not countenance any scandal in the matter of Sir Montague Fowler's death, particularly any suggestion that he had been made away with (they were the Bishop's own words) by his own son, a clerk in Holy Orders.

Timothy was to go to St Faith's, Spanner Lane, a poor dockside parish in Portsmouth, and labour there among the poor and destitute for a period of three years. As he was now a man of considerable substance, he would not receive a stipend. An Anglican bishop had no power to force a cleric into a particular parish, but if Tim refused to do as he was bid, the Bishop would suspend his licence to preach.

Frances could not forbear a smile when her brother expressed his horror at having to serve in a Ritualist parish, 'little better than Rome', with orders from the Bishop that he was not to interfere with the worship and customs of the place.

After this outburst, Tim had rallied a little, and had contrived to eat a light breakfast before she set out for the memorial service. For all that, he still lay under suspicion, and it was clear that Mr Antrobus had singled him out as the man who had murdered his own father for gain. He had faced the disappointment of losing Lord Stevenage's patronage manfully enough. He would now have to respond to the Bishop's challenge, and lie low at Portsmouth for a few years. That is, of course, if he was not arrested for Father's murder, found guilty, and hanged.

When she arrived back at Makin House, she learned that Tim had gone for a walk across the meadow. Throwing off her mourning cloak, she retired to her study, where Trixie brought her a welcome cup of tea. What a cheerful, willing girl she was! She remembered asking her whether Trixie was her real name. 'It's really Patricia, mum,' she'd said, 'but that's not a servant's name.' She'd mentioned this interesting piece of below-stairs etiquette to the Lady Principal of Lady Margaret Hall, who told her that girls christened 'Helen' who wished to go into service had to call themselves Ellen. Ellen was acceptable as a name for a servant. Helen was not.

The Lady Principal ... Elizabeth Wordsworth had not only been the founding Principal of Lady Margaret Hall in 1879, she had gone on to found and endow St Hugh's College. Daughter of one bishop and sister of another, she was a formidable woman, and one of Fanny's heroines. Would she, perhaps, agree to be her confidante? They had met on more than one occasion, and the older woman had shown her approbation of Fanny's determination to succeed in her plan to educate senior girls for entrance to the three Oxford women's colleges.

Fanny sat down at her desk, and began to compose a note to the Lady Principal of Lady Margaret Hall.

The following Wednesday was a hot, sultry day, though the sky seemed innocent of any threatening clouds. Miss Wordsworth had sent a reply by hand to Fanny's note, stating that she would be free that morning, and would look forward to seeing her any time after nine o'clock.

There was a quality of domesticity and warmth about Lady Margaret Hall that Fanny had never found in any of the other colleges of the university. It had started life fifteen years earlier in a yellow-brick, mock-Gothic villa in Norham Gardens, where Miss Wordsworth had opened her college with nine students. The house, known as Old Hall, had received a fine redbrick extension designed by Sir Basil Champneys in the eighties. In a way perhaps unique to Oxford, the new building soon came to be known as New Old Hall.

Fanny walked slowly along the sweep of gravel that would take her to the front entrance of Old Hall. Was she right in bothering the distinguished Lady Principal with what was essentially a domestic matter? Would she lose face by showing Miss Wordsworth the weakness of her regard for Tim?

She mounted the steps under the heavy porch, and rang the bell. The door was opened immediately by a girl wearing the apron and ribboned cap of a parlour-maid.

'Miss Fowler?' she asked. 'Please come this way. Madam Principal is expecting you.'

Elizabeth Wordsworth was sitting at a table in her crowded study, sifting through what appeared to be a pile of examination papers. A woven cane waste-paper basket beside the table was full of balls of crumpled-up paper. The study walls, papered in a heavily floral William Morris style, were covered in framed pictures and portraits.

The Lady Principal rose from the table and came forward to greet her visitor. She was wearing a long dress of some dark material, and her still fair hair was crowned with a somewhat old-fashioned cap of black and white lace. She was an impressive woman, with a firm jaw and piercing eyes that regarded Fanny from beneath dark eyebrows.

'Sit down in that chair, Miss Fowler,' she said, 'and tell me what it is that ails you. You spoke of a "family matter". You compose yourself well for so young a woman, but you cannot hide the desperation that I can see lurking in your eyes.'

'Oh, dear Miss Wordsworth,' Fanny cried, 'it is my brother, the Reverend Timothy Fowler. He is suspected of having – having murdered his father, and I know he did no such thing! Inspector Antrobus will arrest him at any moment. What shall I do? I have no one to turn to....'

Despite a heroic effort to remain calm, Frances Fowler suddenly burst into tears. It was evidently a much-needed catharsis, because she abandoned herself to a bout of pro-longed weeping. Miss Wordsworth sat in silence, watching her. Eventually her young visitor gained her self-control.

'You poor child,' said Miss Wordsworth, 'you have been much tried. I've heard all the rumours, of course, and I flatter myself that I'm not too proud to listen to them. And this police officer has settled upon your brother Timothy as the culprit. Just now, you said that you knew your brother had done no such thing – murdered his father. Do you know that as a fact? You don't, do you? If you knew it as a fact, you could produce that fact as conclusive proof of his innocence.'

'You are right, Miss Wordsworth. I don't know for sure. I don't know at all.'

Fanny sank back in her chair with a feeling of utter wretch-edness. She had made a fool of herself for nothing. She must find an excuse to leave as soon as was decent.

Miss Wordsworth had picked up a pencil, and was drum-ming absently with it on the table. Then she seemed to make up her mind as to a course of action.

'Come, Miss Fowler,' she said, standing up. 'I want you to meet someone who will be very interested to hear your story, someone who, I am sure, will be able to help you. Have you heard of Dr Sophia Jex-Blake?'

Fanny awoke abruptly from her bout of despair. 'She is here?' she cried.

'She is. She and I are exact contemporaries, and we've both

striven long and hard for equal opportunities for women. Her father was a lawyer, you know, a decent man enough, but of a narrow cast of mind. He did not approve much of women's education, but Sophia persuaded him to let her go to the classes at Queen's College for Women in Harley Street. That was in 1858. She was only eighteen. She was always a determined woman, undeterred by ridicule and obstruction – and there was plenty of that. Eventually, she qualified as a doctor at the Irish College of Physicians.'

'And she will help me?'

'She has an acute mind, Miss Fowler, and a penchant for logical thought. Her mind is far superior to mine. She's here as my guest for a few weeks during the long vacation, so she's plenty of time to spare. Tell her the whole story, beginning with the death of your poor father. Leave nothing out. She's having a mid-morning break in the garden. Come, I will take you to her.'

On the few visits that Fanny had made to Lady Margaret Hall, she had felt immediately embraced by the 'country house' quality of the college buildings, and by the understated elegance of the gardens. The close-cropped lawns glowed in the sun, the beds of summer flowers close to the walls of Old and New Old Hall were a riot of colour. The gable end of Champneys' Wren-like extension was covered with Virginia creeper and Wisteria.

Dr Sophia Jex-Blake was sitting in a cane chair drawn up to a cast-iron garden table, upon which some tea things had been set out. She was reading a newspaper, with the aid of small, round, gold-framed spectacles. She was dressed smartly but soberly in a businesslike costume dress. Her fair hair, parted in the middle, was uncovered. She had a round, pleasant face, and was blessed with a flawless complexion.

'Sophia,' said Elizabeth Wordsworth, 'I want you to meet Miss Frances Fowler, Headmistress of Makin House School. She has an intriguing tale to tell. Let me leave you both for a while.

If you agree together, we can all have luncheon at one o'clock.'

'You have been crying, Miss Fowler,' said Dr Jex-Blake. 'This tea is still hot. Let me pour you out a cup, and when you've drunk it, you will tell me your story.'

She put her newspaper down on the grass, and sat watching Frances as she obediently sipped her cup of tea. Did this girl know how beautiful she was? Well, perhaps it was of no import. If she had founded a school, and then became its principal, beauty had only limited relevance. Miss Fowler had chosen her part....

The lawn was bathed in the strong summer sunlight. Somnolent bees drifted past. And everywhere there was the scent of flowers. By the time she had finished her tea, Frances was in full control of herself.

Carefully and accurately, she told Sophia Jex-Blake the whole story of her father's illness, his decline, his death, and the ugly rumours of murder, which had proved to be true. She told her about Inspector Antrobus, her personal regard for him, and his gathering of evidence against her brother. She omitted nothing: the damning letter from silly Kate, the packet of deadly poison and how it had been discovered, and her brother's lame excuse for concealing it in his house.

When she had finished her story, Fanny sat in silence, watching her companion. What would Dr Jex-Blake make of it all? Would she be really interested in the troubles of a young woman whom she had only just met?

'Oh, how I wish that I could see that mysterious packet!' cried Sophia Jex-Blake. 'I suppose this Inspector Antrobus has got it? But your brother picked it up.... Where is your brother, Miss Fowler?'

'He's staying with me at my school – Makin House.'

'Staying?'

The single word was invested with a subtle mockery. Frances blushed.

'Hiding. He's avoiding the public eye, Miss Jex-Blake. But yes, as I told you, he had the packet in his possession.'

'Hm…. Could you persuade your brother to come here, now? I can assure you that the Lady Principal won't mind. I want to see him, and speak to him. But more than that, I want to hear about this pesky packet!'

'You will see him? Oh, Miss Jex-Blake, how very kind of you!'

'Nonsense. There's nothing kind about it, girl. This whole business revolves around that packet, and your brother is one of the few people who have actually seen it. Get him to come here. Miss Wordsworth will send the porter to him with a message, and he can come over here by hackney carriage. It's getting very hot out here. When he comes, we'll find a quiet corner of Old Hall to have our confabulation.'

'Miss Jex-Blake,' cried the Reverend Timothy Fowler, 'I swear….'

'"Swear not at all", Mr Fowler,' said Sophia Jex-Blake, '"neither by heaven, for it is God's throne, nor by the earth, for it is his footstool; neither by Jerusalem, for it is the city of the great king." Give me a simple yea or nay to this question: Did you murder your father?'

'No.'

'Well, then, let us sit back calmly, and consider the position. Vain oaths and righteous outbursts will only cloud the issue. Drink a glass of barley water, and compose yourself.'

When Timothy had arrived at Lady Margaret Hall, he had blundered past the servant who had taken him to the common room, whence the two women had removed from the heat of the garden, and had begun to blurt out a protestation of innocence. Frances was deeply concerned for him, but could not refrain from smiling when her new friend had quoted St Matthew at him to quieten him down. Tim had actually blushed with mortification: it was usually he who quoted scripture for the edification of others.

'Now, Mr Fowler – may I call you Timothy? And you, my dear, will you object if I call you Fanny? We are talking of intimate family matters here, which preclude too much formality. Now, Timothy: describe this packet of poison to me. You have actually seen it and held it. Inspector Antrobus has possession of it, I'm told, but I doubt if he'd show it to me without wanting to know the whys and wherefores. So: the packet.'

'It was about five inches in length, and two inches wide. It was quite heavy, considering its size. It was made of stout blue paper, and sealed at each end with white gummed wafers. It had a printed label stuck to it, on which were written the words "Mercuric Chloride".'

'Excellent. I can see it now, in my mind's eye. Was the name of the chemist written on it?'

'It was printed on it, but I can't recall the name. He practised in Kingston upon Thames – I remember seeing that much before I placed it into the pocket of my frock coat.'

'Placed?'

'Hid. I hid it away. I was horrified. I knew, of course, that *I* had not put it there, and assumed that—'

'He assumed, Miss Jex-Blake,' said Frances hotly, 'that *I* had dropped it there, after having successfully poisoned my father for gain. He pretends that he suspected our elder brother, John, too; but he really thought that *I* had done it!'

'Very well. Dear me, this is all most interesting! Now, supposing – just supposing – that Timothy had done it. Murdered his father, I mean. I am going to put myself into his place. How can I administer this poison without being suspected? Can I spoon it into his medicine during my visits to his sickroom? Most unlikely, because a nurse will be present, and it will be her duty to administer any medicines to the patient. Had you tried to do so, Timothy, the nurse would have said: "Excuse me, Mr Timothy, but why are you putting a spoonful of white powder into Sir Montague's glass of medicine?" It wouldn't do, you know.'

Miss Jex-Blake laughed at the absurdity of this notion.

'So it would have to be in Sir Montague's food. And here, we meet with the same difficulty. The substance that you have chosen to use is one of the cruellest and deadliest poisons known to man: salts of white mercury, known also as corrosive sublimate. How are you going to mix it into your father's food, in full sight of doctors, nurses, and other attendants? I don't know how you managed to do it. I don't know how *anyone* could have managed to do it.'

It had become very quiet in the common room. The sun filtered through the tall window, and threw bright bars of light across the carpet. The only sound came from the rapid ticking of a little china clock on the mantelpiece. The brother and sister listened, fascinated, to their companion's detached analysis of the crime.

'So I don't know how you did it, Timothy,' she continued, 'and I don't understand what you did subsequently. But you were successful, despite the fact that your packet of poison seemed to have been sealed at both ends. Maybe you were able to peel one of the wafers back, and reseal it later. That would certainly be possible.

'Your crime went undetected, despite the fact that you carelessly left behind your poison at the scene. "Ah!" you cried, "I have achieved my nefarious end. So I'll just throw this packet of poison under the bed, and walk away. I can always come back and pick it up later." No, it won't do. It won't do at all. Your crime, Timothy, for crime it was, was committed when you found that packet, and failed to hand it immediately to the police. But you did no murder, and neither did your excellent sister, here. We must look elsewhere. I wonder....'

During Sophia's analysis, Timothy Fowler had regained

some of his old confidence. Colour was returning to his ravaged face.

'I will seek out that man Antrobus, and repeat your arguments to him, Miss Jex-Blake. He will surely see, then, that I am innocent.'

'Perhaps so. But then again, perhaps not. I suggest that you leave this Mr Antrobus to me. He should look more deeply into your late father's colleagues at St Michael's. After all, most of them are resident there, with far more opportunities for villainy than either of you. I shall call upon Mr Antrobus. I have the bit between my teeth, Timothy, and I am going to delve more deeply into this business. Now, I have another question to ask you both. Your father returned to Oxford from a visit, and immediately took to his bed. Whom had he been visiting?'

Brother and sister looked at each other.

'We don't know,' said Fanny. 'Father never told us.'

'Did he tell you where he was going on other occasions?'

'He would tell *me*, occasionally,' said Fanny, 'though usually he would keep his own counsel.'

'Did he tell anyone in college where he had been? His doctors, you see, would want to know that, in case he had caught an infection elsewhere. Who are his doctors? I will call on them – remember, I am a doctor myself.'

'He was attended by old Dr Hope, who had been his physician for all the time that he was at Oxford. When things took a turn for the worse, he called in a young man to assist him, a Dr Chambers.'

'And can you furnish me with the addresses of these doctors?'

'Unfortunately, no,' said Fanny. 'Dr Hope has retired, and gone to live elsewhere in the country. Dr Chambers has accepted a post as a ship's doctor, and is now on the high seas somewhere.'

Miss Jex-Blake sprang from her chair. She clasped her hands

together in a kind of spasm of concentration, and began to pace about the room.

'On the high seas! Can it be?' she muttered. 'Can it possibly be? But surely....'

She turned to face the brother and sister, and they saw that her eyes were shining.

'You have seen something that we have not?' asked Timothy. Both women heard the note of pleading in his voice.

'I believe that I have, but I can't even begin to hint at it yet. Everything now depends on Detective Inspector Antrobus. Will he receive me? Will he take me seriously, or dismiss me as just another female busybody? I should love to work with a professional police detective, but if he declines, then I'll go my own way. You probably won't see me for some time, but remember that I'm going about *your* business. We shall meet again, here, at Lady Margaret Hall, when my quest is accomplished. Pray God that I shall come then bringing good news.'

12

A JOINT VENTURE

'TERRIBLE IT WAS, ma'am,' said the porter at Oxford Station, 'such a civil gentleman he was, and very free with the gratuities, as we say. And then to be poisoned by his own son, and him a clergyman. It doesn't bear thinking of.'

The porter narrowed his eyes and peered down the track. Then he glanced at the clock hanging over the platform. The 10.31 from Paddington would be arriving in four minutes' time. Meanwhile, it was a nice change to be talking to a lady about the late Sir Montague Fowler.

'I suppose he was always travelling up to London?' asked Sophia Jex-Blake.

'Fairly often, ma'am. But it wasn't to London that he travelled the week before he was took ill. No, it was to – well, it were to somewhere else. Whenever he made those particular journeys, he'd give me half-a-crown. Yes, he was a lovely man.'

'And where did he go to? I'm making enquiries on behalf of a friend of his.'

'Well, ma'am, I don't know as how I can tell you that. "Ponder," he'd say – that's my name, Alfred Ponder – "there's no need to tell people where I'm going if they ask you. A man in my position needs a bit of peace and quiet from time to time." And then he'd slip me the half-crown.'

At that moment, the train from Paddington appeared in a haze of smoke and steam. Alfred Ponder excused himself, and joined a little knot of fellow porters in assisting the passengers to alight, and have their luggage carried out to the cab-stand. Then he rejoined Dr Jex-Blake.

'You know, Mr Ponder,' said Sophia, 'this work of yours – this dashing around, and carrying heavy weights – must make you very thirsty. Would you be offended if I offered you a half-crown? You need to drink plenty of liquids on a hot day like this.'

'Why, that's very handsome of you, ma'am, thank you very much.'

'So Sir Montague liked to escape from the burden of his work from time to time? I'm sure that his poor daughter would love to know where he went. She's overcome with grief, you know. Won't you tell me, for her sake? Actually, she was the friend I mentioned.'

'Well, ma'am, I will, seeing as how Sir Montague's dead. He used to go a few times a year to a little place called Elm Ridge, which is a village over the county border in Berkshire, about twenty-five miles on the down line. It's just a few farmhouses, a little inn, and a church. Nobody goes there much. There's a halt there, and you have to let the train driver know that you want to get off.'

'I suppose he'd stay with friends there?'

'Well, maybe so. He stayed at one of the bigger farmhouses, a place called Grange Farm. He mentioned the name to me once.'

'If I decided to go to Elm Ridge, how frequent are the trains?'

'Well, you'd need to catch a train from here to Abingdon – they run three minutes past the hour daily until eight o'clock. Change there for Sutton Wick, and change again at Sutton Wick for Elm Ridge. Ask the driver at Sutton Wick to stop the train at Elm Ridge Halt. If you come into the ticket office, ma'am, I'll write all that down for you.'

'Sir,' said the desk sergeant, coming in from the front office, 'there's a lady to see you. I told her you were very busy this morning, but she said she'll wait.'

James Antrobus sighed. Thursday mornings were usually uneventful, letting him deal with routine matters. Why could he not be left alone?

'What kind of a lady, Sergeant? It's not Mrs Moulton again, is it? We can't go in pursuit of her maid: she left of her own accord, and hadn't stolen anything. Why can I not be left in peace, just for one morning? Can't you deal with this lady yourself?'

'Sir, she knows you by name, and won't see anyone else. She's a regular real London lady, not the type to brook any evasive action from the likes of me. She gave me this calling-card. It says she's a doctor, but I don't see how that can be the case, her being a woman and all.'

Inspector Antrobus looked at the card that the sergeant had given him.

Dr Sophia Jex-Blake, MD ChB
The Edinburgh School of Medicine for Women

'Show the lady in,' he said.

'Inspector,' said Sophia Jex-Blake, after a few initial courtesies had taken place, 'I have no right whatsoever to bother you with my importuning, and I am here simply because I am sorry for a very distressed young lady whom I have only just met, and desire to help. I am relying on your good-will and forbearance to help me in my quest, or at least to hear me out.'

'This young lady, ma'am,' said Antrobus, smiling, 'is she to remain anonymous?'

'By no means. Her name is Miss Frances Fowler, and she is

the headmistress of Makin House School.'

'I know the young lady well, Dr Jex-Blake. She and I have a certain rapport. How can I help you?'

'I am concerned, Inspector, about her brother, the Reverend Timothy Fowler. I gather that he is suspected of his father's murder?'

'I'm sure you'll understand, ma'am, that I can't comment on investigations in progress—'

'I take that to mean that Timothy Fowler is suspected of murder. From what his sister has told me – and she has told me all – I can quite understand that you fear he is guilty. But can you at least admit the possibility that he may be innocent?'

'I can admit the possibility, ma'am, but I must deal in probability. I cannot discuss the case, but I can assure you that I act solely on evidence, and on sifting through facts. If you think him innocent, then you must set out to prove your case. Have you come to me with fresh evidence?'

'I have come with a suggestion of a new line of investigation. Have you thought of finding out where Sir Montague Fowler had been staying before he returned, already fatally ill, to Oxford? Would it not be a good idea to find out?'

'Yes, it would be a good idea, Miss Jex-Blake, but you see, nobody seems to know where Sir Montague went. He never told anybody, you know, and nobody at St Michael's College ever thought of asking him. It would, at least, have been a faux pas to do so, and at the most, an unwelcome impertinence.'

'You say that nobody knows where Sir Montague went, Inspector. Well, *I* do. He went to visit someone at a place called Elm Ridge, in Berkshire, about twenty-five miles away from Oxford. And when he got there, Mr Antrobus, he stayed at a house called Grange Farm.'

'How … how on earth did you find that out?'

'I have my methods, Inspector.'

Antrobus treated his visitor to a good-humoured laugh. He

relaxed in his chair, and surveyed Miss Jex-Blake with a look that betokened a growing regard.

'And do you propose to visit Elm Ridge?' he asked. 'What do you expect to find there?'

'I don't know, Inspector. But we should be able to find out why Sir Montague went there. There may be a family relationship involved, or this Grange Farm may be tenanted by old friends of his who may be able to tell us things about him that we don't yet know.'

'Hmm.... You have a theory, haven't you? Something has made you question what I would call the physical evidence in this case.'

'Yes, Inspector, I have a theory. But I'd rather not tell you what it is just now, because you would dismiss it as absurd.'

'Elm Ridge.... Miss Jex-Blake, I am taking a chance with you, and am going to suggest that you and I should work in tandem over this business. I'm intrigued with this line of enquiry that you have suggested, but I cannot allow you to investigate this matter alone. We shall go together to Elm Ridge, and see what we can unearth. I realize that you will be disappointed that I cannot give you a free hand, but...'

'Say no more, Mr Antrobus,' said Sophia Jex-Blake. 'I came here today prepared for such a possibility.' She opened her reticule, and produced two railway tickets, which she held up for Antrobus's inspection. Before the astonished inspector could say anything, Sophia pressed home her advantage.

'Will you show me that packet of poison that Timothy is supposed to have retrieved from under his father's bed?'

Her tone suggested that she had staked all on his replying in the affirmative, that the whole interview had climaxed in this bold request.

Antrobus rose and opened a safe, which stood in the corner of the office, and took from it the fatal packet of mercuric chloride.

'This is most irregular, ma'am,' he said placing the packet before her on his desk, 'but I feel impelled to do as you ask.'

She threw him a swift glance of gratitude, and examined the packet carefully. Then she uttered a little sigh of satisfaction.

'The chemist's name is printed on the label. Have you been to see him?'

'I sent a constable down to Kingston-upon-Thames to interview the chemist, William Hart, at his premises in Winery Lane. He remembered supplying the poison to a customer, a young man wearing a slouch hat and with a muffler wound around his neck. He was not a regular customer. He signed the poisons register as George Thomas, and gave an address in Kingston. My constable made enquiries and found that no man of that name lived at the address given.'

'Hm.... Decidedly sinister. The odd thing about this package is that I don't think its contents were ever used. It's full of powder, right to the edges. I suppose it really is mercuric chloride?'

'Oh, yes, it is, ma'am. It has been submitted to chemical analysis by a forensic specialist. Somebody went to great lengths to obtain it, and then, apparently, never used it.'

Dr Jex-Blake stood up.

'Will Friday be too early for us to embark on our investigation, Inspector?' she asked.

'Friday will do very nicely, Miss Jex-Blake.'

Sophia turned at the door, and submitted the inspector to a searching glance.

'I can see, Mr Antrobus,' she said, 'that you are suffering from a confirmed phthisis. The stuffy air of this office will do you no good. Try to get out into the fresh air as much as possible. I would also recommend judicious use of the carbolic and menthol inhalers. Goodbye, Inspector. We shall meet again on Friday morning.'

*

159

When Sophia Jex-Blake and Inspector Antrobus alighted from the single-carriage train at Elm Ridge Halt, they found that they were the sole passengers to do so. They watched the little smoky engine clatter along the line until it passed out of sight behind a line of stately elms. Sophia looked about her. Their only companions were a few incurious cows standing in a field bordering the line. Facing her was a sunken road running beside the single track, a road that could only be reached by crossing the line on a series of wooden planks, rather like stepping-stones, place between the rails.

She had come equipped with a generous reticule, and a small leather suitcase, both of which she put down beside her on the wooden platform. She had carefully planned her visit to Elm Ridge, and knew that they would not long be alone.

Presently, she heard the sound of approaching hooves, and within a couple of minutes a horse and trap appeared on the road that ran beside the track. The driver, a young man in a plaid overcoat, and sporting a rakish bowler hat, ran across the track and retrieved their luggage, bidding them follow him on the 'stepping-stones' and so down to the road.

'Miss Jessie Blake?' said the young man. 'And this'll be the gentleman that you said might be coming with you. Good day, Master. I'm Joe Foster, from the White Lion. Let me help you up into the trap, ma'am. It's only half a mile to Elm Ridge, so we'll be there in no time.'

The village of Elm Ridge was just as the porter at Oxford Station had described it. There was a church, very old by the look of it, and partly fallen into ruin. As they passed the churchyard, Sophia told the porter to stop.

'Joe,' she said, 'take Mr Antrobus and the luggage to the White Lion. I want to look in the churchyard. I'll join you in a few minutes.'

Sophia opened the gate into the churchyard. Something had caught her attention as they had passed, a mass of fresh flowers lying on an area of disturbed earth. She felt a little surge of excitement, as she had half expected to see something of the sort.

She picked her way through the long grass growing up around the ancient gravestones, until she came to the patch of colour, which proved to be the cut flowers placed as tributes on three fresh graves. One of the graves possessed a head-stone, with an earlier inscription all but effaced by lichen. But a second inscription had evidently been carved quite recently.

Also Marian, wife of the above, died 25 May 1894, aged 60 years.

The other graves were marked by wooden boards fastened into the loose earth with pegs. One commemorated Victoria Bolt, aged 21, and the other Alison Jacobs, aged 16. Both had died on the same date: 21 May, 1894.

'So, Sophia,' said Sophia Jex-Blake aloud, 'it would seem that my hypothesis was correct. It's time to make my way back to Mr Antrobus.'

Poor woman! Poor girls! What a desolate place this church-yard was!

A string of thatched cottages bordered the single road of beaten earth on the same side as the church, while opposite these stood the White Lion, a single-storey whitewashed build-ing set in what appeared to be a market garden. The landlord, who was Joe Foster's father, was engrossed in conversation with Antrobus, who held a tankard of beer in his hand.

'Welcome, Miss Jessie Blake,' he said cheerfully. 'You'll find your luggage in room 3, along the passage there. Joe, show the lady to her room.'

'I'll be here for two days, I expect. Were you able to accom-modate Mr Antrobus?'

'Oh, yes, miss. The gentleman's got a very snug room above the stables across the yard. Will you excuse me a moment? I must just look into the tap room.'

'So, madam,' said Antrobus sternly, putting down his empty

tankard on the bar, 'you gambled on my agreeing with your madcap scheme, and booked a room for me in advance. It was a bold move, ma'am!'

'I expect it was,' Sophia replied, 'but you're not really angry – I can see that from the twinkle in your eye. In any case, a couple of days in the country will be good for you. Now, will you be content to leave the landlord to me? I'll make him tell us what we want to know.'

'I wouldn't dream of interfering with you,' said Antrobus. 'What did you see in the churchyard?'

'Graves. Ah! Here's Mr Foster back. Landlord, my friend and I are hoping to visit the family of a lady who died here not so long ago. She lived at a place called Grange Farm....'

'Oh! So you knew poor Marian Hughes? What a tragedy! Poor Marian.... Her gentleman friend from Oxford had come to visit, too, which seems to make it even worse. It was gastric stomach, on account of tainted meat. I never serve curry here at the White Lion. Curry covers a multitude of sins in hot weather.'

Mr Forster was a stout, genial man in shirtsleeves, a man with a healthy red face and a shining bald head. He seemed content to stand on the threshold, talking of the village tragedy.

'But there's no family for you to visit, Miss Jessie, ' he said. 'Her husband died what seems a lifetime ago, and she never had no children. No; Grange Farm lies closed and empty, though I hear that her husband had kin living in Northamptonshire, so maybe one of them will come to live in it.'

'Poor dear Marian,' said Sophia. 'I first heard tell of her from that very gentleman who was staying with her at the time – Sir Montague Fowler. He'd known her for a very long time, I believe, and he once told me her maiden name – dear me! I've forgotten it. As I get older, my memory plays me tricks. Can you remember it, Mr Antrobus?'

'Just for the moment I can't recall....'

'Ballard, Miss,' said the landlord, 'that was her name.

Marian Ballard. She was a real beauty when she was a girl, and there was many a lad after her, if you take my meaning. But Arthur Hughes was the lucky one. He was quite well-to-do, and Grange Farm was his own property. He died of a cut from a scythe, which turned to septic – septo....'

'Septicaemia.'

'Yes, that's right. And so she was left alone. But she managed very well, and became a farmer in her own right. Well, I must go about my business. If there's anything you want, ma'am, just call me, and if I'm not here, young Joe will see to you.'

'I don't suppose there was a doctor in the village, was there? I expect they had to send for one from the nearest town.'

'Oh, no, ma'am, we've got our own doctor here, Dr Folliott, he's called. He's always been here – in fact, he delivered me, when I was born, and that's over forty years ago. He lives in that little stone house opposite the church.'

'That was a brilliant interrogation, Miss Jex-Blake,' whispered Antrobus as the landlord left the room. 'So her name was Ballard.... Did you think that would be so?'

'Oh, no, I'm not a seer, you know. I just wanted to know her maiden name because no doubt it was the name by which Sir Montague Fowler would have known her at first. Or so I assume. But Ballard ... are you thinking what I'm thinking?'

'Very likely,' said Antrobus. 'But my training forbids me to make conclusions ahead of the facts.'

'Very commendable. Now, I suggest that we have some luncheon here, and afterwards go and pay a visit to the doctor. What was his name? Folliott.'

They were admitted to Dr Folliott's house by an elderly house-keeper, a woman with a pretty, unlined face, and shrewd grey eyes. She took Sophia's calling-card – Antrobus was content to trail behind her – and led them into a comfortable room at the back of the house, a room that overlooked the ancient, overgrown churchyard. A well-polished grandfather clock ticked away soothingly in a corner.

Dr Folliott rose from a chair to greet them. He was clearly very old, with a stooping gait and a shock of white hair. He still held Sophia's card in his hand.

'Please sit down, Dr – er – Jex-Blake,' he said. 'And you, Mr – er –'

'Antrobus, sir. James Antrobus.'

'Antrobus. Very good. That settee is rather comfortable. Bertha, would you bring us some tea?'

The old doctor lowered himself carefully into his chair, sat back, and surveyed his visitor. His eyes, she noticed, were bright and keen.

'So you are the celebrated Sophia Jex-Blake,' he said. 'I've heard of your struggles, and your triumphs. As a young man, I would probably have fought against you. But not now. Old age brings a certain amount of perspective to issues of that sort. You qualified in Ireland, didn't you? Have you actually practised medicine?'

'Indeed I have. Medicine, and surgery too.'

'And why have you come to see me? I don't believe we are acquainted.'

'It's because of poor Marian Ballard – Hughes, I should say. I heard of her passing, and naturally wanted to talk to the doctor who attended her.'

'Yes, I see. Well, Miss Jex-Blake, it was one of the most virulent cases of food poisoning that I'd ever encountered. I thought it was miraculous that she lasted so long. It was tainted mutton, you know, that had been made up into a curry – people often do that with meat that's on the turn. They were all taken ill in the night – Mrs Hughes, Sir Montague, who, as you know, was staying with her, and the two maids, who shared the same food.'

'Tainted meat?'

'Well, it was more than that. It was botulism – a very severe strain. I did everything possible, and sent for a colleague in Saxon Meadow, two miles from here. We used the pumps, applied white of eggs, and washed out their stomachs with bicarbonate of soda – well, you know all that kind of thing.

'Marian – Mrs Hughes, you know – urged Sir Montague to go back to Oxford at once, which he did. I wanted him to stay here, but he insisted on leaving. He was still extremely sick, and very agitated. It was a Monday, as I recall, the 21 May. Both the maids died just after dawn. A terrible tragedy. One was sixteen, and the other twenty-one. Marian lingered on for several days, but died on the morning of the twenty-fifth. It was not long afterwards that we heard that Sir Montague, too, had died, but that in his case it was murder! Corrosive sublimate, I was told. It's a wicked world, Dr Jex-Blake. A very wicked world. Ah! Here's Bertha with the tea.'

The elderly housekeeper had entered the room carrying a tray upon which reposed a large china teapot, cups and saucers, a tall jug of milk, and a bowl of lump sugar. She put the tray down carefully on a table, and as she left the room she gave Sophia a look which only another woman, perhaps, could have interpreted. It said: *When you've finished with the doctor, come and talk to me in the kitchen.* Without waiting to be asked, Sophia poured out the tea, and handed a cup to the old doctor.

She glanced quickly at Inspector Antrobus, who saw her lips form the words 'your turn!' Evidently she had no thought of using him merely as an audience. They were part of a joint venture.

'Mrs Hughes was comfortably off, I gather?' Antrobus asked.

'She was. She'd been a widow for many years, but still ran the Grange Farm. She had four farmhands who'd been with her for years, and she paid them good wages. She never lacked for money, I'm glad to say.'

'And Sir Montague Fowler would visit her?'

'Yes, he came three or four times a year, on each occasion staying for a few days. I can see from your expression that you're wondering why! Well, I've no idea. But the Oxford don and the farmer's widow were close friends. Perhaps she'd been in service with the Fowlers at some time. They had an estate somewhere in the Home Counties. But I don't know anything for certain.'

'This tea is very good,' said Sophia, 'very sustaining, especially on a hot day like this. Did you wash out the stomachs as a last resort?'

'Yes. As you know, it's what you do when you see that there's really no hope of recovery. It was, of course, a fatal nephritis.'

'That's what Sir Montague Fowler's doctors did, you know: washed out his stomach with bicarbonate of soda. He, too, died of a terminal nephritis.'

Ah! thought Antrobus. Clever! That's the stuff!

Dr Folliott put down his cup and saucer. He looked puzzled.

'Well, of course, Dr Jex-Blake, that was before he was found to have been poisoned. I read in the paper that his organs were pervaded by mercuric chloride. So....'

'Dr Folliott,' said Dr Jex-Blake, 'please listen carefully to what I am going to say. When Sir Montague died, which was on the third of June, no one had heard even a hint of poison in the matter. The two doctors in attendance gave the cause of death as fatal nephritis consequent upon gastroenteritis. He was taken away by the funeral furnishers, and entombed on the twelfth. So he was laid to rest, Doctor, with his stomach quite empty, as it had been washed out as death was approaching. Rumours of poison came later.'

The old doctor sighed, and shook his head. He looked at his guest with a kind of humorous vexation.

'Well, that could not be so,' he said. 'For when he was taken from the tomb – I take it that samples were taken to a police mortuary? Yes, I thought so. When his body was opened, his organs were found to be full of mercuric chloride. So his stomach could not have been washed out before he died.'

'But it was. So where does that fact lead us? Would you like some more tea?'

'What? Yes, yes…. It leads us to an absurdity. An impossibility. Either his stomach was empty, or it wasn't. The autopsy proves that it wasn't. Wasn't empty, I mean.'

'There is a way,' said Sophia, 'in which one can re-think that absurdity to make it more than plausible. I've already thought about it, but I'd be delighted and reassured if you could work it out, too.'

'But it's nonsense!' the old doctor cried. 'If you insist that his stomach was empty when he was buried, then the only way…. The only way for mercuric chloride to be in his organs would be for someone to have put it there – put it in the samples, you know, that were brought back to the mortuary.'

'Precisely! It's an interesting speculation, Doctor. No doubt the police will come to the same conclusion, and set about solving the mystery. Well, we must bid you goodbye. Poor Marian! At least, now, she is at peace.'

When they regained the hallway of the doctor's house, Sophia laid her hand on the inspector's arm.

'That servant-woman, Bertha, wants to speak to me in private. Can you skulk in the garden until I've finished talking to her? I rather think that she'll furnish us with the solution to the mystery of Sir Montague's visits to Elm Rise.'

'Now, ma'am,' said Bertha, as Sophia came into the little kitchen at the rear of the house, 'I thought it would be a good idea if you and I had a little chat before you leave. Mrs Hughes was well-esteemed in this village. She was a woman of substance, and very generous to anyone who was in difficulties. I've known her all my life: she and I were born in Elm Ridge, and never left it.

'Now, in the year 1860, when she was twenty-six, but still single, having rejected a number of local suitors for one reason or another, she formed a liaison with a young gentleman from one of the Oxford colleges. I don't know how they met, or where. Marian Ballard was a very pretty girl, and there'd been many a young man in these parts who hoped to win her heart. But she and this Oxford gentleman fell in love – they really did, you know; but he was already married, with a little boy, and they both knew that it would have to end.'

'This young man from Oxford – you're talking about Sir Montague Fowler, aren't you?'

'I am. So they parted, as was right and proper, and soon afterwards she found that she was with child. It was, of course, illegitimate. With Montague Fowler's help it was put out to adoption, and he made certain that the child – it was a boy – received a sound education. He is now a grown man, and if you mention any of this to the Fowler family, they'll soon realize who he is. All this was a profound secret. Lady Fowler never knew about it, and neither did any other member of the family. The boy himself will not know, though I expect he'll have to be told. Marian married Tom Hughes a year later. He was a good man, who died before his time. After his death, Sir Montague began his regular visits.'

'So Sir Montague never forgot Marian,' said Sophia, 'but when he was taken ill, they both knew it was imperative to avoid scandal for the sake of his family. That's why he left. And that's why he evidently never told his doctors or his servants where he had been, or how he had become ill. No one was to know, even when his own life was in peril. I find that rather touching.'

'Maybe so, ma'am, but secrets of that kind tend to fester, and can break out into a lot of trouble. That's why I've told you all this. You're a lady, and will know what best to do, as, no doubt, will the gentleman standing in the garden. I don't want my old

master here to be burdened with all this suspicion and wicked-
ness. But I know you'll be discreet. I'm sorry for the family, and
I wish them all well, but there have been too many secrets here
in Elm Ridge. I expect they're all clever enough and worldly
enough to cope with an unpleasant truth.'

Sophia Jex-Blake left the doctor's house and, as she and
Antrobus walked back to the White Lion, she told him Bertha's
story. Antrobus nodded, and turned aside for a moment. He
brought out his handkerchief, and when he turned to look at
her, she saw that a thin stream of blood was trickling from the
corner of his mouth.

'I think – I think….'

'Don't try to talk, Inspector,' she said. 'Let's get back to the
inn. You must go to bed at once. We don't need to worry old Dr
Forrest. I've brought all that's necessary in my luggage to treat
you. No, no argument, please! Come, give me your arm.'

Sophia Jex-Blake sat on a chair in Antrobus's room over the
stable, and looked at her new-found friend, who was lying in
bed, propped up by pillows. As a doctor, she was neither intimi-
dated nor frightened by illness. She had subjected the inspector
to a thorough and rigid examination, despite his feeble protests,
and had concluded that the bleeding from his lung would soon
stop. Thankfully, it had not been arterial blood.

She had administered a carbolic spray, and, despite the
warm weather, had had a small fire lit in the grate, upon which
she was burning a lavender shovel.

'In fifteen minutes' time, Mr Antrobus,' she said, 'I shall
turn you on your right side so that you can clear your chest
of phlegm. I've ordered a meal of scrambled eggs for you, followed by a dish of junket.'

Inspector Antrobus groaned.

'I'd rather have a steak, followed by a pint of porter,' he
whispered.

'Well, you can't. Not today, anyway. But you can have a small glass of brandy.

'You'll be quite recovered and fit to travel by tomorrow morning. We should be back in Oxford well before noon. Meanwhile, let us consider a few facts relating to the death of Sir Montague Fowler. Both doctors who attended the Warden in his last illness left Oxford almost immediately. One retired to the country, and the other took a berth as a ship's doctor, and is somewhere half way across the world. So when the rumours began, and the packet of poison appeared in Sir Montague's bedroom, neither physician was in England, so they could not be consulted on the matter. Had they been in Oxford, I'm sure they would have insisted that the Warden's death was natural.'

'But they weren't,' came a whisper from the bed, 'and so an exhumation was inevitable.'

'It was, and that was when some malevolent person gained access to the organs removed for analysis. And we know who that person is.'

'Do we really? Pray enlighten me.'

'We don't know him by name – yet. What we *do* know is that it must be someone who works in the Oxford police mortuary. This was a natural death decked out to look like murder. Let us leave Sir Montague's children alone for a while, and turn our attention to the denizens of St Michael's College, and to Floyd's Row Mortuary.'

13

FOUNDER'S DAY

William Podmore surveyed himself in the full-length mirror attached to the wall of his dressing-room in the Lodgings. Really, he *was* an impressive sight! It would be wonderful when the undergraduates returned in October, and found him installed as Warden. He would watch their awed glances from the corner of his eye as they accosted him in the quadrangles, and when they raised their academic caps, he would raise his in reply, accompanying the action with a grave smile of acknowledgement.

Today was Founder's Day, which was celebrated each year on 21 July. In 1479 it had been a Sunday, but Lord Dorset, beset with many worries, had insisted on his new college being signed into existence on that day. A votive Mass of St Michael had been offered in the nearby church of St Michael at the North Gate.

He had always looked well in full academic dress, with the scarlet gown and velvet bonnet of his doctorate in Civil Law. Today, he would be outshone only by the Vice-Chancellor, a man loaded with honours and gold braid. The college would be filled with guests for the day, and a number of old members would be staying overnight.

There would be a champagne reception and buffet in the Common Room at lunchtime, ably arranged, as always, by Joe Steadman. It would be followed by a concert in hall, given by a talented local string quartet, followed by afternoon tea.

At six o'clock, Latin vespers would be sung in the college chapel, an ancient tradition that had survived both the Reformation and the ejection by Cromwell's men of the Warden and his chaplain, staunch Laudians both, and the installing of a Roundhead regime.

And then would come the Founder's Dinner in hall. He would sit in old Fowler's tall-backed chair at the high table, flanked by the Vice-Chancellor and the Visitor, the Earl of Caernarvon. It would be splendid, and he would be at its centre.

There had been three more of those hideous notes, two pushed under his door, and the third posted from Summertown. Their impact had been just as severe as the first note, the one that he had tried to burn in the flame of the candle. Would they ever stop?

With a final straightening of his white tie, the Warden left the Lodgings, and passed through the arched entrance into the second quadrangle. A gaggle of guests had already assembled on the centre lawn. The champagne had been served, and everybody was clutching a glass, and engaging in animated conversation. There was Steadman, smiling broadly as he engaged an elderly clergyman in conversation.

And there was Stanley Fitzmaurice, chatting to Templar. Fitzmaurice was too much attached to that fellow for his liking. He wanted Fitzmaurice as Bursar when he judged it right for Joe Steadman to go. Templar seemed to be running to seed. He was correctly dressed for once, but he still looked like a bundle of rags. What was the matter with him? He looked pale and drawn, and his eyes moved restlessly over the guests as though he were looking for a ghost.

It was time for the buffet. The guests, as though alerted by a hidden signal, began to drift in the general direction of the senior common room.

'Warden,' said the Vice-Chancellor, the Reverend Henry Boyd, 'do you think I could have a word with you in private?'

The buffet was now just a pleasant memory. The concert in hall had been enjoyable in its own way, though perhaps a trifle too long. In a moment, when the Vice-Chancellor had left him, he would go and lie down in the Lodgings for an hour, before the chapel bell summoned them all to Latin Vespers – and then dinner!

It was a lovely summer's afternoon, with the perfume of wisteria in the air. The two men strolled out of the hall, and made their way through the throng of guests into the first quadrangle. The Vice-Chancellor pointed to the door of the Lodgings.

'Perhaps you would invite me in to your cool hallway,' he said. 'What I have to tell you won't take more than a couple of minutes, but it is rather hot out here.'

The ground floor of the Lodgings had always been a gloomy part of the house. But it was pleasant enough to sit on the two upright Jacobean chairs flanking the hall fireplace.

'I'll come straight to the point, Podmore,' said the Vice-Chancellor. 'Your plagiarizing of another man's work, and passing it off as your own, was a rascally thing to do. Quite frankly, I would not have believed it of you....'

'Sir, that is an outrageous thing to suggest....'

'Oh, it won't do! I tell you I have proof positive of your chicanery, which somebody – never mind who – sent to me earlier this week. You have built your whole career on a lie and a cheat. For goodness sake, man, don't go fainting on me! Your face alone betrays your guilt.'

Podmore's voice, little more than a whisper, came faint and tremulous.

'Did Steadman tell you?'

'Dr Steadman? Certainly not. What a bizarre idea!'

'What will you do?'

'Do? You realize that I can't keep silent about this business? To do so would make me an accessory to your act. When the Founder's Dinner is over tonight, I will tell the Earl of Caernarvon. With luck, His Lordship will be persuaded that discretion in the matter would be preferable to a hideous scandal. You would be advised to resign immediately. Perhaps you could cite ill health as your reason. Yes, that must be your way out. And as for your ambition to succeed me as Vice-Chancellor, you will see that there is now no chance whatever of that. John Magrath will get it, and deservedly so.'

The Vice-Chancellor rose to his feet. He looked at the crumpled figure sunk in the chair opposite. Surely he could find it in his heart to pity the man? Dash it all, no! He was a cad and a hypocrite. But he would help him to leave the college and the university away from the limelight, and as soon as was decent.

When he reached the door, he turned to look at the Warden of St Michael's College.

'You may be able to join the Exchequer in a permanent post,' he said. 'But then again, I don't suppose the Chancellor of the Exchequer will countenance it, once the story gets out. I will do what I can to protect the reputation of the college. Bear up, and face your misfortunes like a man. For you, and you alone, are the author of them.'

At six o'clock, the chapel bell was rung by the porter, and those guests who had elected to attend the Latin Vespers made their way into the chapel. It occupied the same side of the first quadrangle as the Lodgings, and was, in its way, an impressive place. It had been thoroughly restored in the fifties, and some fine stained-glass had been installed. The congregation faced each other, as is the custom in collegiate chapels, and there were two return stalls, each curtained, one for the Warden, and the other for the Vice-Warden.

There was an antechapel, above which stood the organ, and today an organ scholar, borrowed from Exeter College for the occasion, was playing some soft and subtle music. Those with a knowledge of such things recognized it as a work by William Byrd.

Joseph Steadman rested his back on the panelling, and looked around him. Podmore had seemed very proud and happy, as well he might be on his first Founder's Day as Warden. Hypocrite! He had still pretended to drink nothing but bottled spring water, but Steadman had seen the tell-tale tremor that showed he'd been secretly at the bottle.

The Vice-Warden's stall was still empty. When would Podmore make his choice? And would he have the sense to choose Stanley Fitzmaurice? He was an able Senior Tutor, and a man whose modesty made one forget that he was a professor of Arabic.

The organist reached the end of his repertoire. In a moment, no doubt, he'd start up again. Old Theodore Waynefleet was slumped in his stall in the sanctuary, thumbing through his prayer book. He did Latin well, in the old style, but he was getting too old for his office of chaplain. He was said to be eighty-five, and that could well be true.

In a few moments it would be time for 'swish-bang'. This was the ritual that began every service. The Warden by custom waited for the chapel to fill up before he made his entrance. When the bell stopped ringing, he would leave the Lodgings, enter the chapel, climb up into his stall, and close the curtain with an audible swish. This was a signal to the porter to slam the door, which in turn was a signal to the chaplain to begin the service.

Swish-bang.

But not this evening. The organist began to play something by Stainer. The congregation became restless, some going as far as to look at their watches. All eyes gradually turned to the Warden's empty stall. A quarter of an hour passed. And then people began to whisper to each other. Steadman caught Fitzmaurice's eye, and the Senior Tutor rose from his seat opposite and went into the antechapel. Steadman heard him say to the porter, 'Reid, will you go into the Lodgings, and tell the Warden that we are waiting to begin the service.'

Ten minutes passed. Somebody coughed nervously. The organist came down from the loft. Then the door was flung open without ceremony, and the porter gave them the news that death had once again visited the Lodgings.

As the new town hall in St Aldate's was not yet completed, the inquest on the body of Dr William Podmore, MA DCL, was held in a spacious room above the public bar in the King's Arms, Holywell Street. It was the Monday following Founder's Day, and the whole city was agog with the news of a second mysterious death at St Michael's College. It was a very hot day, and the room was packed almost to suffocation. A boisterous knot of reporters stood on the steep staircase, notebooks at the ready.

Joseph Steadman looked around him. He sat on one of a number of uncomfortable chairs, which had been set out to receive those who were to be called to give evidence in the matter of Podmore's death.

Stanley Fitzmaurice sat beside him, looking with evident distaste at the chattering throng on the stairs. Next to him was his young friend Gerald Templar, bearded and wild-eyed. Really, what was wrong with him? He looked as though he was suffering from some inner torture. Templar eked out his meagre salary as Junior Dean by undertaking investigative work at Floyd's Row Mortuary, but Fitzmaurice had told him that he had vehemently refused to do any such work with respect to Podmore.

Next to Templar was a doctor who had been a guest at the Founder's Day celebration, and beside him, the college's head porter, John Reid, wearing his best suit, and looking both shocked and nervous. From the way he sat, it was clear to Steadman that the poor man was acutely embarrassed at having to sit among the Fellows.

And next to Reid, the Vice-Chancellor. What on earth had *he* to do with the matter in hand?

Behind a trestle table placed beneath the open window, sat the coroner, an irascible retired Army officer. Steadman had heard of Major Savage: he'd served with distinction in the West Kents before retiring to a picturesque cottage out at Littlemore. Next to him was his clerk, and beside the clerk Dr Armitage, Chief Anatomist and coroner's officer. On a chair placed beside the coroner's table, sat Detective Inspector Antrobus.

The Major, who had been shuffling through a pile of papers, suddenly pushed them aside, and banged his gavel to bring the assembly to order.

'On this day,' he said, 'Monday, 23 July, 1894, we hold an inquest on the body of one William Podmore, now lying dead. I am cognizant of the details of this case, and, as the law allows, will sit without a jury. It's very hot in here, but we will not be here long, thank goodness, as there are only a few witnesses for me to examine. Let John Reid stand up and approach the table. You are John Reid, head porter at St Michael's College?'

'I am, sir.'

'Tell me what occurred at, or soon after, six o'clock in the evening of Saturday, 11 July last.'

'Sir, I was on duty in the college chapel, where some of the Fellows and their guests were about to attend what is called the Latin Vespers. The Warden, Dr William Podmore, always comes in last. Well, on that night, he didn't, and after a while Captain Fitzmaurice told me to go to the Lodgings to fetch him. I did so, and entered the Lodgings to look for him...'

177

'You say you entered the Lodgings. Did you not knock on the door or ring the bell?'

'No, sir, because I knew that there would be no servants in the house. They were all engaged on various duties around the college in connection with Founder's Day. Besides, sir, it's not the custom in the best-regulated households for servants to knock on the door. A gentleman's house is not a hotel.'

There was a murmur of laughter, and the Major banged his gavel, but there was the trace of a smile on his own face.

'So you entered the Lodgings. What did you find?'

'I found no sign of the Warden on the ground floor, so I went up the stairs. There was a peculiar smell, like fresh peaches, which seemed to be coming from what I knew to be the Warden's bedroom. I went in, and found Dr Podmore lying across the bed. He was still wearing day-clothes, but had taken off his jacket. I could see that he was dead. His eyes and mouth were open, and his face was sort of twisted, sir, as though in agony. I ran back to the chapel, and told the gentlemen what I had seen.'

'Hm.... Very good. You gave your testimony very well, Reid. Did you like Dr Podmore?'

'Like him, sir? Well, he was the Warden of the college. I liked him in what you might call his professional capacity. But since you ask, sir, I didn't like him as a man.'

'Very well. You can go back to your chair. Now, Dr Holmes. You were a guest at the college, and examined the body. It was very fortunate that you were there. These colleges are full of doctors, none of whom knows anything about medicine. What was your conclusion as to the cause of this man's death?'

'Mr Coroner, I could only make a preliminary examination, but I concluded that Dr Podmore had swallowed a lethal quantity of cyanide. I also detected a strong smell of alcohol, or ardent spirits. I made a note of my conclusions on the spot, and later handed it to Detective Inspector Antrobus.'

Stanley Fitzmaurice was called, and confirmed the evidence of Reid and Dr Holmes. Dr Armitage described how he had opened the body of the dead man late on Saturday night, and had found his stomach to contain a lethal quantity of cyanide. It had been taken in liquid form, and another witness would speak about that. The blood samples taken from the body showed evidence of the recent imbibition of a large amount of alcohol.

'And did you draw any conclusion from your findings, Dr Armitage?'

'I concluded, sir, that William Podmore had committed suicide.'

'Thank you. I should think.... What is that noise? Has that man fainted? Some of you carry him downstairs, will you, and give him something to drink. It's this hot weather. Quickly, now.'

Two members of the public came forward, and between them they carried Gerald Templar from the room.

'Now,' said Major Savage, 'let us hear from you, Inspector Antrobus. You look pale, sir, and I gather that you have not been well. Do you feel fit enough to give evidence?'

'Yes, thank you, Mr Coroner. I was taken ill whilst in the country, but returned to Oxford on Saturday, just in time, as it were, to investigate the death of Dr Podmore. On the evening of Saturday, 21 July, I was summoned to St Michael's College, where I was shown the dead body of Dr William Podmore. I provisionally accepted the opinion of a doctor who was present – Dr Holmes, there – that the man had committed suicide. I dismissed everybody from the room....'

'Everybody? Could you be more precise, Inspector?'

'Yes, sir. I was taken into the Lodgings by Mr Reid, the head porter, who preceded me up the stairs and so into Dr Podmore's bedroom. There I found Dr Holmes, and two Fellows of the college, Dr Steadman, the Bursar, and Captain Fitzmaurice, the

Senior Tutor. Also present was Haynes, Dr Podmore's scout, or staircase servant.'

'Thank you. Pray proceed.'

'I asked everybody to leave the room, and then examined it closely. I found an empty gin bottle, capacity one pint, rolled against the skirting board behind the bed. I also found a beer glass, of the ordinary sort that you get in a public house, and beside it an empty half-pint bottle labelled "Stothard's Premium Hair Wash."'

'Stothard's? I use it myself. Surely it isn't poisonous?'

'No, sir. Dr Armitage, the Chief Anatomist at the mortuary, later confirmed that this bottle had contained a quantity of essential oil of bitter almonds, a form of cyanide. The beer glass also contained traces of this poison. The doctor and I both agreed that Dr Podmore must have obtained the essential oil from an unknown source, and that it had been kept in the empty bottle for possible future use.'

'Were you able to ascertain the source from where Podmore obtained this poison?'

'Not as yet, sir. But he or a possible agent would have had to sign the Poisons Register, pursuant to the Pharmacy Act of 1852. I am still pursuing enquiries about that.'

The two empty bottles were produced, and placed upon the table.

'Did you find anything else of significance, Inspector?'

'I did, sir. I found half a sheet of notepaper lying on a writing-table placed near the bed. It was a note in Dr Podmore's handwriting. I transcribed the message on the note, and you have the original as exhibit number 3.'

There was a stir of renewed interest in the room, and the somnolent reporters on the stairs sprang back to life. The coroner asked Antrobus to read the note aloud.

'"It is all up with me. Boyd and Steadman have done for me. I cannot face the shame. Blame no one for my death."'

'Well,' said Major Savage, when the inspector had finished his evidence, 'It's very sad, and very pathetic. I think there can be no doubt in anyone's mind that William Podmore committed suicide, and when these proceedings are over, I will give my verdict to that effect.

'But now, we need to ask a few questions about the role played in this tragedy by the people mentioned by name in the dead man's suicide note. By questioning them, we might be able to arrive at a motive for poor Podmore's action.'

The room fell silent as the Reverend Henry Boyd, Vice-Chancellor of the University of Oxford, was bidden to stand before the coroner's table.

'Now, Vice-Chancellor,' said Major Savage, 'we should like to hear in what way you "did for" the unfortunate Podmore. What did you do?'

'I ... I did nothing, Mr Coroner. But it came to my notice that Podmore had committed a transgression, and I spoke to him about it during the Founder's Day celebrations at St Michael's on Saturday last.'

'And what was the nature of this transgression?'

'It was an offence against academic integrity. It was an act that Dr Podmore should never have permitted himself to perform.'

'And what was that act, Vice-Chancellor? Are you going to tell me?'

'I have already told you, Major Savage. It was something that Dr Podmore should not have done. An offence, as I said, against academic integrity. I don't suppose for a moment that it was a crime in the accepted sense of that word.'

Major Savage's face flushed red with anger.

'So the "transgression" has now become an "offence". Evidently, Vice-Chancellor, you feel yourself entitled to interpret the Law as to what is criminal and what is not. Tell me what Podmore did, or by God, sir, I'll attach you for contempt!'

There was a subdued murmur from the audience. No one had ever heard the Vice-Chancellor so bluntly taken to task. Henry Boyd knew that he had met his match, and submitted to the rebuke with what good grace he could muster.

'Mr Coroner,' he said, 'Dr William Podmore plagiarized a book that had been written by an older colleague. As far as I know, the book had not been submitted to the Oxford University Press at the time of that colleague's death. Podmore got possession of the manuscript, and published it as his own. That was, I believe, in the year 1873. Dr Podmore received his Doctorate in Civil Law on the strength of that book, and his academic reputation rested on it. But it was not his.'

This time the audience remained silent. What the Vice-Chancellor had revealed left no room for words, only shock. Their pity for the dead man was now tinged with contempt. Nobody likes a cheat.

'And how did you come by this knowledge, Vice-Chancellor?'

'A lady living in the country recently sent me a box of papers which included the diary of the true author of that book, Dr Georg Joachim Bosch. An entry in that diary proved Podmore's transgression beyond any doubt.'

The coroner lapsed into gloomy silence for a while. Everybody waited with bated breath to hear what he would say.

'A bit like cheating at cards, would you say?'

'Morally, yes, Mr Coroner. I think your analogy has some merit.'

'Hm…. Well, in the Army, a fellow who cheated at cards was accounted to be a damned scoundrel. And I don't suppose it's any different in this case. Thank you, Vice-Chancellor, you may stand down. And now, Dr Joseph Steadman. Come up here, will you? Tell me what *you* did to make Dr William Podmore take his own life.'

'Sir, like the Vice-Chancellor, I, too was aware of Dr Podmore's defalcation….'

'Were you indeed? Why did you not tell anybody about it? It was the work of a scoundrel. By saying nothing, you condoned his scurrility.'

'I found out the truth of the matter only a few weeks ago. I was still revolving in my mind what to do.'

'Did you tell Dr Podmore that you knew? Come, sir, it's no use blushing like that. We'll have no secrets here. Did you tell him? You must have done.'

'I did not, sir. It was sufficient for me to know that he had founded his reputation on a despicable plagiarism of another man's work. Whenever he decided to lord it over me with his loathsome patronizing, I would derive great satisfaction from knowing that I rose above him as a moralist. Whatever I have achieved, I have done so through my own efforts.'

'Have you really? Very well. You men of the press there, on the stairs. Are you listening? I am appalled at the air of secrecy and corruption that has marked these proceedings. I am appalled at the petty jealousies that I have detected in the witnesses, and the beginnings of an attempt to cover up Podmore's cheating for the sake of so-called academic reputation. I find that the dead man, William Podmore, committed suicide. This court is dismissed.'

14

A BURDEN LIFTED

WHEN INSPECTOR ANTROBUS left the King's Arms, he found Sophia Jex-Blake waiting for him. She was sitting in a hansom cab drawn up at the pavement.

'Were you at the inquest?' he asked.

'I was. I was hidden from sight at the back of the room, where I was sitting with a gaggle of members of the public. As soon as the matter was concluded, I left by a back door. I'd already ordered this cab to wait for me. Would you care to join me? The reporters will be out in a minute.'

Antrobus climbed into the cab and sat down. His companion told the cabbie to take them to Lady Margaret Hall.

'That man who fainted....'

'That man, Miss Jex-Blake, was Dr Gerald Templar, Tutor in Chemistry at St Michael's College. And it was obvious that he regarded himself as being responsible for Dr Podmore's death. I agree with the coroner that Podmore committed suicide. So why was Templar so upset? Upset enough to faint?'

The cab was clattering along the High Street, at the beginning of its long drive into North Oxford. It had been a splendid idea of Miss Jex-Blake to cheat the reporters of their prey.

'Why was Templar so upset? Are you asking me to tell you

the answer, Inspector, or do you know it already? He was upset because he had done something sufficiently serious to send Podmore frantic. Something that had already unsettled the man's equilibrium before ever the Vice-Chancellor had confronted him with his charge of plagiarism.'

'The fountainhead of this secret knowledge,' said Antrobus, 'seems to have been "a lady in the country", who had sent a box of papers to the Vice-Chancellor. Somehow, Templar had access to those papers. And do you recall that the Bursar, Dr Steadman, said that he knew all about Podmore's chicanery? Our immediate task is to confront those two men – Templar and Steadman – and make them tell us all they know. What did Podmore mean when he said, "Boyd and Steadman have done for me"? Not a very elegant expression, but then, his mind was disturbed, poor man.'

'The Boyd reference is clear enough,' said Sophia. 'The Vice-Chancellor had confronted Podmore with his misdeed. But Steadman ... I believe him when he avers that he told poor Podmore nothing. So when the wretched man said that Steadman had "done" for him, he must have received a letter, or a note, telling him that all was known, an anonymous letter of some sort, and assumed that Steadman had sent it.'

'Exactly. I think there was such a note, but I don't think it came from Steadman. It is now quite imperative that we seek out Dr Steadman, and make him tell us how he knew about the plagiarism. And then, Miss Jex-Blake, it will be time to deal with Templar. What did he do, and, more importantly, why did he do it?'

They had left St Giles, and were making their way into the opulent redbrick suburbs of North Oxford.

'This has been a pleasant morning's drive,' said Antrobus. 'Would you mind telling me why we are going to Lady Margaret Hall? My own inclination would have been to go straight to St Michael's.'

'The Reverend Timothy Fowler and his sister will be at Lady Margaret Hall when we arrive there,' said Sophia Jex-Blake. 'They need to be told about Elm Rise and their father's secret lover. Oh, don't blush, man! Can we not speak the honest truth? From what I can gather, none of the Fowlers are exactly pillars of rectitude. Come, here we are. They will be waiting for us in the Lady Principal's sitting room.'

Sophia watched the inspector as he admired some of the pictures hanging on the walls. She herself had provisionally approved of the pink and blue William Morris wallpaper. It had been gracious of Elizabeth Wordsworth to abandon her sanctuary to them for the rest of the morning.

Mr Antrobus looked much better. They had left Elm Rise early on the Saturday morning, and all the time they were on the train she had prayed that the bleeding from his left lung would not recommence. It had not, and he had been rested and ready when the evening summons from St Michael's College had brought him to investigate William Podmore's death.

The door opened, and the Reverend Timothy Fowler and his sister Frances came into the room.

Poor fellow, thought Sophia, he looks utterly desperate, and yet he has brought misfortune on himself through his own folly. Frances is standing up well to her family's ordeal, but then, as far as she knew, Frances had little with which to reproach herself, apart from a certain hardness of heart.

'You have summoned my sister and me here very urgently, madam,' said the Reverend Timothy Fowler. 'I take it that you have news for us? It's becoming more and more scandalous that my poor father's murder has gone unavenged. Is it not time for Scotland Yard to be called in? We....'

Timothy suddenly caught sight of Antrobus. He turned deadly pale, and staggered, as though he were about to faint once more. His sister helped him to a chair.

'Your father, Mr Fowler,' said Antrobus, 'was not murdered. He died of natural causes. All this suggestion of murder was either a cruel imposture, or an appalling misjudgement on someone's part. No, sir,' he cried peremptorily, 'you will be quiet and listen to me. On 18 May this year,' said Antrobus, 'your father, Sir Montague Fowler, paid a visit to an old friend of his, a lady called Marian Hughes, who lived at a place called Elm Ridge, in Berkshire. While staying with her, he contracted gastroenteritis from eating infected meat. Within the space of four days, Marian Hughes and her servants died of the same infection. Your father was able to return to Oxford, and lingered for near on a fortnight before death supervened. He died of natural causes, and for the reasons stated on his death certificate.'

'But how can that be? I found a packet of mercuric chloride....'

'You did indeed, Mr Fowler, and foolishly concealed it, an act that could have had catastrophic consequences for you. But the placing of that poison in your father's bedroom was part of another action on the part of a third party, and was not in any way connected with your father's death. At the moment, you must take my word for that.'

When Antrobus finished speaking, there was a palpable silence in the room. Timothy Fowler seemed stunned by what he had heard, and it was his sister Frances who broke the silence.

'So no one murdered Father?'

'No one, miss. Yourself, and your two brothers, are entirely innocent of any criminal act with respect to your father's death. But grave acts of criminality *have* been committed, and will be punished with the utmost rigour of the law. What those acts are, you will learn in due course. I will leave you both alone with Miss Jex-Blake for a while, as there is something that she wishes to tell you.'

Inspector Antrobus rose and quickly left the room.

'Now, Timothy, and you, Frances,' said Sophia, 'is there no question you want to ask about your father's behaviour while he lay on his sick-bed?'

'There is,' Frances replied. 'Why did Father not tell the doctors where he had been, and what had occurred? He said nothing, you know. Nothing at all.'

'He said nothing, my dear, because he did not want anyone to know of his relationship with Mrs Marian Hughes. He had known her for many years, ever since he was a young man. And the secret that he wanted to keep was that, many years ago, he and Marian had had a child together.'

'What?' Timothy had sprung to his feet. 'A child? A child of wrath? No wonder he said nothing! Oh, the disgrace! This must not be made public. We have suffered enough from Father's peccadilloes over the past few years. But this!'

'Sit down, Mr Fowler,' said Sophia, and there was a steely edge to her voice that made the young clergyman obey. 'Examine your own conscience, and ask yourself is there nothing in *your* past that needs atonement. I have heard from Mr Antrobus the story of you and a young man called Adrian Fortesque.'

'What young man? Timothy, what…?'

Timothy Fowler made no reply to his sister, but he had the grace to blush. He held his head in his hands, and sat in all the misery of overwhelming shame.

'I must leave you both now,' said Sophia. 'But before I do, there is something I wish to tell you about Sir Montague's illegitimate child. In the manner of these things, the child – it was a boy – took its mother's surname. She had not in those days married the man called Hughes, who was to be her husband for many years. Her maiden name was Ballard.'

'A natural death? So Monty wasn't murdered after all!'

Joseph Steadman had received his unexpected visitors with

his usual courtesy, and had sent for coffee to be brought up to the Bursary. Inspector Antrobus seemed much as usual, still clad in the sombre black suit that he had worn at the inquest, though that morning there were hectic spots showing in those parts of his face that were not hidden by his close black beard and moustache.

He had heard of Dr Sophia Jex-Blake by reputation, and was sufficiently impressed by her now, as she sat at the table in the outer Bursary, where he had received them. She was sufficiently sure of herself to dress conventionally, though with a decided dash of style; her shrewd eyes regarded him from behind small, round spectacles.

'No, sir, the Warden was not murdered, and it won't be long now before the whole truth of the matter is laid before the public. The press need to be invited to a conference, in order to spread the truth of the Warden's death as widely as possible.'

'It's such a relief to hear this news, Antrobus,' said Joseph Steadman. 'It was an appalling affront to imagine that anyone who knew Monty – the Warden – would have wanted to do him harm. So his family is entirely exonerated in any complicity – no, I'm not thinking straight! No one is implicated in any crime, because a crime did not take place!'

Steadman's brow grew dark, and a flush of anger suffused his face.

'So the indignity – the sacrilege – of that autopsy was entirely unnecessary.... I confess, Inspector, that I'm beginning to lose the thread of what happened here.'

'Let me ask you a specific question, Bursar,' said Sophia Jex-Blake. 'How did you find out about Dr William Podmore's plagiarism? The coroner took you to task for not making your knowledge public – which was rather fatuous of him, as gentlemen are not in the business of sneaking on each other – but he didn't ask you how you knew about it. The plagiarism, you know.'

Steadman told his visitors of his seeing Podmore hiding Herr Doctor Bosch's manuscript under his coat, and his discovery of the address of the old German scholar's sister and her companion, Mrs Langrish, at Hampton Stonor. He had visited her, and discovered the diary with the damning entry, which he had copied, and brought back to college to examine privately and at leisure.

'The entry in Herr Doctor Bosch's diary proved beyond doubt that Podmore had stolen his work, and published it as his own. I remember that lady asking me who was "in charge" of the university, as she wanted to send all Dr Bosch's papers to him. It was an odd request, so I told her that the Vice-Chancellor was the man to contact. That's how he, too, came to find out about Podmore's – er – defalcation.'

'When you came back to college with your copy of the diary entry, where did you examine it? Was it in here?'

'Yes, Inspector. In the far room, there, what we call "the archive".'

'And was anyone else present when you did so?'

'No. At least, Dr Templar, the Tutor in Chemistry, came to see me about a private matter while I was reading my copy of the diary entry.'

'Could Dr Templar have seen that paper? I have a specific reason for asking you that question.'

'Well…. I left him standing beside the desk on which I'd placed the sheet of paper while I came in here to deal with the business that he'd come about. So yes, he could have seen it. Could have read it, you know.'

'Sir,' said Inspector Antrobus, 'Miss Jex-Blake and I both believe that Dr Templar read that diary entry, and used it to take some kind of revenge on Dr Podmore. We think he sent him anonymous notes, telling him that his secret was known. Dr Podmore evidently thought that it was you who sent them, as he accused you of having "done for" him in his suicide note.'

Joseph Steadman blushed, and pretended to consult one of the papers spread out on his working-table. It was not Antrobus's words that made him uneasy, but the steady, appraising gaze of the woman doctor. Dash it all! It wasn't a crime to think badly of a rotter!

'I did nothing of the sort. It was sufficient for me to know that Podmore was a bad lot – oh, yes, I had always been jealous of him! He pipped me to the post at every position I aspired to. Did you know that he once sent an aged, ailing don up to Scotland in the winter, knowing that the journey would kill him? And in the end he was too weak-willed, too pusillanimous, to face up to the consequences of his actions like a man. There, I've finished.'

'I'm convinced that Dr Templar sent anonymous letters to Dr Podmore,' said Antrobus, 'and I intend to ask him face to face whether he did so. It was almost certainly Dr Templar who concealed that packet of poison under Sir Montague Fowler's bed. I shall ask him about that, too.'

Joseph Steadman had recovered his equanimity. His attention passed from recollected resentment against Podmore to the immediate subject of Gerald Templar.

'Dr Templar had always resented Podmore's refusal to consent to the construction of a chemical laboratory here in St Michael's College. Sir Montague Wheeler had favoured the idea, but Podmore talked him out of it.'

'So his motive for putting that poison where he did was to make Sir Montague's death look like murder,' said Antrobus. 'Why should he do that? The answer is almost embarrassingly obvious. It was to throw suspicion on Podmore. The idea was that Dr Podmore had murdered his predecessor in order to become Warden himself.

'And then there is the business of the post-mortem examination, and the finding of mercuric chloride in the stomach. How do you think that substance got there, Dr Steadman?'

'Are you implying that Templar put it there?' asked Steadman. 'I believe he assisted at the examination of the remains. I think, Inspector, that you had better ask him for answers to these things now. As far as I know, he should be in college today, though he wasn't at breakfast in hall. He's been acting very strangely since the inquest. I think his mind is turning.... In the light of what you've told me this morning, I should think that Templar's now blaming himself for Podmore's death.'

Templar was not in his usual haunts, and the porter at the lodge thought that he had not left the college that morning. His rooms were deserted, and it was seen that his bed had not been slept in. He was not in the Common Room, or in the library.

The Bursar and his two visitors stood on the shale path in the second quad, which seemed to be deserted. All three were beginning to feel a profound unease. It was a bright, warm morning, and the perfume of the wisteria came gratefully to their senses. The gilt clock above the passageway into the first quad struck eleven.

And then a figure emerged from staircase XII. It was the aged chaplain, the Reverend and Honourable Theodore Waynefleet. He caught sight of Joseph Steadman, and greeted him with a kind of glad relief.

'Ah! Joe! Good morning, madam. Good morning, sir. Pleased to meet you. Joe, there's water coming through my ceiling. It's making quite a mess in my sitting-room. Would you have a look at it? I know you're very good at that kind of thing.'

Steadman glanced up at the first floor windows immediately above the chaplain's rooms, three sixteenth-century windows elaborately glazed with frosted glass. He knew instinctively what had happened.

'Dr Jex-Blake,' he said, 'will you stay down here with Mr Waynefleet? Antrobus, come with me.'

*

There were three bathrooms on the first floor, installed in the 1870s for the use of the undergraduates. It was a very advanced feature, much more convenient than the usual hip baths, brought in to the individual rooms, and filled with hot water by the staircase scouts from enormous jugs. The bathrooms were known affectionately as 'The Palace'.

In the second bathroom, Gerald Templar lay fully clothed in the long cast-iron bath. His eyes were closed, and to all appearances he was dead. The water, cascading over the rim, was coloured a faint red. The taps were still running. Steadman turned them off, released the plug, and together he and Antrobus dragged the Junior Dean from the bath, and laid him on the floor. At the same time, Stanley Fitzmaurice burst in to the room.

'What's amiss?' he cried. 'What has the fool done to himself? Here, let me attend to him.'

Fitzmaurice turned the stricken man on to his stomach, and began to apply artificial respiration. A quantity of water poured from Templar's mouth.

'Now for the wrists,' said Fitzmaurice. 'Yes, he's cut them across, so they can be easily stitched and then dressed. Had he thought to cut them vertically, he'd have severed arteries, and would be dead by now.'

'How do you know all this?' asked Steadman.

'From certain Army experiences. There, he's coming round!'

Templar opened his eyes and tried to speak, but his voice came in stertorous agonized gasps. There came the sound of footsteps on the stairs, and Sophia Jex-Blake entered the bathroom. She looked with calm professionalism at Gerald Templar.

'There's a penknife lying on the bottom of the bath,' she said. 'I expect that's what he used. He must be got to a hospital immediately. Could you gentlemen bind his wrists with neckties above and below those gashes? Only three ties? Well, don't be shy of using Mr Templar's own tie!'

Inspector Antrobus looked at their patient with distaste. Attempted suicide was a crime, and he would have to pay for that. But he had done other things, things that had wrought havoc to the college, its members, and the family of its late Warden. He had much to answer for, and he would make sure that no attempts were made to spirit him away to some place were he could not be held to account for his actions.

'Dr Steadman,' he said, 'do you have the electric telephone installed in the college? Good. Please ask someone to ring this number,' he wrote hastily on a scrap of paper torn from a notebook, 'and ask for a police ambulance to be sent here straight away. Mr Templar must be taken at once to the Radcliffe Infirmary, where one of my constables will be present at his bedside.'

Steadman made no reply. He took the piece of paper from Antrobus, and made his way to the lodge, where the electric telephone was kept.

When Templar opened his eyes, he saw that he was lying in a narrow hospital cot. His chest ached, as did his wrists. He vaguely remembered having the wounds on his wrists stitched and covered with dressings. He recalled a brisk young nurse forcing him to swallow raw white of eggs, which made him retch. His throat had been sprayed with carbolic. For most of the time, though, he had dozed fitfully. How wretched he felt!

He was now aware of a number of faces looking down on him. His eyes focused, and he saw the cream-painted walls of the small room, the wooden bedside locker, and the plain deal table placed beneath a barred sash window. The faces became something more than pinkish blobs. There was Joe Steadman, and Stanley Fitzmaurice, and a well-dressed lady wearing a fashionable bonnet. And there was Detective Inspector

Antrobus. He turned his head to the left, and saw an impassive bearded constable sitting beside the bed. After what seemed an age, a voice spoke.

'Why did you attempt suicide? What had you done?'

'It was I who drove Podmore to suicide. I sent him anonymous type-written notes, telling him that his plagiarism was known. How could I have possibly known that he would commit suicide as a result? So I thought I could atone for my crime by following his example.'

'How did you find out about Dr Podmore's plagiarism of Dr Bosch's work?' asked Antrobus.

'I found out about it one day when I went to visit the Bursar. He had left a damning letter or diary entry on his desk. I already hated Podmore – or so I thought – and I saw the opportunity of tormenting him with his guilt, leaving him always uncertain of his security, waiting for exposure....'

'That was a damned wicked thing to do, Templar,' said Stanley Fitzmaurice.

'I know – I know that, now, to my cost. I'd no idea that those notes of mine would have driven the poor man to suicide. And when he blamed not just the Vice-Chancellor but Dr Steadman, in that suicide note of his, I was frantic. It was my fault that the college was being torn apart.'

Templar stirred uneasily, and his pale cheeks flushed with something like anger.

'But.... I was not entirely to blame,' he said. 'Podmore was the kind of dyed-in-the-wool pedant who had no interest whatever in the future. He put paid to my suggestion that laboratories should be constructed at St Michael's, even though the Warden was in favour. Podmore disliked me, and the feeling was mutual. Can you wonder that my resentment of the man festered after that? The idea of revenge came to me as the Warden lay dying in the Lodgings. I secured a quantity of mercuric chloride from a chemist's shop in Kingston upon Thames....'

'Why there?' asked Fitzmaurice.

'Because it was a place that had no connection with me personally, or as far as I knew, with anyone here at St Michael's. I thought I'd have difficulty in obtaining the stuff, but it was frighteningly simple. I left the packet in Sir Montague's bedroom when I paid him a visit, knowing that it would be found. I knew – we all knew – that Podmore would be appointed Warden, and I wanted to give him an uncomfortable time when people began to suspect that he had poisoned Sir Montague Fowler in order to succeed him.'

'Another incredibly wicked idea,' said Fitzmaurice. 'Templar, our friendship ends here.'

The wretched man seemed not to hear. Unheeded tears rolled down his cheeks.

'I tried to play fair,' he whispered, 'I left the packet unopened, and with the chemist's seals intact. I assumed that once the packet was properly examined, Podmore would be cleared of all suspicion very soon. If nothing had happened by the end of the week, I would have started to ask the right questions about that packet myself, so forcing the authorities to examine it.'

Templar suddenly cried out, wringing his hands in despair.

'But there's more – more!' he cried. 'The autopsy on Sir Montague Fowler. I—'

'We know what you did, Templar,' said Inspector Antrobus. 'You can give us your account of the affair when you are recovered. Meanwhile, you must prepare yourself to answer grave charges of law-breaking in court, and I will advise you now to prepare yourself for a long term of imprisonment. When you are well enough to leave here, you will be lodged on remand in Oxford Gaol.'

15

ANOTHER VISITOR TO MAKIN HOUSE

Dʀ Aʀᴍsᴛʀᴏɴɢ ʀᴇᴀᴄʜᴇᴅ up to a high shelf fixed to the wall of the mortuary laboratory, and brought down one of the glass specimen jars stored there.

'This jar,' he said, 'contains the stomach of the late Sir Montague Fowler. You will see his name affixed to the label, together with my signature, and that of Dr Gerald Templar, who assisted me at the autopsy. The lid is secured with a wax seal.'

He stood back from the bench and surveyed his audience. Dr Jex-Blake seemed to be controlling her excitement. Inspector Antrobus stood a little apart from the others, as though conscious of the fact that he was not a medical expert.

What would Armstrong make of Dr Evan Pincent, a forensic specialist brought in by Dr Jex-Blake from London to re-examine the stomach? He was a gloomy-looking man in his forties, with a straggling moustache, rheumy eyes, and a prominent Adam's apple.

Armstrong removed the crepe cover, revealing the stomach, submerged in a preservative liquor. Inspector Antrobus leaned forward and surveyed it with interest. It was about twelve inches long and six inches wide, and had assumed a yellowish

197

hue. It was hard to imagine that it had once been part of a living man.

'Remind me, if you will, Doctor,' said Antrobus. 'You removed that stomach from Sir Montague's body with the assistance of Dr Gerald Templar of St Michael's?'

'Yes, that's right. We detached it from the duodenum and the oesophagus, and placed it in that jar. We did that in an old stable in the village of Lynham Hill, in Wiltshire, where Sir Montague was buried.'

'And did you personally examine the contents of the stomach?' asked Antrobus.

'No. The stomach, and other organs, were conveyed back to Oxford, and examined here by Dr Templar, who was able to confirm the presence of large quantities of mercuric chloride in the rugae and mucus membrane. I have looked out his report for you, in case you would like to consult it.'

They had come straight from the Radcliffe Infirmary to the mortuary. Dr Armstrong knew nothing of the dramatic events of that morning.

'When you removed the stomach at Lynham Hill,' asked Sophia Jex-Blake, 'did you notice that it was apparently empty? The attendant physicians had swilled out the stomach with bicarbonate of soda as a final measure before the patient died.'

'You will understand, Dr Jex-Blake,' said Armstrong somewhat testily, 'that our purpose was to remove organs for careful examination in a laboratory. To both of us the stomach looked empty. It was, of course, immediately irrigated when we placed it in the formalin solution.'

Dr Evan Pincent came forward and placed a little shagreen case on the bench beside the jar. Without saying a word, he removed his coat and rolled back his shirtsleeves away from the wrists. Dragging a tall stool towards him, he sat down, broke the wax seal, and unscrewed the jar. A wide, deep enamel tray had been set out by the laboratory steward, and

Antrobus winced as the doctor slid the stomach out of the jar. The smell of formalin filled the room. Pincent opened his little case, and removed some kind of metal probe, and what seemed to Antrobus to be a long, narrow brass telescope. He bent over the stomach, and began to use his probe.

They all watched in silence as he worked. Sometimes he peered through his telescope at a particular locus of tissue inside the grim mass, at other times he wielded a scalpel. After thirty minutes or so, he straightened up from the bench, and addressed himself to Sophia Jex-Blake. He spoke with a slightly belligerent London accent.

'Miss Jex-Blake, it's obvious that this stomach was empty at the time of Sir Montague's death. There is no trace of any food or of any foreign body adhering to the rugae or in the pylorus. I have detected some traces of the sodium bicarbonate used to flush out the stomach: a very strong solution, virtually saturated in this case, had been used, and some particles have adhered to the stomach wall.'

He handed his telescope to Sophia, who examined the stomach wall, and nodded her agreement.

'That adhesion should have been mentioned in Dr Templar's report,' she said. 'I have read that report, and there is no mention of the fact. Pray continue, Doctor.'

'When I looked more deeply beneath the surface, penetrating both the mucosa and the sub-mucosa, I found large quantities of mercuric chloride crystals pressed deeply into the tissue. Not lodged, but pressed. There are similar deposits virtually jammed into the opening of the oesophagus, and beyond the pylorus in the surgically severed part of the duodenum. In two places, the probe – probably the flat end of a chemical spatula – had actually pierced the serosa, the fibrous outer cover of the stomach wall.'

Dr Pincent looked at his audience. They were waiting for him to announce his conclusion.

'When this man died, his stomach was empty. It remained in that state until it was brought back here to Oxford Mortuary. Once here, someone "doctored" it, if I may use that word, so that it looked as though the man had been poisoned. It is a crude physical attack on a dead organ, which any trained doctor would notice immediately. To find out who did it, you must question the doctor who examined this organ and produced the report detailing what he had discovered.'

Dr Armitage made no reply, but left the room, returning after a couple of minutes with a young man in a brown laboratory coat.

'This is John Maitland,' he said, 'who is one of the technicians employed here in the mortuary. Maitland, I want you to cast your mind back to that day in July when the specimen organs of the late Sir Montague Fowler were brought here for examination. I want you to tell us what occurred here on that day.'

The young man cleared his throat nervously.

'Sir,' he said, 'The specimens arrived here by railway courier late on the afternoon of 5 July, which was a Wednesday. They'd been sent straight here after the exhumation proceedings on the day before. Well, you know that, Dr Armitage, because you despatched them yourself.'

'I did indeed, Maitland,' said Armitage, a ghost of a smile playing round his lips. 'And of what did this consignment consist?'

'There were three sealed jars, sir. One contained the stomach, one held the liver, and the third the kidneys of the deceased subject. I brought them in here to the laboratory, and left them on that bench for Dr Templar.'

'Did you unseal them, or remove the crepe masks?'

'No, sir. I left them just as they were. I would not have touched them until Dr Templar arrived from St Michael's College.' The lad licked his lips. 'I hope I did nothing wrong, sir. I followed the standard procedures as usual.'

'And when did Dr Templar arrive?'

'He came in quite late, sir, just after seven o'clock. It was getting dark, and when I heard his cab stopping outside I lit the gas mantle over the bench.'

'What happened then?'

'Dr Templar came in, and sat down at the bench. He'd brought his own doctor's bag with him, which he placed beside the jars. Dr Templar seemed nervous and uneasy. He was very pale, and his brow was covered in sweat. I don't think he was very well. He knew me, of course, because I'd worked with him before. But that night he said that he wished to work alone. He told me to go home, and as I left the laboratory I heard him lock the door behind me.'

'What did you find when you came in on Friday morning? Was everything in order?'

'Yes, sir. The jars were all properly signed and sealed, and Dr Templar's written report was lying in a cardboard folder on the bench. He must have worked very late into the night to have completed it.'

'Well, Maitland,' said Dr Armitage, 'I have one final question that I want to put to you. What did you think when Dr Templar told you to leave him alone and go home?'

'Well, sir, I thought it was irregular, if you don't mind me saying so. We've always had two or more medical staff present when these investigations are carried out. Yes, I thought it was most irregular.'

'Antrobus,' said Dr Armitage, when he had dismissed young Maitland, 'what does this mean? Surely Dr Templar would not stoop to such wicked fabrication?'

Antrobus told him of the dramatic events of that morning at St Michael's College, and of Templar's hospital confession.

'I'm shocked, Inspector,' said Armitage, 'shocked and horrified.' He glanced at the row of jars arrayed on the shelf above the bench. 'When time serves, I'll examine Sir Montague's liver and kidneys, for signs of similar contamination. But what we've seen here, in the stomach, is all you will need to confirm your suspicions.'

'I must go now,' said Antrobus, 'to secure the necessary warrants. Templar may imagine that there was some justification for what he did, but the law will think otherwise, and he will most certainly have to serve a term of imprisonment. His days as a Fellow of St Michael's College are over.'

The re-examination of the post-mortem specimens took place on Thursday, 26 July. By that weekend, the whole of Oxford had heard the sensational news, thanks to the assiduous reporters of *Jackson's Journal*. The London papers took the matter up, and reports of what The *Daily Telegraph* described as 'the villainy of an Oxford don' ensured that Gerald Templar was firmly established as the villain of the piece. The *Morning Post*, noted for its even-handed reporting, printed as its third leader a persuasive summary of what had come to be known as 'the St Michael's College Affair' in its issue of Monday, 30 July:

> Since Thursday last we have all become familiar with the appalling villainy of Dr Gerald Templar, who, apparently out of mean jealousy, contrived to make the sad passing of Sir Montague Fowler, a victim of gastroenteritis, appear to have been murder. Then Templar, having discovered evidence of an unethical act committed by Dr William Podmore, Sir Montague Fowler's successor as Warden of St Michael's, proceeded to send that unfortunate gentleman a series of anonymous notes, so cruel and gloating in their import, presumably, as to drive Podmore to suicide.
>
> St Michael's College will have to cope with these tragedies as well as it may, and we have no doubt that, as an institution, it will survive this injurious epoch in its

202

long history. It is to the family of the late Sir Montague Fowler that most harm has been done, harm that the wretched Templar can do nothing to alleviate. The dark shadow of suspicion – suspicion of parricide – has hung over Fowler's three innocent children for too long. They must now be left in peace to resume their avocations with our hearty best wishes for their continued success. As for Gerald Templar, let the Law fall heavily upon him. A disgrace to his profession, he is not fit to form the minds of the young gentlemen who are entrusted to his care. Let the Law act. Let us hear no more of him.

'Sergeant Maxwell,' said Inspector Antrobus, 'I've decided to let that business of the Reverend Mr Fowler's concealing the packet of mercuric chloride to lie on the file. Or to put it more plainly, to forget about it. It was an innocent man's blind panic that made him do it. But you're dressed up for battle this morning, Joe, buttoned up like that, and with your best bowler on display. Are you going to tell me what you're up to?'

'Do you mind if I tell you when I've come back, sir?' said Maxwell. 'It'll be a nice surprise for you. I'm going to St Michael's College, to have a word with that scout, Haynes, the one who looked after poor Mr Podmore. I have a little theory about him.'

Maxwell found Haynes washing up cups and saucers in a sort of cupboard leading off the first-floor landing on Staircase IV. The man gave him a surly nod, but before he could ask why the sergeant had come to disturb him at his work, Maxwell attacked.

'I'll not beat about the bush, Haynes,' he said, in his loud, intimidating voice. 'I want to know why you forged this suicide note.' From the inside pocket of his coat he took the half sheet of note paper that Antrobus had discovered in Podmore's bedroom, and slammed it down on the drain-board. The cups and saucers rattled in protest.

'What do you mean, forged? I never....'

'Why deny it? What's the point? It's a very good forgery of Mr Podmore's handwriting, but forgery it is, my friend. You and your master were a precious pair, weren't you? He was a plagiarist, by which we mean a copier of other people's efforts, and you were a forger. Maybe you caught it from him. Forgery, I mean. So, listen. You can tell me here and now, here in this little cubby-hole, why you did it, or you can come down to the police station and—'

'He was not my "master", Mr Maxwell. This is a college, not a private residence. But then, you wouldn't know that, would you? He was my gentleman, who lived on my staircase, and I looked after his needs. Why are you accusing me of forgery?'

'Because of what it says in that note. Look at it! "It is all up with me. Boyd and Steadman have done for me. I cannot face the shame. Blame no one for my death." Someone as learned as Dr Podmore wouldn't write "Boyd and Steadman have done for me." *Done for me*? Gentlemen don't speak like that. He'd have used some fancy phrase or other.'

'He said "Boyd and Steadman between them have secured my downfall." I only remembered his exact words later. Yes, I wrote that note, because he never wrote one himself, and I wanted everyone to know who'd driven him to his death.'

Tears rose to the man's eyes. He dashed them away angrily.

'I'll tell you what happened, and then you can do as you like. It was late in the afternoon of Founder's Day. I'd been out to buy Dr Podmore a bottle of gin. He drank heavily, and so did I, though everybody here thought he was a total abstainer. He was very generous to me, but the dons here despised him. Curse them! What secrets were *they* concealing from the light of day?'

'So you'd been out to buy him a bottle of gin? What happened next?'

'Well, I'm telling you, aren't I? I went into the Lodgings. He must have heard the door open, because he called down from upstairs. I found him in his bedroom, in a terrible state. He'd drunk a whole bottle of spirits, he told me, but it couldn't drown his sorrows. He hadn't changed for dinner, and was still in his day clothes. "In God's name, what's the matter, sir?" I cried. And then he gave me such a look as almost froze my blood in my veins. "Oh, Haynes," he said, "Boyd and Steadman between them have secured my downfall." I said a few soothing words, and left him.

'Not long afterwards, the chapel bell was rung by Mr Reid, the Head Porter, and you know what happened then. It was after Mr Reid discovered the body, and before Inspector Antrobus arrived, that I slipped into the Lodgings and wrote that note. He'd not written one himself, you see, and I wanted everybody to know who'd driven him to his death. He was lying there, across the bed, and I knew that he'd poisoned himself. He'd talk about poison sometimes, when he was low, and under the influence. He was *my* gentleman! I wasn't going to let him go to his grave with no one knowing who'd put him there. So what are you going to do about it?'

The man's voice had become tremulous, and he had turned pale. Maxwell knew that he feared the loss of his livelihood.

'I'm going to do nothing, Mr Haynes,' said Maxwell. 'I just wanted to satisfy my curiosity, that's all. This note will go back into the case-file, and that's the last anyone will hear of it. So dry those cups and saucers, and put your mind at rest.'

Frances Fowler stood on the pavement in Scrivener's Court, a discreet little square between George Street and Friar's Entry, and in the purlieus of Worcester College, looking up at a freshly painted sign above a bow-fronted shop:

HENRY BALLARD, UNIVERSITY STATIONER

The dark shadow of murder hanging over the family had lifted, but it would be quite wrong to leave Father's secretary in the dark as to his parentage. Now was the time to let him know that he was their half-brother. It would be difficult for all concerned to adjust to the idea, but she and her brothers had always led independent lives, and no doubt Ballard would do the same. The approach that she had planned would probably save all four of them embarrassment.

She entered the shop, setting a bell jangling behind the door. The shelves were still not filled, and there was a pile of shavings left by a joiner at the side of the long mahogany counter. A neat stack of leaflets had been placed in a tray, announcing that Mr Henry Ballard sought the patronage of the colleges and institutions of Oxford University for the supplying of the highest quality stationery.

A door at the back of the shop opened, and Ballard appeared, carrying a pile of exercise books. His normally austere face was transformed by a smile of welcome.

'Why, Miss Frances!' he exclaimed. 'How kind of you to look in! I wonder.... Have you come to favour me with an order for Makin House School?'

'I will certainly do that, Ballard,' she said. 'The sign above the door reads "University Stationer". Is that an official title?'

Henry Ballard smiled and shook his head.

'No, miss, I fear I awarded it to myself. But I have many contacts among the colleges, and I've already been promised large orders from Balliol and Trinity.'

'You seem in your element here.'

'I am, Miss Frances. I always hoped, if Sir Montague had dispensed with my services, that I could seek employment in this kind of business. Of course, it means that I am now in trade, but it's a dignified, clean-handed business. And this shop is my own: I was even able to buy the lease. I open for business in two weeks' time. Yes, I am very happy, miss. And it goes without saying that I am happy for the family, now that you have emerged from the shadow cast upon you by that appalling man.'

'Ballard,' said Frances, 'I haven't come here today to place an order, though you can be sure of my custom. I am here to tell you an intimate secret concerning my – concerning the late Sir Montague Fowler.'

She told him all that Inspector Antrobus and Miss Jex-Blake had discovered in their visit to Elm Ridge. While she spoke, Ballard did not raise his eyes from the counter. He stood perfectly still, though it was obvious that he was greatly agitated. It was only when she had finished speaking that he looked up and met her eyes. He had gone very pale, but there was a faint smile hovering about his lips.

'So what do you think, Ballard?' said Frances quickly, before he could reply. 'That was the tale told to Inspector Antrobus and Miss Jex-Blake, by an old country doctor and his housekeeper. What do you think?' she repeated.

Henry Ballard's shoulders sagged in evident relief.

'Well, Miss Frances,' he said, 'that is a very curious tale, not very – well, not very *nice*, if I may put it like that. Quite frankly, I don't believe a word of it. Oh, I'm not doubting your word, miss – God forbid! I can understand my late dear employer having a friend in the country in whom he could confide. But all this suggestion of a child – well, that can only be speculation. Country folk, I believe, are often avid for sensation, living as they do such humdrum lives, and what won't come to them by way of fact, they conjure up from their imagination.'

Francis laughed.

'I'm sure you're quite right, Ballard,' she said. 'And the fact that Sir Montague's lady friend had been named Ballard before her marriage is nothing more than coincidence. Yes, I'm sure you're quite right.'

Both she and Ballard knew that it was vital to adhere to his interpretation of the facts. If Ballard was publicly recognized as a son of Sir Montague Fowler, and so the blood-brother of herself, John, and Timothy, he would be regarded as a gentleman, and therefore unsuitable to be in trade. None of the colleges would put business his way, and he would find himself dwelling in a half-world somewhere between gentility and the servant class, and accepted by neither.

'Yes, Ballard,' she repeated, 'I'm sure you're quite right, and we'll forget what I have told you today. As you quite rightly said, the subject is not very nice. Could you come out to Makin House some time next week? We can discuss the school's stationery requirements over a cup of tea.'

'I should be delighted to attend on you at your convenience any time next week, Miss Frances,' said Ballard. 'How is Mr Timothy? I had contemplated calling on him at Makin House, but thought that he might consider me forward in doing so.'

'Timothy is rapidly recovering from his ordeal. And he would not have considered a visit from you as something forward. You were our Father's faithful servant and friend, and you are welcome to see us anytime.'

She saw how Ballard blushed with pleasure at her remark. They were all now safe from scandal, and Father's disgusting fall from grace could be forgotten. He had begotten a child of wrath, and had ultimately paid a terrible price.

One week later, Frances stood in the hallway of Makin House School, recalling the frightful events of the previous two months. She had just come in from the garden at the rear of the house, where her newly-appointed gardener had wanted to discuss various matters horticultural. She had pleased him by agreeing to everything he had suggested; she liked gardens, but shied away from actually working in them.

The encaustic tiles by De Morgan glowed yellow and brown in the strong August sunlight. The polished woodwork gleamed, and the brass stair-rods shone. As always, when she stood at that particular spot, she could hear the low voices of her staff and their charges in the adjacent rooms.

She had nearly lost all this! But now it was safe, all outstanding debts paid, and an endowment fund established. That had been Miss Graves' idea. She was proving to be an outstanding teacher. In Michaelmas Term, she would appoint her Deputy Headmistress.

Trixie, her cheerful parlour maid, came through from the kitchen passage into the hall.

'Oh, miss,' she said, 'a lady has called to see you. She wouldn't give her name. I took her upstairs to the study.'

A lady? Could it be Miss Jex-Blake? She was returning to London in a few days' time. Perhaps she had called to make her farewells. Whatever the reason, she was more than welcome.

She opened the study door, and saw Ursula Forrest standing at the window, looking out across Port Meadow. The blood raced to her head, and she thought for a moment that she was going to faint. But it was not pleasure that caused such a reaction. Ursula Forrest's presence in her school seemed to violate its sanctity. Ursula turned from the window, and smiled. The strong sunlight illuminated her face, and Frances could see the heavily-applied powder and rouge that were not apparent in the discreetly shaded boudoir in Old Bond Street.

'My sweet ring-dove,' said Ursula Forrest, 'how delightful to see you. I knew you wouldn't mind my coming down here to visit you. As a matter of fact, I'm very interested in one of your dear girls – perhaps you favour her yourself? Her name is Julia Trefusis. Her mother tells me that she's eighteen, and I suggested that she could perhaps visit me unaccompanied at Old Bond Street? What do you think?'

'Really, Ursula, I don't think that would be wise....'

'No, I thought you'd counsel caution. Well, I'm not prepared to wait. The coterie lacks young members of Julia's type. I know that she's here, Frances, hidden away in some dreary classroom, learning Latin or Greek. Send for her, will you? I want to look her over. Why have you turned so pale? Do as I tell you!'

Ursula was wearing a beautifully cut morning suit and a hat of dark green silk adorned with dyed feathers. She looked very handsome, and very imperious. It took Frances all her courage to summon up the words of her reply.

'I think not, Miss Forrest. While Julia is here, I am *in loco parentis*. London and Oxford don't mix. I must ask you to leave at once.'

Ursula's face flushed crimson with fury. She all but ran across the room and seized Frances by the arm.

'You little fool!' she hissed. 'Do you dare bandy words with me? Send for the girl. Remember this: I have photographs of you, my ring-dove, and letters, too. Once those pictures are shown to Julia's mother – or to the parents of any of your girls – you will be finished as a school mistress.'

Her voice suddenly lost its refinement. She renewed her grasp of Frances's arm, and she cried out in pain.

'You'll be finished entirely, dearie. Remember what happened to our little mistle thrush. She tried to fly the nest, and found that the only way out was suicide. Nobody leaves the swan's nest without the swan's permission. You have far more to lose than she had. For the last time: fetch the girl.'

Frances crossed to the fireplace and pulled the bell three times. That would summon the porter, but Ursula didn't know that. How had she ever allowed herself to be lured into this woman's trap? She had yielded to her own physical impulses, and had fallen into the clutches of a procuress. Oh, God, what was she to do?

The door opened, and a grey-haired man in a porter's uniform came into the study.

'Johnson,' said Frances, 'this lady is just leaving. Please see her off the premises.'

Ursula Forrest gave her a look of implacable fury, a look which said more loudly than mere words: 'You will regret this!'

Johnson held the door open, and Ursula Forrest swiftly left the room without looking behind her. Frances collapsed, weeping, into an armchair.

How could she free herself from this nightmare? Should she confess everything to Timothy, and ask him to intervene? No. How could she confess her wicked deeds to such a righteous man as her clergyman brother? And what, in practical terms, could he do? She dare not tell Inspector Antrobus, and watch his obvious regard for her turn to secret contempt.

John.... Yes, she would go up to London and tell John everything. Somehow, she knew that he would not judge her, but try to help her. He was a man of business, a practical man. He would do everything in his power to rid her of Ursula. Until that woman was silenced, she would never know a single minute's peace.

16

THE WELL IN THE SPINNEY

'My poor, dear Fanny! What a foolish, reckless girl you are.'

She had been lucky to find her brother alone in his fine house in a quiet square near Clarence Gate. Margaret and the children, he'd told her, were visiting the South Kensington Museum. She had flung herself at his feet in a welter of misery and despair, and had told him everything. He had not interrupted her confession, but had stroked her hair as he had done when she was a little girl.

'John,' she whispered, 'I know that you will despise me as an unnatural woman, and may not wish to know me in the future.'

'Rot! What I need to do now is to deal with this harpy, and make sure she does you no more harm. These albums, and the letters that you wrote to her – where does she keep them? And this other woman, the photographer – she will have the glass negatives.'

She remained kneeling at her brother's feet, too ashamed to lift her eyes to his face.

'Oh, get up, will you, Fanny!' John exclaimed. 'It looks as though you and me are chips off the old block. Father was no angel, from what we hear, and we are his children. Go over to that desk and write me the addresses of this Ursula and the other woman, Rosalie. Then leave the matter to me.'

Frances looked up at her brother, and saw that his lips had set in an almost vicious line of determination. She obeyed him without speaking, and wrote the names of her tormentors on a sheet of notepaper.

'John,' she whispered, 'what will you do? How can...?'

'Never mind what I shall do. By tomorrow morning, Fanny, those albums and letters, and the photographic negatives, will all have been destroyed. And I can guarantee that you will never hear from those two women again. No, don't say anything, dear girl. Go back to Oxford, to your school, and to your bright future there. By this time tomorrow, you will be free.'

It was long after closing time, but Ursula Forrest still lingered in her show room, admiring the newly set out display of shawls and bonnets, fresh from Milan. There was plenty there for her discerning clients to discuss, appreciate, and then buy.

It was eight o'clock on the evening of 9 August, and she had lit the shaded oil lamps that she favoured. Soon, she would retire to her private quarters.

What was that noise? The sound of heavy boots clattering up the stairs from the street entrance. They were accompanied by what sounded like howls and imprecations. She felt her heart pounding with fear. What could it mean? What...?

Crash! The door of the show room was kicked open, sending both lock and bolts flying across the room. Her scream of fear was drowned by the shouts and curses of the frightful men who had invaded her privacy. A huge giant of a man with scarred fists and a mouthful of broken teeth seized her by the throat and threw her to the floor. Behind him she saw a fierce black man, who was wielding an open razor. A third man, bent and bow-legged, began to use an iron bar to smash the glazed cabinets lining the walls.

The giant with the broken teeth began to scream at her, his heavy Irish accent making it difficult, in her terror, for her to understand what he was saying.

'Where are the albums?' he shrieked. 'Where are the letters from our friend Fanny Fowler? Where are they? Give them to me!'

The bow-legged man with the iron bar heaved one of the cabinets to the floor. The black man, she saw to her horror, had begun to cut the heavy velvet curtains to ribbons with his flashing, slashing razor.

'We're Fanny Fowler's friends!' the Irishman bellowed. 'You thought she was easy meat, didn't you? Well, she isn't. Give me the albums and the letters!'

The man with the razor suddenly darted across the room and held the gleaming blade to her throat. With a tremendous effort of will, Ursula Forrest got to her feet. She staggered into her private room, followed by the giant Irishman and the razor-man. The bow-legged man stayed behind in the show room, and she could hear him smashing up what displays remained with his iron bar.

She unlocked a cupboard, and with trembling hands withdrew two large photographic albums, fastened with brass clasps.

'Here,' she cried, 'take them! But don't hurt me!'

She all but collapsed in a chair. Was her heart going to burst with this endless terror?

The giant Irishman tore open the albums, glanced briefly at the contents, and then demanded the letters. The razor-man suddenly slashed the skirts of her dress, and in his turn demanded the letters. Almost fainting now, she eagerly opened a drawer, and produced a bundle of letters tied with blue tape.

'Here! Here!' she cried. 'Take them! But don't hurt me! What is that flickering light? What...?'

In the show room, the bow-legged man had lit a fire in the centre of the room, using some of her stock, and pages torn from catalogues. It was already burning fiercely, making a dark circle of destruction on the carpet. The Irishman tore the albums apart with his great, scarred hands, and threw them, with the letters, on to the fire. The room filled with pungent smoke. Once again, the big Irishman seized her by the throat, and pushed her against the wall.

'Remember this, Ursula Forrest. We are Fanny's friends. If you try to contact her, or persecute her in any way, we'll be back. We're always here, in good old London Town, and we'll always find you. We've spared you this time. Next time, you'll not be so lucky.'

The gang waited until the albums and letters had all been burned to ashes, and then left the premises as quickly as they had come. Soon, a little crowd of neighbours poured into the street. Someone had sent for the fire brigade. The neighbours carried Ursula Forrest, now in a dead faint, from the ruined salon.

Later that night, in her photographic studio above a fashionable print gallery in Regent Street, Rosalie sat on the floor among the ruins of her cameras and broken tripods, dry-eyed with shock and fear. The stone hearth lay thick with broken glass, where a big, hulking thug of an Irishman had trampled the glass negatives that he had demanded, to tiny pieces. He had screamed to her, while his accomplices had been jumping on her cameras and equipment, that he was Frances Fowler's friend and protector, and that if she ever bothered her again, he would come back with his razor-wielding friend, and spoil her beauty for her. Well, a few hundred pounds would make good this damage. But the time had come for her to seek new friends elsewhere.

So much for Ursula. Being her friend was just not worth the candle.

*

John Fowler sat in the back bar of a public house near Covent Garden market, and sipped his glass of sherry. His three companions preferred beer. It was very early morning, and they were the only customers in the bar.

'Well, gentlemen', he said, 'I'm very much obliged to you. And so is my sister. I've brought you all a little present.'

He handed each of his companions a small canvas purse.

'There's a hundred sovereigns for each of you. One for you, Mr O'Brian, one for you, Mr Delgado, and one for you, Mr Sime. Perhaps we can do business again in the future. I'll bid you good day. Please give my compliments to Captain Macdonald.'

'Mr Fowler, sir,' said Mr O'Brian, 'you've been very generous to us today. I hope you bear no ill will for past disagreements? Please give Miss Fowler our kind regards.'

'I will indeed. As for past disagreements, let's forget about them completely.'

The big Irishman fumbled in a pocket, and withdrew a gold watch and chain. He pushed it, rather shamefacedly, across the table.

'I believe this is your watch, Mr Fowler, which you left with us as a pledge? I'm happy to return it to you.'

John Fowler thought to himself: it's money that talks, and money that makes the world go round. I'll never stop gambling, but I'll curb my excesses at Paulet's tables in future. I've had enough of debt, and the fear of visits from villains like this precious lot.

He swept watch and chain into his pocket, threw half a sovereign on the table, and stood up. 'The drinks are on me, gentlemen,' he said. 'I must go, now. Business calls.'

Dear, silly Fanny! She'd never see or hear from those harpies again.

*

Sophia Jex-Blake walked through the sunlit gardens of Lady Margaret Hall, deep in conversation with Inspector Antrobus. It was 16 August, the day before her planned return to London.

'A remarkable business,' she said, 'with a remarkable outcome. Wouldn't you agree that you and I made a very effective team?'

James Antrobus laughed. How he had enjoyed the unlikely partnership with the intrepid lady doctor! Yes, they *had* made a good team. Even Sergeant Maxwell had admitted as much. He would be sorry to see her leave Oxford.

Sophia opened her reticule, and after a little rummaging produced a calling-card.

'There, Inspector,' she said, 'that is where you will find me should the need arise. Who knows, we might work together again, some time, if the right kind of case comes your way. Something medical, you know, where we can investigate together, and I can keep a professional eye on your health.'

The two partners shook hands.

'I'll bear in mind what you suggest, ma'am,' said Antrobus, raising his hat. 'I was going to say "goodbye", but maybe "au revoir" is more in order.'

'Au revoir, Inspector,' said Sophia Jex-Blake. She stood for a while in the sun-drenched garden of Lady Margaret Hall, shading her eyes with her hand, and watching her erstwhile colleague as he walked away swiftly along the path that would take him to the gate out into Norham Gardens.

It had not taken long for St Michael's College to settle down once again into its summer routine. True, the Lodgings were vacant, and no Warden had been appointed. Joseph Steadman had heard from a friend in London that the Queen herself had suggested that some decent period of time should elapse before a permanent appointment was made.

Stanley Fitzmaurice came striding across the lawn in the

second quad, and joined the Bursar, who was standing in the open passageway that joined the two quadrangles.

'Well, Bursar,' said Fitzmaurice, 'I think St Michael's is going to survive all the tragedy and scandal of the last few months. How do you feel about being made Regent?'

'I suppose I'm flattered that anyone at Court thought fit to appoint me as the temporary administrator of St Michael's until the great ones in London have made their decision. But I get no joy from it, Fitzmaurice. For me, the loss of Monty – Sir Montague Fowler – is irreparable. And if I had not stirred up the whole hornet's nest of *The Boethian Apices*, Podmore would be alive today.'

'True, but life must go on, Bursar. In a couple of months' time the undergraduates will be back, clamouring to be taught. I very much hope that a new Warden will be appointed before Christmas.'

'I hope so, too,' Steadman replied. 'I hope it may be you, Fitzmaurice. But if not, then let it be an outsider, someone who's not yet tainted by all our squalid secrets and petty conspiracies. I'm running the college from the Bursary, not the Lodgings, and you'll have noticed that I don't presume to lord it over you all by sitting in the Warden's chair.'

'I'm flattered that you should think me eligible,' said Fitzmaurice, 'but what we need at St Michael's is a new broom.'

'Yes, a new broom,' said Joseph Steadman. 'And when he's swept the place clean, I shall retire, and go to live in a house that I've purchased out at Headington.'

Stanley Fitzmaurice laughed.

'That's what you say, Bursar, but I bet that when a new Warden asks for our invaluable help and support in his heavy task, and so forth – heads of houses always say things like that – you'll be the first to pledge undying loyalty to him personally, as well as to the college. Somehow, I think that future generations of undergraduate will still benefit from the unique skills of "Joe the Plumber" whenever a pipe bursts, or a washer fails on a tap!'

The Reverend Timothy Fowler emerged from a beech wood covering the flank of a gentle hill, and saw at once the object of his pilgrimage, the isolated cemetery belonging to the village church at Highfield St Mary. It was odd, and rather unnerving, to find a graveyard sitting alone among tilled fields, a mile or so from its church.

He had put off his pilgrimage for so long that he had wondered whether he would ever be able to pluck up the courage to make it. And so it was only now, on 25 August, that he had ventured so far from home into what was virtually unknown territory to him: the remote hills and vales of Dorset.

No one here would know him, and he had thought it judicious to don secular clothing for his visit. Heaven had smiled upon him, clearing his name of all stain, and miraculously restoring to him not only his wife – he had known in his heart that she would come back to him – but also the parish of Clapton Parva.

As soon as his name was cleared, Kate had returned to him, clinging and weeping, and protesting her undying love. Initially, she had forborne to tell him that her father, losing all patience with her, had declared that if she did not return to her husband, he would deliver her personally to Clapton Parva like a parcel sent through the Royal Mail. After a day or two back home, though, she had told him what her father had said, and he had laughed at her confusion and embarrassment. It mattered little to him how she came home, as long as she was there with him.

Within days of the revelation of Gerald Templar's villainy, Timothy had received a letter from the Bishop of Winchester.

My dear Fowler,

I must confess that I was too precipitate in my plan to banish you to what I know would have been an uncongenial parish in Portsmouth. Your reputation as a first-rate clergyman remains unblemished, and I have written urgently to Lord Stevenage, asking him to renew his offer to sell you the advowson of Clapton Parva. As you may have heard, the present incumbent has been obliged to resign the living by reason of frailty, so the parish is vacant.

My congratulations on this 'happy issue out of all your afflictions'. I shall follow your career with lively interest.

Well, the grovelling tone of that letter had raised his spirits considerably. The Bishop had too readily believed the worse, and would atone for that by helping Timothy in every way, and possibly to higher preferment, such as that of archdeacon, in future years.

Soon afterwards, Lord Stevenage, evidently fretting at the absence of his favourite parson, had immediately renewed his offer of the advowson, and Timothy had purchased it without more ado. They had begun their move into the gracious Queen Anne vicarage within days of his receiving the Bishop's letter. Yes, Heaven had been kind....

Timothy descended the hill and opened the wicket gate in the fence surrounding the churchyard. It was a hot, oppressive day towards the end of August, and unnervingly quiet, as though the very birds were too exhausted to sing. A few sheep were nibbling the grass, but they moved away as he walked along the narrow, overgrown paths between the monuments.

He found the grave almost immediately, one of three all belonging to the same family, surrounded by railings, and marked by granite headstones. He read the inscription on the third stone; the letters still looked fresh, although they had been carved some seven years ago.

Also Adrian,
only son of James Fortesque, Esq.,
died 29 July, 1887,
aged 24.
'For so He giveth His beloved sleep.'
Psalm 127.

'Adrian,' said the Reverend Timothy Fowler, aloud, 'I know that by now you will have forgiven me for standing by and letting you drown. I make no excuse for what I did. Like you, I was a strong swimmer, and could so easily have plunged in and brought you safe to the bank. But you see, I was so in love with Kate that I could not bear the thought of another winning her. They say "all's fair in love and war", and there's some truth in that.'

A dark cloud obscured the sun, and a deep shadow rushed across Adrian Fortescue's grave. Timothy seemed not to notice.

'I have been living in the dark shadow of despair recently,' he said, 'but all that is past, and my future is assured. I can devote myself once more to the needs of my little flock at Clapton Parva, doing so much good, and by works of charity, combined with preaching of the Word, bringing them to Salvation. I feel that God has forgiven me, though He has never let me forget that terrible day by the river in '87. That, I suppose, is to be part of my penance.

'So have you, too, forgiven me? I am sure that you have, and that you will look down from Heaven with compassion for my youthful folly. Goodbye, Adrian. May you rest in the sleep of peace. For now I have made my peace with God, and, I am sure, with you!'

Timothy turned his back on the three granite stones, and made his way out of the churchyard. It was near noon, and very hot. Far away, he heard the faint, low rumbling of thunder, presage of a gathering storm. It was time to regain the village inn, and order a conveyance to take him to the railway station in the neighbouring town. There was much to be done at Clapton Parva, and now that his mind was free of the burden of guilt, he could give full attention to his ministry.

'Oh, Timothy,' cried Kate Fowler, 'how wonderful it is to have left that dreadful hovel! Had we stayed there much longer, I'm sure I would have died! And now – look at this beautiful dining room! When the new furniture arrives from Maple's, this room will rival Lord Stevenage's. When shall we hold the house-warming?'

'When all is ready, my dear, and the whole house is redecorated. Mid-September would be a good time. We'll have a full complement of servants by then, including two resident gardeners. Did you know that the advowson included three neat cottages beyond the spinney? That's where we'll house some of our staff.'

'They say there's a freshwater well by those cottages,' said Kate. 'I saw some men with plumb-lines – or do I mean theodolites? They were doing something near the well, yesterday. You can see the cottages from the upstairs drawing-room windows.'

'Those men were surveyors, Kate. I got them down from London to examine that well with a view to taking it through a conduit, and to look at the site with a view to building a decent coach house there. We'll need a good carriage, you know, and a dog-cart. The present stables will suffice, at least for a while. I'm going down there now, to have a look at that well. They told me that they've begun exploratory work there. I'll see you in an hour's time.'

Timothy left the house by one of the back doors, and made his way down the long rear lawn of the gracious old house. The grass was roughly trimmed, but in a week's time a new gardener, with a modern lawn mower, would transform it into something disciplined and beautiful.

There was a low wall at the bottom of the lawn, with a little iron gate that took him into the spinney where the cottages lay. The wall around the old well had been partly demolished, and a pile of new bricks lay nearby, together with a number of workmen's tools. Timothy could hear the rushing of water from the hidden spring that fed the well.

The sky had become overcast, and suddenly there came a clap of thunder. Within less than a minute, heavy rain had begun to fall. Tall oaks overarched the well, and Timothy moved closer to them to shelter beneath their branches. Looking back across the lawn, he could see the rear elevation of the vicarage, and the face of his wife Kate, who was standing at the drawing-room window.

The rain fell heavier, and he turned up the collar of his morning coat. Confound the rain! Why had he not brought an umbrella with him? From the area of the well, the sound of its feeding stream became louder. He suddenly thought of Adrian, and the expression on his face when he had beseeched him to save him from drowning. His feet suddenly felt cold, and when he glanced down, he saw that a stream of water was pouring down on to the path from the well. At the same time, the earth seemed to shift beneath his feet. He heard the sound of falling bricks as the rest of the well-head collapsed.

Kate stood in the long, well-lit drawing room on the first floor, and admired the Italian marble fireplace that had been brought from Florence by the first vicar to inhabit the house. She would have a Turkey carpet laid in here, with tapestried armchairs on either side of the fireplace. They had already purchased a Venetian mirror to stand above the mantelpiece.

The old oil lamps suspended from the ceiling would soon be replaced by new gas chandeliers: the necessary pipes had already been brought in to the loft above.

Kate crossed to one of the rear windows, and looked out

at the summer storm. Beyond the garden wall she could see Timothy apparently executing a little dance on the path. Was he, too, so excited by their new home that he felt the need to leap for joy?

She saw him suddenly fall, and fling his hands to Heaven as though crying for help, and then the ground beneath him seemed to burst asunder as a raging torrent of water broke free from some underground restraint.

Kate Fowler stood transfixed at the window, unable to move through shock, and watched, motionless, as her husband disappeared beneath the waters of a long-imprisoned stream intent on finding a new course for itself. After some minutes, the storm abated, and the sun struggled out from the clouds. The initial shock had passed, but Kate still stood motionless, because she knew, before ever the news was brought to her, that her husband had drowned.

Author's Note:

Sophia Jex-Blake (1840 – 1912) was one of a group of remarkable women who laboured for the right of their sex to become doctors. Two of her fellow students at Queen's College, Harley Street, in 1858 were Dorothea Beale, who became Head of Cheltenham Ladies' College, and Frances May Buss, founder of the North London Collegiate School for Girls. Sophia's elder brother, Thomas Jex-Blake, became Headmaster of Rugby in 1874. One of his daughters, Henrietta, succeeded Elizabeth Wordsworth as principal of Lady Margaret Hall in 1909.